SPECTRUM TWO

SPECTRUM TWO

Modern Short Stories

Edited by
BRUCE BENNETT
PETER   COWAN
JOHN HAY

LONGMAN

LONGMAN GROUP LIMITED
Longman House
Burnt Mill, Harlow, Essex CM20 2JE, England
and Associated Companies throughout the World

First published 1970
Eleventh impression 1984

ISBN 0 582 34314 3

Printed in Hong Kong by
Wing King Tong Co Ltd

PREFACE

Writing short stories is a comparatively modern art. It was first given serious consideration in the early part of the nineteenth century and is still, today, undergoing radical experiment and change. Yet paradoxically, the short story derives from the ancient and unsophisticated tradition of the prose tale, the earliest of which, *The Shipwrecked Sailor*, was recorded in Egyptian papyri about 4000 B.C.

The transition from the predominantly oral tradition of the prose tale, to the written tradition of the short story, is recent and complex, and, like the short story itself, resists simple definition. Perhaps the most useful descriptive criterion for the short story is the criterion of limitation. To the inexperienced this can be deceptive. The relative brevity of the short story, its traditional focus upon a single episode, and its radical limitation of detail in both characterization and setting, might suggest simplicity. In fact it requires the exercise of the fullest capacity of the conscious artist. Short stories, however simple they may appear to be, reveal an awareness of technique on the part of the author. The American writer, Edgar Allan Poe, discussing his fellow writer, Nathaniel Hawthorne, insisted that in Hawthorne's stories 'every word *tells*, and there is not a word which does not *tell*'.

In this two volume anthology we have included stories which are intrinsically interesting, and which illustrate the diversity of themes and techniques used by short story writers. We have arranged the stories in an order which begins with simple reportage of an anecdote by a detached narrator, and ends with the complexity of symbolic short stories in which plot seems to have vanished. As much as other works of art, short stories resist classification, and forcing them into categories according to theme, or to specific technical characteristics limits the ways in which different readers might respond to them. By calling the anthology *Spectrum* we hope to emphasize the relationships which exist between apparently different stories.

In providing prefatory notes to each story, our intention has been to offer enough brief biographical and critical comments, and suggestions for further reading, to provide a perspective which will increase the reader's understanding and enjoyment of the stories.

CONTENTS

Preface   v

Introduction   ix

Anton Chekhov
VANKA   1

Anton Chekhov
GRIEF   7

Katherine Mansfield
THE FLY   13

D. H. Lawrence
ODOUR OF CHRYSANTHEMUMS   19

Franz Kafka
A HUNGER ARTISTE   37

James Joyce
CLAY   47

Thomas Wolfe
THE FAR AND THE NEAR   53

James Thurber
THE CATBIRD SEAT   57

Katherine Anne Porter
ROPE   67

Eudora Welty
DEATH OF A TRAVELLING SALESMAN   75

William Carlos Williams
THE USE OF FORCE   87

Ernest Hemingway
OLD MAN AT THE BRIDGE   93

Douglas Stewart
THE THREE JOLLY FOXES   97

CONTENTS *(continued)*

Peter Cowan
THE RED-BACKED SPIDERS   107

Angelica Gibbs
THE TEST   115

Shirley Jackson
AFTER YOU, MY DEAR ALPHONSE   119

Ray Bradbury
THE PEDESTRIAN   123

Philip K. Dick
IMPOSTOR   129

Albert Camus
THE GUEST   143

Daniel Keyes
FLOWERS FOR ALGERNON   155

Joseph Conrad
AMY FOSTER   181

INTRODUCTION

The stories in this volume suggest something of the range and variety of the modern short story. In subject, this variety is obvious, and leads to an assumption that any subject may make a good short story. However, an examination of these stories indicates just how carefully the writers have chosen their subject matter.

What all the stories have in common in this respect is a preference for a subject that reveals more than itself—that is, however strong the narrative interest may be in these stories, it is not the main focus. The narrative, or anecdote, is used as a frame to enable the writer to explore deeper levels of meaning, to imply more than he states. It is this refusal to rely primarily, or at all, on narrative and neatly rounded plot structures, which gives the stories their main interest, and their real power. And which is the mark of the contemporary short story.

The most obvious difference among the stories lies, at least at first glance, in their length. The brevity of a story like OLD MAN AT THE BRIDGE, or THE TEST, contrasts with the much greater length of ODOUR OF CHRYSANTHEMUMS or AMY FOSTER. Some subjects seem to enforce brevity, some stories gain great impact from the compression they achieve. But clearly there is little point in trying to assess the very brief story on exactly the same basis as one as long as AMY FOSTER. The longer form offers the writer some advantage—greater freedom to explore character, setting, range of incident. A greater discursiveness. All of which show to some degree in AMY FOSTER. But it also leads the writer away from the short story. It may lead him to smother the impact of his story, to labour its implications, to explain the whole thing away. But the short story does not lead to the novel. It is a form in its own right, and too great a reliance on mere length is usually suspect.

Through the range of stories there run wide differences of technique. Differences in the point of view the writer adopts, in the use of narrators who are deeply involved or who stand apart from what they relate. Stories that use a narrator to act as a commentator to assist the reader, involving him while yet making his task a little easier, or stories that work towards the objectivity of finely edged dialogue, where the reader is left to act as his own interpreter. Differences in presentation, from the dramatic form of THE TEST, or AFTER YOU, MY DEAR ALPHONSE, where the characters speak for themselves and the incidents are not explained, to the quiet, narrated form of THE FAR AND THE NEAR. Obvious differences in the extent to which writers establish setting and background, in the ways in which the stories establish their own mood and tone.

All these stories offer experience and insight, they order this and present it in their own ways, with their own degree of emphasis. And in the end they are alike in seeking the co-operation of the reader, they would involve him as a collaborator rather than explain to him, invite him to interpret rather than present him with neatly packaged solutions.

ACKNOWLEDGEMENTS

We are grateful to the following for permission to include copyright material:
Robert P. Mills Ltd for 'Flowers for Algernon' by Daniel Keyes; New Directions Publishing Corporation, New York for 'The Use of Force' from *The Farmers' Daughters* by William Carlos Williams, Copyright 1938 by William Carlos Williams; Jonathan Cape Limited and the Executors of the Ernest Hemingway Estate for 'Old Man at the Bridge' from *The First Forty-nine Stories* by Ernest Hemingway; The Society of Authors as the literary representative of the Estate of Katherine Mansfield for 'The Fly' by Katherine Mansfield; A. D. Peters & Co. for 'The Pedestrian' from *The Golden Apples of the Sun* by Ray Bradbury (Rupert Hart-Davis); A. M. Heath & Company Ltd for 'Death of a Travelling Salesman' by Eudora Welty; Scott Meredith Literary Agency (London) for 'Impostor' by Philip K. Dick; William Heinemann Ltd for 'The Far and the Near' from *From Death to Morning* by Thomas Wolfe; Hamish Hamilton Ltd for 'The Guest' from *Exile and the Kingdom* by Albert Camus © 1958 The Estate of Albert Camus, Translation by Justin O'Brien © 1957, 1958 Alfred Knopf Inc. (Hamish Hamilton London); Angus & Robertson Ltd for 'The Red-Backed Spiders' by Peter Cowan and for 'The Three Jolly Foxes' by Douglas Stewart; Laurence Pollinger Limited and the Estate of the late Mrs Frieda Lawrence for 'Odour of Chrysanthemums' by D. H. Lawrence from *The Complete Short Stories* (William Heinemann Ltd); Jonathan Cape Ltd and the Executors of the James Joyce Estate for 'Clay' from *The Dubliners* by James Joyce; Martin Secker & Warburg Limited for 'A Hunger Artiste' from *In the Penal Settlement* by Franz Kafka; Jonathan Cape Ltd on behalf of Katherine Anne Porter for 'Rope' from *The Collected Stories of Katherine Anne Porter*; J. M. Dent & Sons Ltd for 'Amy Foster' by Joseph Conrad'; Hamish Hamilton Ltd for 'The Catbird Seat' from *Vintage Thurber* by James Thurber © 1963 Hamish Hamilton, London; The New Yorker Magazine, Inc. for 'The Test' by Angelica Gibbs © 1940, 1968 *The New Yorker Magazine, Inc.*; Brandt & Brandt, New York, for 'After You, My Dear Alphonse' by Shirley Jackson.

Anton Chekhov born in Taganrog, Russia, in 1860. The son of a poor shop-keeper and the grandson of a serf, he took up writing in order to support himself while studying medicine. He did not conclude his studies, but became a writer, and is known as a dramatist for such plays as THE CHERRY ORCHARD, UNCLE VANYA, *and* THE THREE SISTERS.

His attempts at the novel never satisfied himself or critics. In the short story his output was vast, and uneven, but through his best work he helped create the modern form of the short story. He was not concerned with narrative as the main interest or aim of his stories. In fact his stories have been called formless, lacking in plot or important event. And they seemed to lack definite conclusion. Yet though he avoids 'big' themes, his choice of incident, his use of contrast, his dialogue, are so brilliantly achieved that his stories attain great insight and power. The formlessness of the stories is seen to be an illusion, we find they have been, in fact, very precisely put together. Selections of his stories are in many editions, a good sample of his work may be found in the Viking: PORTABLE CHEKHOV.

Chekhov died in 1904.

VANKA

Anton Chekhov

NINE-YEAR-OLD VANKA JUKOV, WHO HAS BEEN APPRENTICE TO THE shoemaker Aliakhine for three months, did not go to bed the night before Christmas. He waited till the master and mistress and the assistants had gone out to an early church-service, to procure from his employer's cupboard a small phial of ink and a penholder with a rusty nib; then, spreading a crumpled sheet of paper in front of him, began to write.

Before, however, deciding to make the first letter, he looked furtively at the door and at the window, glanced several times at the sombre ikon, on either side of which stretched shelves full of lasts, and heaved a heart-rending sigh. The sheet of paper was spread on a bench, and he himself was on his knees in front of it.

'Dear Grandfather Constantin Makaritch,' he wrote, 'I am writing you a letter. I wish you a Happy Christmas and all God's holy best. I have no father or mamenka, you are all I have.'

Vanka gave a look towards the window in which shone the reflection of his candle, and vividly pictured to himself his grandfather, Constantin Makaritch, who was night-watchman at Messrs. Jivarevev. He was a small, lean, unusually lively and active old man of sixty-five, always smiling and blear-eyed. All day he slept in the servant's kitchen or trifled with the cooks. At night, enveloped in an ample sheep-skin coat, he strayed round the domain, tapping with his cudgel. Behind him, each hanging its head, walk the old bitch Kashtanka, and Viune, so named because of his black coat and long body, and his resemblance to a loach. Viune is an unusually civil and friendly dog, looking as kindly at a stranger as at his masters, but he is not to be trusted. Beneath his deference and humbleness is hid the most inquisitorial maliciousness. No one better than he knows how to sneak up and take a bite at a leg, to slip into the larder or steal a moujik's chicken. More than once they have nearly broken his hindlegs, twice he has been hung up, every week he is nearly flogged to death, but he recovers from it all.

At this moment, for certain, his grandfather is standing at the gate, blinking his eyes at the bright red windows of the village church, stamping his feet in their high-felt boots, and jesting with the people in the yard; his cudgel will be hanging from his belt, he will be hugging himself with cold, giving a little dry, old man's cough, and at times pinching a servant girl or a cook.

'Won't we take some snuff?' he asks, holding out his snuff box to the women. The women take a pinch of snuff, and sneeze.

The old man goes into indescribable ecstasies, breaks into loud laughter, and cries:

1

'Off with it, it will freeze to your nose!'

He gives his snuff also to the dogs. Kashtanka sneezes, twitches her nose, and very offended walks away. Viune deferentially refuses to sniff, and wags his tail. It is glorious weather, not a breath of wind, clear, and frosty; it is a dark night, but the whole village, its white roofs, and streaks of smoke from the chimneys, the trees silvered with hoar-frost, and the snow-drifts, you can see it all. The sky scintillates with bright twinkling stars, and the Milky Way stands out so clearly that it looks as if it had been polished and rubbed over with snow for the holidays. . . .

Vanka sighs, dips his pen in the ink, and continues to write.

'Last night I got a thrashing, the patron dragged me by my hair into the yard, belaboured me with a shoemaker's stirrup, because, while I was rocking their brat in its cradle, I unfortunately fell asleep. And during the week, my mistress told me to clean a herring, and I began by its tail, so she took the herring and thrust its phiz into my face. The assistants tease me, send me to the tavern for vodka, make me steal the patron's cucumbers, and the patron beats me with whatever is handy. Food there is none; in the morning it's bread, at dinner "gruel," and in the evening again bread, as for tea or sour-cabbage soup, the patrons themselves guzzle that. They make me sleep in the vestibule, and when their brat cries I don't sleep at all, but have to rock the cradle. Dear Grandpapa, for Heaven's sake take me away from here, home to our village, I can't bear this any more. . . . I bow to the ground to you, and will pray to God for ever and ever, take me from here or I shall die. . . .'

The corners of Vanka's mouth went down, he rubbed his eyes with his dirty fist, and sobbed.

'I'll grate your tobacco for you,' he continued, 'I pray to God for you, and if there is anything wrong, then flog me like the grey goat. And if you really think I shan't find work, then I'll ask the manager, for Christ's sake, to let me clean the boots, or I'll go instead of Fedia as underherdsman. Dear Grandpapa, I can't bear this any more, it'll kill me. . . . I wanted to run away to our village, but I have no boots, and I was afraid of the frost. And when I grow up I'll look after you, no one shall harm you, and when you die I'll pray for the repose of your soul, just like I do for mamma Pelagea.

'As for Moscow, it is a large town, there are all gentlemen's houses, lots of horses, no sheep, and the dogs are not vicious. The children don't come round at Christmas with a star, no one is allowed to sing in the choir, and once I saw in a shop window hooks on a line and fishing rods, all for sale, and for every kind of fish, awfully convenient. And there was one hook which would catch a sheat-fish weighing a pound. And there are shops with guns, like the master's, and I am sure they must cost 100 roubles each. And in the meatshops there are woodcocks, partridges, and hares, but who shot them or where they come from the shopman won't say.

'Dear Grandpapa, and when the masters give a Christmas tree take a golden walnut and hide it in my green box. Ask the young lady, Olga Ignatievna, for it, say it's for Vanka.'

Vanka sighed convulsively, and again stared at the window. He remembered that his grandfather always went through the forest to the Christmas tree, and took his grandson with him. What happy times! The frost crackled, his grandfather crackled, and as they both did Vanka did the same. Then before cutting down the Christmas tree his grandfather smoked his pipe, took a long pinch of snuff, and made fun of poor frozen little Vanka. . . . The young fir trees, wrapt in hoar-frost, stand motionless and wait; which of them will die? Suddenly a hare springing from somewhere darts over the snowdrift. . . . His grandfather could not help shouting:

'Catch it, catch it, catch it! Ah, short-tailed devil!'

When the tree was down, his grandfather dragged it to the master's house, and there they set about decorating it. The young lady, Olga Ignatievna, Vanka's great friend, busied herself most about it. When little Vanka's mother, Pelagea, was still alive, and was servant-woman in the house, Olga Ignatievna used to stuff him with sugar-candy, and, having nothing to do, taught him to read, write, count up to one hundred, and even to dance the quadrille. When Pelagea died, they placed the orphan Vanka in the kitchen with his grandfather, and from the kitchen he was sent to Moscow, to Aliakhine, the shoemaker.

'Come quick, dear Grandpapa,' continued Vanka, 'I beseech you for Christ's sake take me from here. Have pity on a poor orphan, for here they all beat me, and I am frightfully hungry, and so bored that I can't tell you, I cry all the time. The other day the patron hit me on the head with a last; I fell to the ground, and only just returned to life. My life is a disaster, worse than any dog's. . . . I send greetings to Aliona, to one-eyed Egor, and the coachman, and don't let anyone have my harmonium. I remain, your grandson, Ivan Jukov, dear Grandpapa, do come.'

Vanka folded his sheet of paper in four, and put it into an envelope, purchased the night before for a kopeck. He thought a little, dipped the pen into the ink, and wrote the address:

'The village, to my grandfather.' He then scratched his head, thought again, and added: 'Constantin Makaritch.' Pleased at having been able to write without disturbance, he put on his cap, and, omitting his sheep-skin coat, ran out in his shirt-sleeves into the street.

The shopman at the poulterer's, from whom he had inquired the night before, had told him that letters were to be put into post-boxes, and from thence they were conveyed over the whole earth in mail troikas by drunken post-boys and to the sound of bells. Vanka ran to the first post-box and slipped his precious letter into the slit.

An hour afterwards, lulled by hope, he was sleeping soundly. In his dreams he saw a stove, by the stove sat his grandfather with his legs dangling down, barefooted, and reading a letter to the cooks. . . . Around the stove walks Viune wagging his tail. . . .

Anton Chekhov born in Taganrog, Russia, in 1860. The son of a poor shop-keeper and the grandson of a serf, he took up writing in order to support himself while studying medicine. He did not conclude his studies, but became a writer, and is known as a dramatist for such plays as THE CHERRY ORCHARD, UNCLE VANYA, and THE THREE SISTERS.

His attempts at the novel never satisfied himself or critics. In the short story his output was vast, and uneven, but through his best work he helped create the modern form of the short story. He was not concerned with narrative as the main interest or aim of his stories. In fact his stories have been called formless, lacking in plot or important event. And they seemed to lack definite conclusion. Yet though he avoids 'big' themes, his choice of incident, his use of contrast, his dialogue, are so brilliantly achieved that his stories attain great insight and power. The formlessness of the stories is seen to be an illusion, we find they have been, in fact, very precisely put together. Selections of his stories are in many editions, a good sample of his work may be found in the Viking: PORTABLE CHEKHOV.

Chekhov died in 1904.

GRIEF

Anton Chekhov

IT IS TWILIGHT. A THICK WET SNOW IS SLOWLY TWIRLING AROUND THE newly lighted street-lamps, and lying in soft thin layers on the roofs, the horses' backs, people's shoulders and hats. The cab-driver, Iona Potapov, is quite white, and looks like a phantom; he is bent double as far as a human body can bend double; he is seated on his box, and never makes a move. If a whole snowdrift fell on him, it seems as if he would not find it necessary to shake it off. His little horse is also quite white, and remains motionless; its immobility, its angularity, and its straight wooden-looking legs, even close by give it the appearance of a ginger-bread horse worth a kopeck. It is, no doubt, plunged in deep thought. If you were snatched from the plough, from your usual grey surroundings, and were thrown into this slough full of monstrous lights, unceasing noise and hurrying people, you too would find it difficult not to think.

Iona and his little horse have not moved from their place for a long while. They left their yard before dinner, and, up to now, not a 'fare'. The evening mist is descending over the town, the white lights of the lamps are replacing brighter rays, and the hubbub of the street is getting louder. 'Cabby, for Viborg way!' suddenly hears Iona. 'Cabby!'

Iona jumps, and through his snow-covered eyelashes, sees an officer in a greatcoat, with his hood over his head.

'Viborg way!' the officer repeats. 'Are you asleep, eh? Viborg way!'

With a nod of assent Iona picks up the reins, in consequence of which layers of snow slip off the horse's back and neck. The officer seats himself in the sleigh, the cab-driver smacks his lips to encourage his horse, stretches out his neck like a swan, sits up, and, more from habit than necessity, brandishes his whip. The little horse also stretches his neck, bends his wooden-looking legs, and makes a move undecidedly.

'What are you doing, were-wolf!' is the exclamation Iona hears, from the dark mass moving to and fro as soon as they started.

'Where the devil are you going? To the r-r-right!'

'You do not know how to drive. Keep to the right!' calls the officer angrily.

A coachman from a private carriage swears at him; a passer-by, who has run across the road and rubbed his shoulders against the horse's nose, looks at him furiously as he sweeps the snow from his sleeve. Iona shifts about on his seat as if he were on needles, moves his elbows as if he were trying to keep his equilibrium, and gapes about like someone suffocating, and who does not understand why and wherefore he is there.

'What scoundrels they all are!' jokes the officer; 'one would think they had all entered into an agreement to jostle you or fall under your horse.'

Iona looks round at the officer, and moves his lips. He evidently wants to say something, but the only sound that issues is a snuffle.

'What?' asks the officer.

Iona twists his mouth into a smile, and with an effort says hoarsely: 'My son, barin, died this week.'

'Hm! What did he die of?'

Iona turns with his whole body towards his fare, and says: 'And who knows! They say high fever. He was three days in hospital, and then died. . . . God's will be done.'

'Turn round! The devil!' sounded from the darkness. 'Have you popped off, old doggie, eh? Use your eyes!'

'Go on, go on,' said the officer, 'otherwise we shall not get there by to-morrow. Hurry a bit!'

The cab-driver again stretches his neck, sits up, and, with a bad grace, brandishes his whip. Several times again he turns to look at his fare, but the latter had closed his eyes, and apparently is not disposed to listen. Having deposited the officer in the Viborg, he stops by the tavern, doubles himself up on his seat, and agains remains motionless, while the snow once more begins to cover him and his horse. An hour, and another. . . . Then, along the footpath, with a squeak of goloshes, and quarrelling, came three young men, two of them tall and lanky, the third one short and hump-backed.

'Cabby, to the Police Bridge!' in a cracked voice calls the hump-back. 'The three of us for two griveniks!' (20 kopecks).

Iona picks up his reins, and smacks his lips. Two griveniks is not a fair price, but he does not mind if it is a rouble or five kopecks—to him it is all the same now, so long as they are wayfarers. The young men, jostling each other and using bad language, approach the sleigh, and all three at once try to get on to the seat; then begins a discussion which two shall sit and who shall be the one to stand. After wrangling, abusing each other, and much petulance, it was at last decided that the hump-back should stand, as he was the smallest.

'Now then, hurry up!' says the hump-back in a twanging voice, as he takes his place, and breathes in Iona's neck. 'Old furry. Here, mate, what a cap you have got, there is not a worse one to be found in all Petersburg! . . .'

'Hi—hi,—hi—hi,' giggles Iona. 'Such a . . .'

'Now you, "such a," hurry up, are you going the whole way at this pace? Are you? . . . Do you want it in the neck?'

'My head feels like bursting,' says one of the lanky ones. 'Last night at the Donkmasovs, Vaska and I drank the whole of four bottles of cognac.'

'I don't understand what you lie for,' said the other lanky one angrily; 'you lie like a brute.'

'God strike me, it's the truth!'

'It's as much a truth as that a louse coughs!'

'Hi, hi,' grins Iona, 'what gay young gentlemen!'

'Pshaw, go to the devil!' indignantly says the hump-back.

'Are you going to get on or not, you old pest? Is that the way to drive? Use the whip a bit! Go on, devil, go on, give it him well!'

Iona feels at his back the little man wriggling, and the tremble in his voice. He listens to the insults hurled at him, sees the people, and little by little the feeling of loneliness leaves him. The hump-back goes on swearing until he gets mixed up in some elaborate six-foot oath, or chokes with coughing. The lankies begin to talk about a certain Nadejda Petrovna. Iona looks round at them several times; he waits for a temporary silence, then, turning round again, he murmurs:

'My son—died this week.'

'We must all die,' sighed the hump-back, wiping his lips after an attack of coughing. 'Now, hurry up, hurry up! Gentlemen, I really cannot go any farther like this! When will he get us there?'

'Well, just you stimulate him a little in the neck!'

'You old pest, do you hear, I'll bone your neck for you! If one treated the like of you with ceremony one would have to go on foot! Do you hear, old serpent Gorinytch! Or do you not care a spit?'

Iona hears rather than feels the blows they deal him.

'Hi, hi,' he laughs. 'They are gay young gentlemen, God bless 'em!'

'Cabby, are you married?' asks a lanky one.

'I? Hi, hi, gay young gentlemen! Now I have only a wife: the moist ground. . . . Hi, ho, ho . . . that is to say, the grave! My son has died, and I am alive. . . . A wonderful thing, death mistook the door . . . instead of coming to me, it went to my son. . . .'

Iona turns round to tell them how his son died, but at this moment the hump-back, giving a little sigh, announces, 'Thank God, they have at last reached their destination,' and Iona watches them disappear through the dark entrance. Once more he is alone, and again surrounded by silence. . . . His grief, which had abated for a short while, returns and rends his heart with greater force. With an anxious and a hurried look, he searches among the crowds passing on either side of the street to find if there is just one person who will listen to him. But the crowds hurry by without noticing him or his trouble. Yet it is such an immense, illimitable grief. Should his heart break and the grief pour out, it would flow over the whole earth it seems, and yet, no one sees it. It has managed to conceal itself in such an insignificant shell that no one can see it even by day and with a light.

Iona sees a hall-porter with some sacking, and decides to talk to him. 'Friend, what sort of time is it?' he asks.

Anton Chekov

'Past nine. What are you standing here for? Move on.'

Iona moves on a few steps, doubles himself up, and abandons himself to his grief. He sees it is useless to turn to people for help. In less than five minutes he straightens himself, holds up his head as if he felt some sharp pain, and gives a tug at the reins: he can bear it no longer, 'The stables,' he thinks, and the little horse, as if he understood, starts off at a trot.

About an hour and a half later Iona is seated by a large dirty stove. Around the stove, on the floor, on the benches, people are snoring; the air is thick and suffocatingly hot. Iona looks at the sleepers, scratches himself, and regrets having returned so early.

'I have not even earned my fodder,' he thinks. 'That's what's my trouble. A man who knows his job, who has had enough to eat, and his horse too, can always sleep peacefully.'

A young cab-driver in one of the corners half gets up, grunts sleepily, and stretches towards a bucket of water.

'Do you want a drink?' Iona asks him.

'Don't I want a drink!'

'That's so? Your good health! But listen, mate—you know, my son is dead. . . . Did you hear? This week, in hospital. . . . It's a long story.'

Iona looks to see what effect his words have, but sees none—the young man has hidden his face, and is fast asleep again. The old man sighs, and scratches his head. Just as much as the young one wanted to drink, the old man wanted to talk. It will soon be a week since his son died, and he has not been able to speak about it properly to anyone. One must tell it slowly and carefully; how his son fell ill, how he suffered, what he said before he died, how he died. One must describe every detail of the funeral, and the journey to the hospital to fetch the defunct's clothes. His daughter Anissia remained in the village—one must talk about her too. Was it nothing he had to tell? Surely the listener would gasp and sigh, and sympathize with him? It is better, too, to talk to women; although they are stupid, two words are enough to make them sob.

'I'll go and look at my horse,' thinks Iona; 'there's always time to sleep. No fear of that!'

He puts on his coat, and goes to the stables to his horse; he thinks of the corn, the hay, the weather. When he is alone, he dare not think of his son; he could speak about him to anyone, but to think of him, and picture him to himself, is unbearably painful.

'Are you tucking in?' Iona asks his horse, looking at his bright eyes; 'go on, tuck in, though we've not earned our corn, we can eat hay. Yes! I am too old to drive—my son could have, not I. He was a first-rate cab-driver. If only he had lived!'

Iona is silent for a moment, then continues:

'That's how it is, my old horse. There's no more Kuzma Ionitch. He

10

has left us to live, and he went off pop. Now let's say, you had a foal, you were that foal's mother, and suddenly, let's say, that foal went and left you to live after him. It would be sad, wouldn't it?'

The little horse munches, listens, and breathes over his master's hand. . . .

Iona's feelings are too much for him, and he tells the little horse the whole story.

Katherine Mansfield born (*Kathleen Beauchamp*) in 1888, in Wellington, New Zealand, where, apart from four years in a neighbouring village, Karori, she spent her early years, aspects of which appear in her short stories. Her wealthy businessman father sent her to England to 'finish' her education. She so enjoyed life in England that, after the age of twenty, she never re-visited New Zealand. A brief disastrous marriage to a singer was followed by a more successful marriage to John Middleton Murry, a well known critic of art and literature.

Her stories reflect her alternating moods of elation and despair, particularly in the period following her brother's death, when she suffered increasingly from chronic pleurisy. Her writing reflects her delight in life and her sensitivity to passing impressions, illustrated in a letter to her husband: 'This morning a robin flew into my room. I caught it. It did not seem at all frightened but lay still and very warm. I carried it to the window and I cannot tell you what a strange joyful feeling—when the little bird flew out of my hands.' It is interesting to compare this mood and attitude to the complex situation in which the businessman in 'THE FLY' finds himself. 'THE FLY' was written in 1922, towards the end of five years' illness. She died in 1922.

Suggested further reading: 'THE GARDEN PARTY', 'THE LADY'S MAID', 'THE VOYAGE', and other stories in COLLECTED SHORT STORIES, 1957.

THE FLY

Katherine Mansfield

'Y'ARE VERY SNUG IN HERE,' PIPED OLD MR WOODIFIELD, AND HE PEERED OUT of the great, green leather armchair by his friend the boss's desk as a baby peers out of its pram. His talk was over; it was time for him to be off. But he did not want to go. Since he had retired, since his . . . stroke, the wife and girls kept him boxed up in the house every day of the week except Tuesday. On Tuesday he was dressed up and brushed and allowed to cut back to the City for the day. Though what he did there the wife and girls couldn't imagine. Made a nuisance of himself to his friends, they supposed. . . . Well, perhaps so. All the same, we cling to our last pleasures as the tree clings to its last leaves. So there sat old Woodifield, smoking a cigar and staring almost greedily at the boss, who rolled in his office chair, stout, rosy, five years older than he, and still going strong, still at the helm. It did one good to see him.

Wistfully, admiringly, the old voice added, 'It's snug in here, upon my word!'

'Yes, it's comfortable enough,' agreed the boss, and he flipped the *Financial Times* with a paper-knife. As a matter of fact he was proud of his room; he liked to have it admired, especially by old Woodifield. It gave him a feeling of deep, solid satisfaction to be planted there in the midst of it in full view of that frail old figure in the muffler.

'I've had it done up lately,' he explained, as he had explained for the past—how many?—weeks. 'New carpet,' and he pointed to the bright red carpet with a pattern of large white rings. 'New furniture,' and he nodded towards the massive bookcase and the table with legs like twisted treacle. 'Electric heating!' He waved almost exultantly towards the five transparent, pearly sausages glowing so softly in the tilted copper pan.

But he did not draw old Woodifield's attention to the photograph over the table of a grave-looking boy in uniform standing in one of those spectral photographers' parks with photographers' storm-clouds behind him. It was not new. It had been there for over six years.

'There was something I wanted to tell you,' said old Woodifield, and his eyes grew dim remembering. 'Now what was it? I had it in my mind when I started out this morning.' His hands began to tremble, and patches of red showed above his beard.

Poor old chap, he's on his last pins, thought the boss. And, feeling kindly, he winked at the old man, and said jokingly, 'I tell you what. I've got a little drop of something here that'll do you good before you go out into the cold again. It's beautiful stuff. It wouldn't hurt a child.' He took a key off his watch-chain, unlocked a cupboard below his desk, and drew forth a dark, squat bottle. 'That's the medicine,' said he. 'And the man from whom I got it told me on the strict Q.T. it came from the cellars at Windsor Cassel.'

Old Woodifield's mouth fell open at the sight. He couldn't have looked more surprised if the boss had produced a rabbit.

'It's whisky, ain't it?' he piped, feebly.

The boss turned the bottle and lovingly showed him the label. Whisky it was.

'D'you know,' said he, peering up at the boss wonderingly, 'they won't let me touch it at home.' And he looked as though he was going to cry.

'Ah, that's where we know a bit more than the ladies,' cried the boss, swooping across for two tumblers that stood on the table with the water-bottle, and pouring a generous finger into each. 'Drink it down. It'll do you good. And don't put any water with it. It's sacrilege to tamper with stuff like this. Ah!' He tossed off his, pulled out his handkerchief, hastily wiped his moustaches, and cocked an eye at old Woodifield, who was rolling his in his chaps.

The old man swallowed, was silent a moment, and then said faintly, 'It's nutty!'

But it warmed him; it crept into his chill old brain—he remembered.

'That was it,' he said, heaving himself out of his chair. 'I thought you'd like to know. The girls were in Belgium last week having a look at poor Reggie's grave, and they happened to come across your boy's. They're quite near each other, it seems.'

Old Woodifield paused, but the boss made no reply. Only a quiver in his eyelids showed that he heard.

'The girls were delighted with the way the place is kept,' piped the old voice. 'Beautifully looked after. Couldn't be better if they were at home. You've not been across, have yer?'

'No, no!' For various reasons the boss had not been across.

'There's miles of it,' quavered old Woodifield, 'and it's all as neat as a garden. Flowers growing on all the graves. Nice broad paths.' It was plain from his voice how much he liked a nice broad path.

The pause came again. Then the old man brightened wonderfully.

'D'you know what the hotel made the girls pay for a pot of jam?' he piped. 'Ten francs! Robbery, I call it. It was a little pot, so Gertrude says, no bigger than a half-crown. And she hadn't taken more than a spoonful when they charged her ten francs. Gertrude brought the pot away with her to teach 'em a lesson. Quite right, too; it's trading on our feelings. They think because we're over there having a look around we're ready to pay anything. That's what it is.' And he turned towards the door.

'Quite right, quite right!' cried the boss, though what was quite right he hadn't the least idea. He came around by his desk, followed the shuffling footsteps to the door, and saw the old fellow out. Woodifield was gone.

For a long moment the boss stayed, staring at nothing, while the grey-haired office messenger, watching him, dodged in and out of his cubbyhole like a dog that expects to be taken for a run. Then: 'I'll see nobody for half an hour, Macey,' said the boss. 'Understand? Nobody at all.'

'Very good, sir.'

The door shut, the firm heavy steps recrossed the bright carpet, the fat body plumped down in the spring chair, and leaning forward, the boss covered his face with his hands. He wanted, he intended, he had arranged to weep. . . .

It had been a terrible shock to him when old Woodifield sprang that remark upon him about the boy's grave. It was exactly as though the earth had opened and he had seen the boy lying there with Woodifield's girls staring down at him. For it was strange. Although over six years had passed away, the boss never thought of the boy except as lying unchanged, unblemished in his uniform, asleep for ever. 'My son!' groaned the boss. But no tears came yet. In the past, in the first months and even years after the boy's death, he had only to say those words to be overcome by such grief that nothing short of a violent fit of weeping could relieve him. Time, he had declared then, he had told everybody, could make no difference. Other men perhaps might recover, might live their loss down, but not he. How was it possible? His boy was an only son. Ever since his birth the boss had worked at building up this business for him; it had no other meaning if it was not for the boy. Life itself had come to have no other meaning. How on earth could he have slaved, denied himself, kept going all those years without the promise for ever before him of the boy's stepping into his shoes and carrying on where he left off?

And that promise had been so near being fulfilled. The boy had been in the office learning the ropes for a year before the war. Every morning they had started off together; they had come back by the same train. And what congratulations he had received as the boy's father! No wonder; he had taken to it marvellously. As to his popularity with the staff, every man jack of them down to old Macey couldn't make enough of the boy. And he wasn't in the least spoilt. No, he was just his bright, natural self, with the right word for everybody, with that boyish look and his habit of saying, 'Simply splendid!'

But all that was over and done with as though it never had been. The day had come when Macey had handed him the telegram that brought the whole place crashing about his head. 'Deeply regret to inform you . . .' And he had left the office a broken man, with his life in ruins.

Six years ago, six years . . . How quickly time passed! It might have happened yesterday. The boss took his hands from his face; he was puzzled. Something seemed to be wrong with him. He wasn't feeling as he wanted to feel. He decided to get up and have a look at the boy's photograph. But it wasn't a favourite photograph of his; the expression was unnatural. It was cold, even stern-looking. The boy had never looked like that.

At that moment the boss noticed that a fly had fallen into his broad inkpot, and was trying feebly but desperately to clamber out again. Help! help! said those struggling legs. But the sides of the inkpot were wet and slippery; it fell back again and began to swim. The boss took up a pen, picked the fly out of the ink, and shook it on to a piece of blotting-paper. For a fraction of a second it lay still on the dark patch that oozed round it. Then the front legs waved, took hold, and, pulling its small sodden body up it began the immense task of cleaning the ink from its wings. Over and under, over and under, went a leg along a wing, as the stone goes over and under the scythe. Then there was a pause, while the fly, seeming to stand on the tips of its toes, tried to expand first one wing and then the other. It succeeded at last, and, sitting down, it began, like a minute cat, to clean its face. Now one could imagine that the little front legs rubbed against each other lightly, joyfully. The horrible danger was over; it had escaped; it was ready for life again.

But just then the boss had an idea. He plunged his pen back into the ink, leaned his thick wrist on the blotting paper, and as the fly tried its wings down came a great heavy blot. What would it make of that? What indeed! The little beggar seemed absolutely cowed, stunned, and afraid to move because of what would happen next. But then, as if painfully, it dragged itself forward. The front legs waved, caught hold, and, more slowly this time, the task began from the beginning.

He's a plucky little devil, thought the boss, and he felt a real admiration for the fly's courage. That was the way to tackle things; that was the right spirit. Never say die; it was only a question of . . . But the fly had again finished its laborious task, and the boss had just time to refill his pen, to shake fair and square on the new-cleaned body yet another dark drop. What about it this time? A painful moment of suspense followed. But behold, the front legs were again waving; the boss felt a rush of relief. He leaned over the fly and said to it tenderly, 'You artful little b . . .' And he actually had the brilliant notion of breathing on it to help the drying process. All the same, there was something timid and weak about its efforts now, and the boss decided that this time should be the last, as he dipped the pen into the inkpot.

It was. The last blot on the soaked blotting-paper, and the draggled fly lay in it and did not stir. The back legs were stuck to the body; the front legs were not be be seen.

'Come on,' said the boss. 'Look sharp!' And he stirred it with his pen—in vain. Nothing happened or was likely to happen. The fly was dead.

The boss lifted the corpse on the end of the paper-knife and flung it into the waste-paper basket. But such a grinding feeling of wretchedness seized him that he felt positively frightened. He started forward and pressed the bell for Macey.

'Bring me some fresh blotting-paper,' he said, sternly, 'and look sharp about it.' And while the old dog paddled away he fell to wondering what it was he had been thinking about before. What was it? It was . . . He took out his handkerchief and passed it inside his collar. For the life of him he could not remember.

D. H. Lawrence born in Eastwood, Nottinghamshire. His father was a coal miner, and his mother a former school-teacher. An element of autobiography is noticeable in most of his writing. He has written, in relation to this, that 'the novels and stories come unwatched out of one's pen' and that 'one sheds one's sicknesses in books, repeats and presents again one's emotions, to be master of them.' In 'ODOUR OF CHRYSANTHEMUMS', written in his early twenties, Lawrence portrays aspects of the life he knew as a boy in the coal mining village where he was born.

The wife in the story, Elizabeth Bates, is modelled on one of Lawrence's aunts, who lost her first husband in a mining disaster, but the strained relationship on which the wife looks back also parallels the unhappy married life of the author's father and mother. Typically, the situation is presented mainly from the woman's point of view. 'ODOUR OF CHRYSANTHEMUMS' exemplifies Lawrence's ability to set a scene convincingly and economically and to represent with great immediacy the complex network of feelings within the Bates household and between the Bates family and their neighbours. Lawrence's third novel, SONS AND LOVERS, also deals with aspects of his early life and shows his creative powers at their height.

In 1917 Lawrence and his German wife were ordered out of Cornwall as suspected spies. They left England after the war for six years of world travel, during which novels, short stories, poems, and essays were written in places as far apart as Italy, Australia, and Mexico. Lawrence died of tuberculosis in France, 1930.

Suggested further reading: Plays. THE WIDOWING OF MRS HOLROYD, 1914, —an expansion of the situation in 'ODOUR OF CHRYSANTHEMUMS'. Short Stories: 'DAUGHTERS OF THE VICAR', 'THE CHRISTENING', 'YOU TOUCHED ME'. Novels: SONS AND LOVERS, THE RAINBOW, KANGAROO.

ODOUR OF CHRYSANTHEMUMS

D. H. Lawrence

I

THE SMALL LOCOMOTIVE ENGINE, NUMBER 4, CAME CLANKING, STUMBLING down from Selston with seven full wagons. It appeared round the corner with loud threats of speed, but the colt that it startled from among the gorse, which still flickered indistinctly in the raw afternoon, out-distanced it at a canter. A woman, walking up the railway line to Underwood, drew back into the hedge, held her basket aside, and watched the foot-plate of the engine advancing. The trucks thumped heavily past, one by one, with slow inevitable movement, as she stood insignificantly trapped between the jolting black wagons and the hedge; then they curved away towards the coppice where the withered oak leaves dropped noiselessly, while the birds, pulling at the scarlet hips beside the track, made off into the dusk that had already crept into the spinney. In the open, the smoke from the engine sank and cleaved to the rough grass. The fields were dreary and forsaken, and in the marshy strip that led to the whimsey, a reedy pit-pond, the fowls had already abandoned their run among the alders, to roost in the tarred fowl-house. The pit-bank loomed up beyond the pond, flames like red sores licking its ashy sides, in the afternoon's stagnant light. Just beyond rose the tapering chimneys and the clumsy black headstocks of Brinsley Colliery. The two wheels were spinning fast up against the sky, and the winding engine rapped out its little spasms. The miners were being turned up.

The engine whistled as it came into the wide bay of railway lines beside the colliery, where rows of trucks stood in harbour.

Miners, single, trailing and in groups, passed like shadows diverging home. At the edge of the ribbed level of sidings squats a low cottage, three steps down from the cinder track. A large bony vine clutched at the house, as if to claw down the tiled roof. Round the bricked yard grew a few wintry primroses. Beyond, the long garden sloped down to a bush-covered brook course. There were some twiggy apple trees, winter-crack trees, and ragged cabbages. Beside the path hung dishevelled pink chrysanthemums, like pink cloths hung on bushes. A woman came stooping out of the felt-covered fowl-house, half-way down the garden. She closed and padlocked the door, then drew herself erect, having brushed some bits from her white apron.

She was a tall woman of imperious mien, handsome, with definite black eyebrows. Her smooth black hair was parted exactly. For a few moments she stood steadily watching the miners as they passed along the railway: then she turned towards the brook course. Her face was calm and set, her mouth was closed with disillusionment. After a moment she called:

'John!' There was no answer. She waited, and then said distinctly: 'Where are you?'

'Here!' replied a child's sulky voice from among the bushes. The woman looked piercingly through the dusk.

'Are you at that brook?' she asked sternly.

For answer the child showed himself before the raspberry-canes that rose like whips. He was a small, sturdy boy of five. He stood quite still, defiantly.

'Oh!' said the mother, conciliated. 'I thought you were down at that wet brook—and you remember what I told you—'

The boy did not move or answer.

'Come, come on in,' she said more gently, 'it's getting dark. There's your grandfather's engine coming down the line!'

The lad advanced slowly, with resentful, taciturn movement. He was dressed in trousers and waistcoat of cloth that was too thick and hard for the size of the garments. They were evidently cut down from a man's clothes.

As they went slowly towards the house he tore at the ragged wisps of chrysanthemums and dropped the petals in handfuls along the path.

'Don't do that—it does look nasty,' said his mother. He refrained, and she, suddenly pitiful, broke off a twig with three or four wan flowers and held them against her face. When mother and son reached the yard her hand hesitated, and instead of laying the flower aside, she pushed it in her apron-band. The mother and son stood at the foot of the three steps looking across the bay of lines at the passing home of the miners. The trundle of the small train was imminent. Suddenly the engine loomed past the house and came to a stop opposite the gate.

The engine-driver, a short man with round grey beard, leaned out of the cab high above the woman.

'Have you got a cup of tea?' he said in a cheery, hearty fashion.

It was her father. She went in, saying she would mash. Directly, she returned.

'I didn't come to see you on Sunday,' began the little grey-bearded man.

'I didn't expect you,' said his daughter.

The engine-driver winced; then, reassuming his cheery, airy manner, he said:

'Oh, have you heard then? Well, and what do you think—?'

'I think it is soon enough,' she replied.

At her brief censure the little man made an impatient gesture, and said coaxingly, yet with dangerous coldness:

'Well, what's a man to do? It's no sort of life for a man of my years, to sit at my own hearth like a stranger. And if I'm going to marry again it may as well be soon as late—what does it matter to anybody?'

The woman did not reply, but turned and went into the house. The man in the engine-cab stood assertive, till she returned with a cup of tea and a piece of bread and butter on a plate. She went up the steps and stood near the footplate of the hissing engine.

'You needn't 'a' brought me bread an' butter,' said her father. 'But a cup of tea'—he sipped appreciatively—'it's very nice.' He sipped for a moment or two, then: 'I hear as Walter's got another bout on,' he said.

'When hasn't he?' said the woman bitterly.

'I heerd tell of him in the "Lord Nelson" braggin' as he was going to spend that b—— afore he went: half a sovereign that was.'

'When?' asked the woman.

'A' Sat'day night—I know that's true.'

'Very likely,' she laughed bitterly. 'He gives me twenty-three shillings.'

'Aye, it's a nice thing, when a man can do nothing with his money but make a beast of himself!' said the grey-whiskered man. The woman turned her head away. Her father swallowed the last of his tea and handed her the cup.

'Aye,' he sighed, wiping his mouth. 'It's a settler, it is—'

He put his hand on the lever. The little engine strained and groaned, and the train rumbled towards the crossing. The woman again looked across the metals. Darkness was settling over the spaces of the railway and trucks: the miners, in grey sombre groups, were still passing home. The winding engine pulsed hurriedly, with brief pauses. Elizabeth Bates looked at the dreary flow of men, then she went indoors. Her husband did not come.

The kitchen was small and full of firelight; red coals piled glowing up the chimney mouth. All the life of the room seemed in the white, warm hearth and the steel fender reflecting the red fire. The cloth was laid for tea; cups glinted in the shadows. At the back, where the lowest stairs protruded into the room, the boy sat struggling with a knife and a piece of whitewood. He was almost hidden in the shadow. It was half-past four. They had but to await the father's coming to begin tea. As the mother watched her son's sullen little struggle with the wood, she saw herself in his silence and pertinacity; she saw the father in her child's indifference to all but himself. She seemed to be occupied by her husband. He had probably gone past his home, slunk past his own door, to drink before he came in, while his dinner spoiled and wasted in waiting. She glanced at the clock, then took the potatoes to strain them in the yard. The garden and fields beyond the brook were closed in uncertain darkness. When she rose with the saucepan, leaving the drain steaming into the night behind her, she saw the yellow lamps were lit along the high road that went up the hill away beyond the space of the railway lines and the field.

Then again she watched the men trooping home, fewer now and fewer.

Indoors the fire was sinking and the room was dark red. The woman put her saucepan on the hob, and set a batter-pudding near the mouth of the oven. Then she stood unmoving. Directly, gratefully, came quick young steps to the door. Someone hung on the latch a moment, then a little girl entered and began pulling off her outdoor things, dragging a mass of curls, just ripening from gold to brown, over her eyes with her hat.

Her mother chid her for coming late from school, and said she would have to keep her at home the dark winter days.

'Why, mother, it's hardly a bit dark yet. The lamp's not lighted, and my father's not home.'

'No, he isn't. But it's a quarter to five! Did you see anything of him?'

The child became serious. She looked at her mother with large, wistful blue eyes.

'No, mother, I've never seen him. Why? Has he come up an' gone past, to Old Brinsley? He hasn't, mother, 'cos I never saw him.'

'He'd watch that,' said the mother bitterly, 'he'd take care as you didn't see him. But you may depend upon it, he's seated in the "Prince o' Wales". He wouldn't be this late.'

The girl looked at her mother piteously.

'Let's have our teas, mother, should we?' she said.

The mother called John to table. She opened the door once more and looked out across the darkness of the lines. All was deserted: she could not hear the winding-engines.

'Perhaps,' she said to herself, 'he's stopped to get some ripping done.'

They sat down to tea. John, at the end of the table near the door, was almost lost in the darkness. Their faces were hidden from each other. The girl crouched against the fender slowly moving a thick piece of bread before the fire. The lad, his face a dusky mark on the shadow, sat watching her who was transfigured in the red glow.

'I do think it's beautiful to look in the fire,' said the child.

'Do you?' said her mother. 'Why?'

'It's so red, and full of little caves—and it feels so nice, and you can fair smell it.'

'It'll want mending directly,' replied her mother, 'and then if your father comes he'll carry on and say there never is a fire when a man comes home sweating from the pit. A public-house is always warm enough.'

There was silence till the boy said complainingly: 'Make haste, our Annie.'

'Well, I am doing! I can't make the fire do it no faster, can I?'

'She keeps wafflin' it about so's to make 'er slow,' grumbled the boy.

'Don't have such an evil imagination, child,' replied the mother.

Soon the room was busy in the darkness with the crisp sound of crunching. The mother ate very little. She drank her tea determinedly, and sat thinking. When she rose her anger was evident in the stern unbending of her head. She looked at the pudding in the fender, and broke out:

'It is a scandalous thing as a man can't even come home to his dinner! If it's crozzled up to a cinder I don't see why I should care. Past his very door he goes to get to a public-house, and here I sit with his dinner waiting for him—'

She went out. As she dropped piece after piece of coal on the red fire, the shadows fell on the walls, till the room was almost in total darkness.

'I canna see,' grumbled the invisible John. In spite of herself, the mother laughed.

'You know the way to your mouth,' she said. She set the dustpan outside the door. When she came again like a shadow on the hearth, the lad repeated, complaining sulkily:

'I canna see.'

'Good gracious!' cried the mother irritably, 'you're as bad as your father if it's a bit dusk!'

Nevertheless, she took a paper spill from a sheath on the mantelpiece and proceeded to light the lamp that hung from the ceiling in the middle of the room. As she reached up, her figure displayed itself just rounding with maternity.

'Oh, mother—!' exclaimed the girl.

'What?' said the woman, suspended in the act of putting the lamp-glass over the flame. The copper reflector shone handsomely on her, as she stood with uplifted arm, turning to face her daughter.

'You've got a flower in your apron!' said the child, in a little rapture at this unusual event.

'Goodness me!' exclaimed the woman, relieved. 'One would think the house was afire.' She replaced the glass and waited a moment before turning up the wick. A pale shadow was seen floating vaguely on the floor.

'Let me smell!' said the child, still rapturously, coming forward and putting her face to her mother's waist.

'Go along, silly!' said the mother, turning up the lamp. The light revealed their suspense so that the woman felt it almost unbearable. Annie was still bending at her waist. Irritably, the mother took the flowers out from her apron-band.

'Oh, mother—don't take them out!' Annie cried, catching her hand and trying to replace the sprig.

D. H. Lawrence

'Such nonsense!' said the mother, turning away. The child put the pale chrysanthemums to her lips, murmuring:

'Don't they smell beautiful!'

Her mother gave a short laugh.

'No,' she said, 'not to me. It was chrysanthemums when I married him, and chrysanthemums when you were born, and the first time they ever brought him home drunk, he'd got brown chrysanthemums in his button-hole.'

She looked at the children. Their eyes and their parted lips were wondering. The mother sat rocking in silence for some time. Then she looked at the clock.

'Twenty minutes to six!' In a tone of fine bitter carelessness she continued. 'Eh, he'll not come now till they bring him. There he'll stick! But he needn't come rolling in here in his pit-dirt, for *I* won't wash him. He can lie on the floor—Eh, what a fool I've been, what a fool! And this is what I came here for, to this dirty hole, rats and all, for him to slink past his very door. Twice last week—he's begun now—'

She silenced herself, and rose to clear the table.

While for an hour or more the children played, subduedly intent, fertile of imagination, united in fear of the mother's wrath, and in dread of their father's home-coming, Mrs Bates sat in her rocking-chair making a 'singlet' of thick cream-coloured flannel, which gave a dull wounded sound as she tore off the grey edge. She worked at her sewing with energy, listening to the children, and her anger wearied itself, lay down to rest, opening its eyes from time to time and steadily watching, its ears raised to listen. Sometimes even her anger quailed and shrank, and the mother suspended her sewing, tracing the footsteps that thudded along the sleepers outside; she would lift her head sharply to bid the children 'hush', but she recovered herself in time, and the footsteps went past the gate, and the children were not flung out of their play-world.

But at last Annie sighed, and gave in. She glanced at her wagon of slippers, and loathed the game. She turned plaintively to her mother.

'Mother!'—but she was inarticulate.

John crept out like a frog from under the sofa. His mother glanced up.

'Yes,' she said, 'just look at those shirt-sleeves!'

The boy held them out to survey them, saying nothing. Then somebody called in a hoarse voice away down the line, and suspense bristled in the room, till two people had gone by outside, talking.

'It is time for bed,' said the mother.

'My father hasn't come,' wailed Annie plaintively. But her mother was primed with courage.

'Never mind. They'll bring him when he does come—like a log.' She meant there would be no scene. 'And he may sleep on the floor till he wakes himself. I know he'll not go to work tomorrow after this!'

24

The children had their hands and faces wiped with a flannel. They were very quiet. When they had put on their nightdresses, they said their prayers, the boy mumbling. The mother looked down at them, at the brown silken bush of intertwining curls in the nape of the girl's neck, at the little black head of the lad, and her heart burst with anger at their father, who caused all three such distress. The children hid their faces in her skirts for comfort.

When Mrs Bates came down, the room was strangely empty, with a tension of expectancy. She took up her sewing and stitched for some time without raising her head. Meantime her anger was tinged with fear.

II

The clock struck eight and she rose suddenly, dropping her sewing on her chair. She went to the stairfoot door, opened it, listening. Then she went out, locking the door behind her.

Something scuffled in the yard, and she started, though she knew it was only the rats with which the place was over-run. The night was very dark. In the great bay of railway lines, bulked with trucks, there was no trace of light, only away back she could see a few yellow lamps at the pit-top, and the red smear of the burning pit-bank on the night. She hurried along the edge of the track, then, crossing the converging lines, came to the stile by the white gates, whence she emerged on the road. Then the fear which had led her shrank. People were walking up to New Brinsley; she saw the lights in the houses; twenty yards farther on were the broad windows of the 'Prince of Wales', very warm and bright, and the loud voices of men could be heard distinctly. What a fool she had been to imagine that anything had happened to him! He was merely drinking over there at the 'Prince of Wales'. She faltered. She had never yet been to fetch him, and she never would go. So she continued her walk towards the long straggling line of houses, standing back on the highway. She entered a passage between the dwellings.

'Mr Rigley?—Yes! Did you want him? No, he's not in at this minute.'

The raw-boned woman leaned forward from her dark scullery and peered at the other, upon whom fell a dim light through the blind of the kitchen window.

'Is it Mrs Bates?' she asked in a tone tinged with respect.

'Yes. I wondered if your Master was at home. Mine hasn't come yet.'

''Asn't 'e! Oh, Jack's been 'ome an' 'ad 'is dinner an' gone out. 'E's just gone for 'alf an hour afore bed-time. Did you call at the "Prince of Wales"?'

'No—'

'No, you didn't like—! It's not very nice.' The other woman was indulgent. There was an awkward pause. 'Jack never said nothink about—about your Mester,' she said.

'No!—I expect he's stuck in there!'

Elizabeth Bates said this bitterly, and with recklessness. She knew that the woman across the yard was standing at her door listening, but she did not care. As she turned:

'Stop a minute! I'll just go and ask Jack if 'e knows anythink,' said Mrs Rigley.

'Oh no—I wouldn't like to put—!'

'Yes, I will, if you'll just step inside an' see as th' childer doesn't come downstairs and set theirselves afire.'

Elizabeth Bates, murmuring a remonstrance, stepped inside. The other woman apologized for the state of the room.

The kitchen needed apology. There were little frocks and trousers and childish undergarments on the squab and on the floor, and a litter of play-things everywhere. On the black American cloth of the table were pieces of bread and cake, crusts, slops, and a teapot with cold tea.

'Eh, ours is just as bad,' said Elizabeth Bates, looking at the woman, not at the house. Mrs Rigley put a shawl over her head and hurried out, saying:

'I shanna be a minute.'

The other sat, noting with faint disapproval the general untidiness of the room. Then she fell to counting the shoes of various sizes scattered over the floor. There were twelve. She sighed and said to herself: 'No wonder!'—glancing at the litter. There came the scratching of two pairs of feet on the yard, and the Rigleys entered. Elizabeth Bates rose. Rigley was a big man, with very large bones. His head looked particularly bony. Across his temple was a blue scar, caused by a wound got in the pit, a wound in which the coal-dust remained blue like tattooing.

''Asna 'e come whoam yit?' asked the man, without any form of greeting, but with deference and sympathy. 'I couldna say wheer he is—'e's non ower theer!'—he jerked his head to signify the 'Prince of Wales'.

''E's 'appen gone up to th' "Yew",' said Mrs Rigley.

There was another pause. Rigley had evidently something to get off his mind.

'Ah left 'im finishin' a stint,' he began. 'Loose-all 'ad bin gone about ten minutes when we com'n away, an' I shouted: "Are ter comin', Walt?" an' 'e said: "Go on, Ah shanna be but a'ef a minnit," so we com'n ter th' bottom, me an' Bowers, thinkin' as 'e wor just behint, an' 'ud come up i' th' next bantle—'

He stood perplexed, as if answering a charge of deserting his mate. Elizabeth Bates, now again certain of disaster, hastened to reassure him:

'I expect 'e's gone up to th' "Yew Tree", as you say. It's not the first time. I've fretted myself into a fever before now. He'll come home when they carry him.'

'Ay, isn't it too bad!' deplored the other woman.

'I'll just step up to Dick's an' see if 'e *is* theer,' offered the man, afraid of appearing alarmed, afraid of taking liberties.

'Oh, I wouldn't think of bothering you that far,' said Elizabeth Bates, with emphasis, but he knew she was glad of his offer.

As they stumbled up the entry, Elizabeth Bates heard Rigley's wife run across the yard and open her neighbour's door. At this, suddenly all the blood in her body seemed to switch away from her heart.

'Mind!' warned Rigley, 'Ah've said many a time as Ah'd fill up them ruts in this entry, sumb'dy 'll be breakin' their legs yit.'

She recovered herself and walked quickly along with the miner.

'I don't like leaving the children in bed, and nobody in the house.' she said.

'No, you dunna!' he replied courteously. They were soon at the gate of the cottage.

'Well, I shanna be many minnits. Dunna you be frettin' now, 'e'll be all right,' said the butty.

'Thank you very much, Mr Rigley,' she replied.

'You're welcome!' he stammered, moving away. 'I shanna be many minnits.'

The house was quiet. Elizabeth Bates took off her hat and shawl, and rolled back the rug. When she had finished, she sat down. It was a few minutes past nine. She was startled by the rapid chuff of the winding-engine at the pit, and the sharp whirr of the brakes on the rope as it descended. Again she felt the painful sweep of her blood, and she put her hand to her side, saying aloud: 'Good gracious!—it's only the nine o'clock deputy going down,' rebuking herself.

She sat still, listening. Half an hour of this, and she was wearied out. 'What am I working myself up like this for?' she said pitiably to herself. 'I s'll only be doing myself some damage.'

She took out her sewing again.

At a quarter to ten there were footsteps. One person! She watched for the door to open. It was an elderly woman, in a black bonnet and a black woollen shawl—his mother. She was about sixty years old, pale, with blue eyes, and her face all wrinkled and lamentable. She shut the door and turned to her daughter-in-law peevishly.

'Eh, Lizzie, whatever shall we do, whatever shall we do!' she cried.

Elizabeth drew back a little, sharply.

'What is it, mother?' she said.

The elder woman seated herself on the sofa.

'I don't know, child, I can't tell you!'—she shook her head slowly. Elizabeth sat watching her, anxious and vexed.

'I don't know,' replied the grandmother, sighing very deeply. 'There's no end to my troubles, there isn't. The things I've gone through, 'm sure it's enough—!' She wept without wiping her eyes, the tears running.

'But, mother,' interrupted Elizabeth, 'what do you mean? What is it?'

The grandmother slowly wiped her eyes. The fountains of her tears were stopped by Elizabeth's directness. She wiped her eyes slowly.

'Poor child! Eh, you poor thing!' she moaned. 'I don't know what we're going to do, I don't—and you as you are—it's a thing, it is indeed!' Elizabeth waited.

'Is he dead?' she asked, and at the words her heart swung violently, though she felt a slight flush of shame at the ultimate extravagance of the question. Her words sufficiently frightened the old lady, almost brought her to herself.

'Don't say so, Elizabeth! We'll hope it's not as bad as that; no, may the Lord spare us that, Elizabeth. Jack Rigley came just as I was sittin' down to a glass afore going to bed, an' 'e said: "'Appen you'll go down th' line, Mrs Bates. Walt's had an accident. 'Appen you'll go an' sit wi' 'er till we can get him home." I hadn't time to ask him a word afore he was gone. An' I put my bonnet on an' come straight down, Lizzie. I thought to myself: "Eh, that poor blessed child, if anybody should come an' tell her of a sudden, there's no knowin' what'll 'appen to 'er." You mustn't let it upset you, Lizzie—or you know what to expect. How long is it, six months—or is it five, Lizzie? Ay!'—the old woman shook her head— 'time slips on, it slips on! Ay!'

Elizabeth's thoughts were busy elsewhere. If he was killed—would she be able to manage on the little pension and what she could earn?— she counted up rapidly. If he was hurt—they wouldn't take him to the hospital—how tiresome he would be to nurse!—but perhaps she'd be able to get him away from the drink and his hateful ways. She would— while he was ill. The tears offered to come to her eyes at the picture. But what sentimental luxury was this she was beginning? She turned to consider the children. At any rate she was absolutely necessary for them. They were her business.

'Ay!' repeated the old woman, 'it seems but a week or two since he brought me his first wages. Ay—he was a good lad, Elizabeth, he was, in his way. I don't know why he got to be such a trouble, I don't. He was a happy lad at home, only full of spirits. But there's no mistake he's been a handful of trouble, he has! I hope the Lord'll spare him to mend his ways. I hope so, I hope so. You've had a sight o' trouble with him, Elizabeth, you have indeed. But he was a jolly enough lad wi' me, was, I can assure you. I don't know how it is. . . .'

The old woman continued to muse aloud, a monotonous irritating sound, while Elizabeth thought concentratedly, startled once, when she heard the winding-engine chuff quickly, and the brakes skirr with a shriek. Then she heard the engine more slowly, and the brakes made no sound. The old woman did not notice. Elizabeth waited in suspense. The mother-in-law talked, with lapses into silence.

'But he wasn't your son, Lizzie, an' it makes a difference. Whatever he was, I remember him when he was little, an' I learned to understand him and to make allowances. You've got to make allowances for them—'

It was half-past ten, and the old woman was saying: 'But it's trouble from beginning to end; you're never too old for trouble, never too old for that—' when the gate banged back, and there were heavy feet on the steps.

'I'll go, Lizzie, let me go,' cried the old woman, rising. But Elizabeth was at the door. It was a man in pit-clothes.

'They're bringin' 'im, Missis,' he said. Elizabeth's heart halted a moment. Then it surged on again, almost suffocating her.

'Is he—is it bad?' she asked.

The man turned away, looking at the darkness:

'The doctor says 'e'd been dead hours. 'E saw 'im i' th' lamp-cabin.'

The old woman, who stood just behind Elizabeth, dropped into a chair, and folded her hands, crying: 'Oh, my boy, my boy!'

'Hush!' said Elizabeth, with a sharp twitch of a frown. 'Be still, mother, don't waken th' children: I wouldn't have them down for anything!'

The old woman moaned softly, rocking herself. The man was drawing away. Elizabeth took a step forward.

'How was it?' she asked.

'Well, I couldn't say for sure,' the man replied, very ill at ease. "E wor finishin' a stint an' th' butties 'ad gone, an' a lot o' stuff come down atop 'n 'im.'

'And crushed him?' cried the widow, with a shudder.

'No,' said the man, 'it fell at th' back of 'im. 'E wor under th' face, an' it niver touched 'im. It shut 'im in. It seems 'e wor smothered.'

Elizabeth shrank back. She heard the old woman behind her cry:

'What?—what did 'e say it was?'

The man replied, more loudly: "E wor smothered!'

Then the old woman wailed aloud, and this relieved Elizabeth.

'Oh, mother,' she said, putting her hand on the old woman, 'don't waken th' children, don't waken th' children.'

She wept a little, unknowing, while the old mother rocked herself and moaned. Elizabeth remembered that they were bringing him home, and she must be ready. 'They'll lay him in the parlour,' she said to herself, standing a moment pale and perplexed.

Then she lighted a candle and went into the tiny room. The air was cold and damp, but she could not make a fire, there was no fireplace.

She set down the candle and looked round. The candlelight glittered on the lustre-glasses, on the two vases that held some of the pink chrysanthemums, and on the dark mahogany. There was a cold, deathly smell of chrysanthemums in the room. Elizabeth stood looking at the flowers. She turned away and calculated whether there would be room to lay him on the floor, between the couch and the chiffonier. She pushed the chairs aside. There would be room to lay him down and to step around him. Then she fetched the old red tablecloth, and another old cloth, spreading them down to save her bit of carpet. She shivered on leaving the parlour; so, from the dresser drawer she took a clean shirt and put it at the fire to air. All the time her mother-in-law was rocking herself in the chair and moaning.

'You'll have to move from there, mother,' said Elizabeth. 'They'll be bringing him in. Come in the rocker.'

The old mother rose mechanically, and seated herself by the fire, continuing to lament. Elizabeth went into the pantry for another candle, and there, in the little pent-house under the naked tiles, she heard them coming. She stood still in the pantry doorway, listening. She heard them pass the end of the house, and come awkwardly down the three steps, a jumble of shuffling footsteps and muttering voices. The old woman was silent. The men were in the yard.

Then Elizabeth heard Matthews, the manager of the pit, say: 'You go in first, Jim. Mind!'

The door came open, and the two women saw a collier backing into the room, holding one end of a stretcher, on which they could see the nailed pit-boots of the dead man. The two carriers halted, the man at the head stooping to the lintel of the door.

'Wheer will you have him?' asked the manager, a short, white-bearded man.

Elizabeth roused herself and came from the pantry carrying the unlighted candle.

'In the parlour,' she said.

'In there, Jim!' pointed the manager, and the carriers backed round the tiny room. The coat with which they had covered the body fell off as they awkwardly turned through the two doorways, and the women saw their man, naked to the waist, lying stripped for work. The old woman began to moan in a low voice of horror.

'Lay th' stretcher at th' side,' snapped the manager, 'an' put 'im on th' cloths. Mind now, mind! Look you now—!'

One of the men had knocked off a vase of chrysanthemums. He stared awkwardly, then they set down the stretcher. Elizabeth did not look at her husband. As soon as she could get in the room, she went and picked up the broken vase and the flowers.

'Wait a minute!' she said.

The three men waited in silence while she mopped up the water with a duster.

'Eh, what a job, what a job, to be sure!' the manager was saying, rubbing his brow with trouble and perplexity. 'Never knew such a thing in my life, never! He'd no business to ha' been left. I never knew such a thing in my life! Fell over him clean as a whistle, an' shut him in. Not four foot of space, there wasn't—yet it scarce bruised him.'

He looked down at the dead man, lying prone, half naked, all grimed with coal-dust.

'"'Sphyxiated", the doctor said. It is the most terrible job I've ever known. Seems as if it was done o' purpose. Clean over him, an' shut 'im in, like a mouse-trap'—he made a sharp, descending gesture with his hand.

The colliers standing by jerked aside their heads in hopeless comment. The horror of the thing bristled upon them all.

Then they heard the girl's voice upstairs calling shrilly: 'Mother, mother—who is it? Mother, who is it?'

Elizabeth hurried to the foot of the stairs and opened the door:

'Go to sleep!' she commanded sharply. 'What are you shouting about? Go to sleep at once—there's nothing—'

Then she began to mount the stairs. They could hear her on the boards, and on the plaster floor of the little bedroom. They could hear her distinctly:

'What's the matter now?—what's the matter with you, silly thing?' —her voice was much agitated, with an unreal gentleness.

'I thought it was some men come,' said the plaintive voice of the child. 'Has he come?'

'Yes, they've brought him. There's nothing to make a fuss about. Go to sleep now, like a good child.'

They could hear her voice in the bedroom, they waited whilst she covered the children under the bedclothes.

'Is he drunk?' asked the girl, timidly, faintly.

'No! No—he's not! He—he's asleep.'

'Is he asleep downstairs?'

'Yes—and don't make a noise.'

There was silence for a moment, then the men heard the frightened child again:

'What's that noise?'

'It's nothing, I tell you, what are you bothering for?'

The noise was the grandmother moaning. She was oblivious of everything, sitting on her chair rocking and moaning. The manager put his hand on her arm and bade her 'Sh—sh!!'

The old woman opened her eyes and looked at him. She was shocked by this interruption, and seemed to wonder.

'What time is it?' the plaintive thin voice of the child, sinking back unhappily into sleep, asked this last question.

'Ten o'clock,' answered the mother more softly. Then she must have bent down and kissed the children.

Matthews beckoned to the men to come away. They put on their caps and took up the stretcher. Stepping over the body, they tiptoed out of the house. None of them spoke till they were far away from the wakeful children.

When Elizabeth came down she found her mother alone on the parlour floor, leaning over the dead man, the tears dropping on him.

'We must lay him out,' the wife said. She put on the kettle, then returning knelt at the feet, and began to unfasten the knotted leather laces. The room was clammy and dim with only one candle, so that she had to bend her face almost to the floor. At last she got off the heavy boots and put them away.

'You must help me now,' she whispered to the old woman. Together they stripped the man.

When they arose, saw him lying in the naïve dignity of death, the women stood arrested in fear and respect. For a few moments they remained still, looking down, the old mother whimpering. Elizabeth felt countermanded. She saw him, how utterly inviolable he lay in himself. She had nothing to do with him. She could not accept it. Stooping, she laid her hand on him, in claim. He was still warm, for the mine was hot where he had died. His mother had his face between her hands, and was murmuring incoherently. The old tears fell in succession as drops from wet leaves; the mother was not weeping, merely her tears flowed. Elizabeth embraced the body of her husband, with cheek and lips. She seemed to be listening, inquiring, trying to get some connection. But she could not. She was driven away. He was impregnable.

She rose, went into the kitchen, where she poured warm water into a bowl, brought soap and flannel and a soft towel.

'I must wash him,' she said.

Then the old mother rose stiffly, and watched Elizabeth as she carefully washed his face, carefully brushing the big blond moustache from his mouth with the flannel. She was afraid with a bottomless fear, so she ministered to him. The old woman, jealous, said:

'Let me wipe him!'—and she knelt on the other side drying slowly as Elizabeth washed, her big black bonnet sometimes brushing the dark head of her daughter-in-law. They worked thus in silence for a long time. They never forgot it was death, and the touch of the man's dead body gave them strange emotions, different in each of the women; a great dread possessed them both, the mother felt the lie was given to her womb, she was denied; the wife felt the utter isolation of the human soul, the child within her was a weight apart from her.

At last it was finished. He was a man of handsome body, and his face showed no traces of drink. He was blond, full-fleshed, with fine limbs. But he was dead.

'Bless him,' whispered his mother, looking always at his face, and speaking out of sheer terror. 'Dear lad—bless him!' She spoke in a faint sibilant ecstasy of fear and mother love.

Elizabeth sank down again to the floor, and put her face against his neck, and trembled and shuddered. But she had to draw away again. He was dead, and her living flesh had no place against his. A great dread and weariness held her: she was so unavailing. Her life was gone like this.

'White as milk he is, clear as a twelve-month baby, bless him, the darling!' the old mother murmured to herself. 'Not a mark on him, clear and clean and white, beautiful as ever a child was made,' she murmured with pride, Elizabeth kept her face hidden.

'He went peaceful, Lizzie—peaceful as sleep. Isn't he beautiful, the lamb? Ay—he must ha' made his peace, Lizzie. 'Appen he made it all right, Lizzie, shut in there. He'd have time. He wouldn't look like this if he hadn't made his peace. The lamb, the dear lamb. Eh, but he had a hearty laugh. I loved to hear it. He had the heartiest laugh, Lizzie, as a lad—'

Elizabeth looked up. The man's mouth was fallen back, slightly open under the cover of the moustache. The eyes, half shut, did not show glazed in the obscurity. Life with its smoky burning gone from him, had left him apart and utterly alien to her. And she knew what a stranger he was to her. In her womb was ice of fear, because of this separate stranger with whom she had been living as one flesh. Was this what it all meant—utter, intact separateness, obscured by heat of living? In dread she turned her face away. The fact was too deadly. There had been nothing between them, and yet they had come together, exchanging their nakedness repeatedly. Each time he had taken her, they had been two isolated beings, far apart as now. He was no more responsible than she. The child was like ice in her womb. For as she looked at the dead man, her mind, cold and detached, said clearly: 'Who am I? What have I been doing? I have been fighting a husband who did not exist. *He* existed all the time. What wrong have I done? What was that I have been living with? There lies the reality, this man.' And her soul died in her for fear: she knew she had never seen him, he had never seen her, they had met in the dark and had fought in the dark, not knowing whom they met nor whom they fought. And now she saw, and turned silent in seeing. For she had been wrong. She had said he was something he was not; she had felt familiar with him. Whereas he was apart all the while, living as she never lived, feeling as she never felt.

In fear and shame she looked at his naked body, that she had known falsely. And he was the father of her children. Her soul was torn from her body and stood apart. She looked at his naked body and was ashamed, as if she had denied it. After all, it was itself. It seemed awful to her, She looked at his face, and she turned her own face to the wall. For his look was other than hers, his way was not her way. She had denied him what he was—she saw it now. She had refused him as himself. And this had been her life, and his life. She was grateful to death, which restored the truth. And she knew she was not dead.

And all the while her heart was bursting with grief and pity for him. What had he suffered? What stretch of horror for this helpless man! She was rigid with agony. She had not been able to help him. He had been cruelly injured, this naked man, this other being, and she could make no reparation. There were the children—but the children belonged to life. This dead man had nothing to do with them. He and she were only channels through which life had flowed to issue in the children. She was a mother—but how awful she knew it now to have been a wife. And he, dead now, how awful he must have felt it to be a husband. She felt that in the next world he would be a stranger to her. If they met there, in the beyond, they would only be ashamed of what had been before. The children had come, for some mysterious reason, out of both of them. But the children did not unite them. Now he was dead, she knew how eternally he was apart from her, how eternally he had nothing more to do with her. She saw this episode of her life closed. They had denied each other in life. Now he had withdrawn. An anguish came over her. It was finished then: it had become hopeless between them long before he died. Yet he had been her husband. But how little!

'Have you got his shirt, 'Lizabeth?'

Elizabeth turned without answering, though she strove to weep and behave as her mother-in-law expected. But she could not, she was silenced. She went into the kitchen and returned with the garment.

'It is aired,' she said, grasping the cotton shirt here and there to try. She was almost ashamed to handle him; what right had she or anyone to lay hands on him: but her touch was humble on his body. It was hard work to clothe him. He was so heavy and inert. A terrible dread gripped her all the while: that he could be so heavy and utterly inert, unresponsive, apart. The horror of the distance between them was almost too much for her—it was so infinite a gap she must look across.

At last it was finished. They covered him with a sheet and left him lying, with his face bound. And she fastened the door of the little parlour, lest the children should see what was lying there. Then, with peace sunk heavy on her heart, she went about making tidy the kitchen. She knew she submitted to life, which was her immediate master. But from death, her ultimate master, she winced with fear and shame.

Franz Kafka born in Prague, in 1883, to rich Czech Jewish parents. *After commencing studies in literature and medicine, he completed a doctorate in law. The burden of routine work in an insurance office, and then as a clerk with the Worker's Compensation Bureau of the Austrian government resulted in a nervous breakdown. He fled to Berlin, to begin a life of writing. He broke off an engagement to be married, became ill with tuberculosis and went to a sanatorium, and was tormented by an acute sensitivity to his father's indifference to his literary aspirations. After suffering the 'hunger years' in post-war Berlin, he died in 1924. Although a Czech, his novels and short stories were all written in German, and were not published until after his death. The first English translations of his work appeared in 1930 and 1937.*

His short stories, especially 'METAMORPHOSIS', 'A HUNGER ARTISTE', 'IN THE PENAL SETTLEMENT', *and* 'THE GIANT MOLE', *and his major novels,* THE CASTLE *and* THE TRIAL *demonstrate his astonishing technical skills. Apparently simple tales reveal symbolic and allegorical subtleties, and the allusiveness of parables. His main characters, who usually narrate the stories, are emblems of the anguish of the contemporary man. In their unsuccessful struggles to understand the world they raise the metaphysical questions of what is right or wrong, real or illusory, true or false. Of Kafka W. H. Auden once said: 'Had one to name the artist who comes nearest to bearing the same kind of relation to our age as Dante, Shakespeare, and Goethe bore to theirs, Kafka is the first we would think of.'*

A HUNGER ARTISTE

Franz Kafka

DURING THESE LAST DECADES THE INTEREST IN PROFESSIONAL FASTING HAS markedly diminished. It used to pay very well to stage such great performances under one's own management, but to-day that is quite impossible. We live in a different world now. At one time the whole town took a lively interest in the fasting showman; from day to day of his fast the excitement mounted; everybody wanted to see him at least once a day; there were people who bought season tickets for the last few days and sat from morning till night in front of his small barred cage; even in the night-time there were visiting hours, when the whole effect was heightened by torch flares; on fine days the cage was set out in the open air, and then it was the children's special treat to see the fasting showman; for their elders he was often just a joke that happened to be in fashion, but the children stood open-mouthed, holding each other's hands for greater security, marvelling at him as he sat there pallid in black tights, with his ribs sticking out so prominently, not even on a seat but down among straw on the ground, sometimes giving a courteous nod, answering questions with a constrained smile, or perhaps stretching an arm through the bars so that one might feel how thin it was, and then again withdrawing deep into himself, paying no attention to anyone or anything, not even to the striking of the clock that was the only piece of furniture in his cage, but merely staring into vacancy with half-shut eyes, now and then taking a sip from a tiny glass of water to moisten his lips.

Besides casual onlookers there were also relays of permanent watchers selected by the public, usually butchers, strangely enough, and it was their task to watch the fasting showman day and night, three of them at a time, in case he should have some secret recourse to nourishment. This was nothing but a formality, instituted to reassure the masses, for the initiates knew well enough that during his fast the artiste would never in any circumstances, not even under forcible compulsion, swallow the smallest morsel of food; the honour of his profession forbade it. Not every watcher, of course, was capable of understanding this, there were often groups of night watchers who were very lax in carrying out their duties and deliberately huddled together in a retired corner to play cards with great absorption obviously intending to give the fasting showman the chance of a little refreshment, which they supposed he could draw from some private hoard. Nothing annoyed the artiste more than such watchers; they made him miserable; they made his fast seem unendurable; sometimes he mastered his feebleness sufficiently to sing during their watch for as long as he could keep going, to show them how unjust their suspicions were. But that was of little use; they only wondered at his cleverness in being able to fill his mouth even while singing. Much more to his taste were the watchers who sat close up to the bars, who were not content with the dim night lighting of the hall but focused him in the full glare of the electric pocket-torch given them by the impresario. The harsh light did not trouble him at all, in any case he could never sleep properly, and he could always drowse a little, whatever the light, at any hour, even when the hall was thronged with noisy onlookers. He was quite happy at the prospect of spending a sleepless night with such watchers; he was ready to exchange jokes with them, to tell them stories out of his nomadic life, anything at all to keep them awake and demonstrate to them again that he had no eatables in his cage and that he was fasting as not one of them could fast. But his happiest moment was when the morning came and an enormous breakfast was brought them, at his expense, on which they flung themselves with the keen appetites of healthy men after a weary night of wakefulness. Of course there were people who argued that this breakfast was an unfair attempt to bribe the watchers, but that was going rather too far, and when they were invited to take on a night's vigil without a breakfast, merely for the sake of the cause, they made themselves scarce, although they stuck stubbornly to their suspicions.

Such suspicions, anyhow, were a necessary accompaniment to the profession of fasting. No one could possibly watch the fasting showman continuously, day and night, and so no one could produce first hand evidence that the fast had really been rigorous and continuous; only the artiste himself could know that, he was, therefore, bound to be the sole completely satisfied spectator of his own fast. Yet for other reasons he was never satisfied; it was not perhaps mere fasting that had brought him to such skeleton thinness that many people had regretfully to keep away from his exhibitions because the sight of him was too much for them, perhaps it was dissatisfaction with himself that had worn him down. For he alone knew, what no other initiate knew, how easy it was to fast. It was the easiest thing in the world. He made no secret of this, yet people did not believe him, at the best they set him down as modest, most of them however thought he was out for publicity or else was some kind of cheat who found it easy to fast because he had discovered a way of getting round it, and then had the impudence to admit the fact, more or less. He had to put up with all that, and in the course of time had got used to it, but his inner dissatisfaction always rankled, and never yet, after any term of fasting—this must be granted to his credit—had he left the cage of his own free will. The longest time he could fast was fixed by his impresario at forty days, beyond that term he was not allowed to go—not even in great cities, and there was good reason for it, too. Experience had proved that for about forty days the interest of the public could be stimulated by steady pressure of advertisement, but after that the town began to lose interest, sympathetic support began notably to fall off; there were, of course, local variations as between one town and another or one country and another, but as a general rule forty days marked the limit. So on the fortieth day the flower-bedecked cage was opened, enthusiastic spectators filled the hall, a military band played, two doctors entered the cage to measure the results of the fast, which were announced through a megaphone, and finally two young ladies appeared, blissful at having been selected for the honour, to help the fasting showman down the few steps leading to a small table on which was spread a carefully chosen invalid repast. And at this very moment the artiste always turned stubborn. True, he would entrust his bony arms to the outstretched helping hands of the ladies bending over him, but stand up he would not. Why stop fasting at this particular moment, after forty days of it? He had held out for a long time, an illimitably long time; why stop now, when he was in his best fasting form, or rather, not yet quite in his best fasting form? Why should he be cheated of the fame he would get for fasting longer, for being not only the record fasting showman of all time—which presumably he was already—but for beating his own record by a performance beyond human imagination, since he felt that there were no limits to his capacity for fasting. His public pretended to admire him so much, why should it have so little patience with him; if he could endure fasting longer, why shouldn't the public endure it? Besides, he was tired, he was comfortable sitting in the straw, and now he was supposed to lift himself to his full height and go down to a meal the very thought of which gave him a nausea that only the presence of the ladies kept him from betraying, and even that with an effort. And he looked up into the eyes of the ladies who were apparently so friendly and in reality so cruel, and shook his head, which felt too heavy on its strengthless neck. But then there happened yet again what always happened. The impresario came forward, without a word—for the band made speech impossible—lifted his arms in the air above the artiste, as if inviting Heaven to look down upon its creature here in the straw, this suffering martyr, which indeed he was, although in quite another sense; grasped him round the emaciated waist, with exaggerated caution, so that the frail condition he was in might be appreciated; and committed him to the care of the blenching ladies, not without secretly giving him a shaking so that his legs and body tottered and swayed. The artiste now submitted completely; his head lolled on his breast as if it had landed there by chance, his body was hollowed out, his legs in a spasm of self-preservation clung close to each other at the knees, yet scraped on the ground as if it were not really solid ground, as if they were only trying to find solid ground; and the whole weight of his body, a featherweight after all, relapsed on to one of the ladies, who, looking round for help and panting a little—this post of honour was not at all what she had expected it to be—first stretched her neck as far as she could to keep her face at least free from contact with the artiste, then finding this impossible, and her more fortunate companion not coming to her aid but merely holding extended on her own trembling hand the little bunch of knuckle bones that was the artiste's, to the great delight of the spectators burst into tears and had to be replaced by an attendant who had long been stationed in readiness. Then came the food, a little of which the impresario managed to get between the artiste's lips, while he sat in a kind of half-fainting trance, to the accompaniment of cheerful patter designed to distract the public's attention from the artiste's condition; after that, a toast was drunk to the public, supposedly prompted by a whisper from the artiste in the impresario's ear; the band confirmed it with a mighty flourish, the spectators melted away, and no one had any cause to be dissatisfied with the proceedings, no one except the fasting showman himself, he only, as always.

So he lived for many years, with small regular intervals of recuperation, in visible glory, honoured by the world, yet in spite of that troubled in spirit, and all the more troubled because no one would take his trouble seriously. What comfort could he possibly need? What more could he possibly wish for? And if some good-natured person, feeling sorry for him, tried to console him by pointing out that his melancholy was probably caused by fasting, it could happen, especially when he had been fasting for some time, that he reacted with an outburst of fury and to the general alarm began to shake the bars of his cage like a wild animal. Yet the impresario had a way of punishing these outbreaks which he rather enjoyed putting into operation. He would apologize publicly for the artiste's behaviour, which was only to be excused, he admitted, because of the irritability caused by fasting; a condition hardly to be understood by well-fed people; then by natural transition he went on to mention the artiste's equally incomprehensible boast that he could fast for much longer than he was doing; he praised the high ambition, the goodwill, the great self-denial undoubtedly implicit in such a statement; and then quite simply countered it by bringing out photographs, which were also on sale to the public, showing the artiste on the fortieth day of a fast lying in bed almost dead from exhaustion. This perversion of the truth, familiar to the artiste though it was, always unnerved him afresh and proved too much for him. What was a consequence of the premature ending of his fast was here presented as the cause of it! To fight against this lack of under-standing, against a whole world of non-understanding, was impossible. Time and again in good faith he stood by the bars listening to the impresario, but as soon as the photographs appeared he always let go and sank with a groan back on to his straw, and the reassured public could once more come close and gaze at him.

A few years later when the witnesses of such scenes called them to mind, they often failed to understand themselves at all. For meanwhile the aforementioned change in public interest had set in; it seemed to happen almost overnight; there may have been profound causes for it, but who was going to bother about that? At any rate the pampered fasting show-man suddenly found himself deserted one fine day by the amusement seekers, who went streaming past him to other more favoured attractions. For the last time the impresario hurried him over half Europe to discover whether the old interest might still survive here and there; all in vain; everywhere, as if by secret agreement, a positive revulsion from pro-fessional fasting was in evidence. Of course it could not really have sprung up so suddenly as all that, and many premonitory symptoms which had not been sufficiently remarked or suppressed during the rush and glitter of success now came retrospectively to mind, but it was now too late to take any counter-measures. Fasting would surely come into fashion again at some future date, yet that was no comfort for those living in the present. What, then, was the fasting showman to do? He had been applauded by thousands in his time and could hardly come down to showing himself in a street booth at village fairs, and as for adopting another profession, he was not only too old for that but too fanatically devoted to fasting. So he took leave of the impresario, his partner in an unparalleled career, and hired himself to a large circus; in order to spare his own feelings he avoided reading the conditions of his contract.

A large circus with its enormous traffic in replacing and recruiting men, animals and apparatus, can always find a use for people at any time, even for a fasting showman, provided, of course, that he does not ask too much, and in this particular case anyhow it was not only the artiste who was taken on but his famous and long-known name as well, indeed, consider-ing the peculiar nature of his performance, which was not impaired by advancing age, it could not be objected that here was an artiste past his prime, no longer at the height of his professional skill, seeking a refuge in some quiet corner of a circus; on the contrary, the fasting showman averred that he could fast as well as ever, which was entirely credible, he even alleged that if he were allowed to fast as he liked, and this was at once promised him without more ado, he could astound the world by establishing a record never yet achieved, a statement which certainly provoked a smile among the other professionals, since it left out of account the change in public opinion, which the fasting showman in his zeal conveniently forgot.

He had not, however, actually lost his sense of the real situation and took it as a matter of course that he and his cage should be stationed, not in the middle of the ring as a main attraction, but outside, near the animal cages, on a site that was after all easily accessible. Large and gaily painted placards made a frame for the cage and announced what was to be seen inside it. When the public came thronging out in the intervals to see the animals, they could hardly avoid passing the fasting showman's cage and stopping there for a moment, perhaps they might even have stayed longer had not those pressing behind them in the narrow gangway, who did not understand why they should be held up on their way towards the excitements of the menagerie, made it impossible for anyone to stand gazing quietly for any length of time. And that was the reason why the fasting showman, who had of course been looking forward to these visiting hours as the main achievement of his life, began instead to shrink from them. At first he could hardly wait for the intervals; it was exhilarating to watch the crowds come streaming his way, until only too soon—not even the most obstinate self-deception, clung to almost consciously, could hold out against the fact—the conviction was borne in upon him that these people, most of them, to judge from their actions, again and again, without exception, were all on their way to the menagerie. And the first sight of them from the distance remained the best. For when they reached his cage he was at once deafened by the storm of shouting and abuse that arose from the two contending factions, which renewed themselves continuously, of those who wanted to stop and stare at him—he soon began to hate them more than the others—not out of real interest but only out of obstinate self-assertiveness, and those who wanted to go straight on to the animals. When the first great rush was past, the stragglers came along, and these, whom nothing could have prevented from stopping to look at him as long as they had breath, raced past with long strides, hardly even glancing at him, in their haste to get to the menagerie in time. And all too rarely did it happen that he had a stroke of luck, when some father of a family fetched up before him with his children, pointed a finger at the fasting showman and explained at length what the phenomenon meant, telling stories of earlier years when he himself had watched similar but much more thrilling performances, and the children, still rather incomprehending, since neither inside nor outside school had they been sufficiently prepared for this lesson—fasting was a commonplace to them—yet showed by the brightness of their intent eyes that new and better times might be coming. Perhaps, said the fasting showman to himself many a time, things would be a little better if his cage were set not quite so near the menagerie. That made it too easy for people to make their choice—to say nothing of what he suffered from the stench of the menagerie, the animals' restlessness by night, the carrying past of raw lumps of flesh for the beasts of prey, the roaring at feeding times, which depressed him continually. But he did not dare to present himself in person to the management; after all, he had the animals to thank for the troops of people who passed his cage, among whom there might always be one here and there to take an interest in him, and who could tell where they might seclude him if he called attention to his existence and thereby to the fact that, strictly speaking, he was only an impediment on the way to the menagerie?

A small impediment, to be sure, one that grew steadily less. People grew familiar with the strange idea that they could be expected, in times like these, to take an interest in a fasting showman, and with this familiarity the verdict went out against him. He might fast as much as he could, and he did so; but nothing could save him now, people passed him by. Just try to explain to anyone the art of fasting! Anyone who has no feeling for it cannot be made to understand it. The fine placards grew dirty and illegible, they were torn down; the little noticeboard telling the number of fast-days achieved, which at first was changed carefully every day, had long stayed at the same figure, for after the first few weeks even this small task seemed pointless to the staff; and so the artiste simply fasted on and on, as he had once dreamed of doing, and it was no trouble to him, just as he had always foretold, but no one counted the days, no one, not even the artiste himself, knew what records he was already breaking, and his heart grew heavy. And when once in a time some leisurely passer-by stopped, made merry over the old figure on the board and spoke of swindling, that was in its way the stupidest lie ever invented by indifference and inborn malice, since it was not the fasting showman who was cheating, he was working honestly, but the world was cheating him of his reward.

More days went by, however, and that too came to an end. An overseer's eye fell on the cage one day and he asked the attendants why this perfectly good cage should be left standing there unused with dirty straw inside it; nobody knew, until one man, helped out by the noticeboard, remembered about the fasting showman. They poked into the straw with sticks and found him in it. 'Are you still fasting?' asked the overseer. 'When on earth do you mean to stop?' 'Forgive me, everybody,' whispered the fasting showman; only the overseer, who had his ear to the bars, understood him. 'Of course,' said the overseer and tapped his forehead with a finger to let the attendants know what state the man was in, 'we forgive you.' 'I always wanted you to admire my fasting,' said the fasting showman. 'We do admire it,' said the overseer, affably. 'But you shouldn't admire it,' said the fasting showman. 'Well then we don't admire it,' said the overseer, 'but why shouldn't we admire it?' 'Because I have to fast, I can't do anything else,' said the fasting showman. 'What a fellow you are,' said the overseer, 'and why can't you do anything else?' 'Because,' said the fasting showman, lifting his head a little and speaking with his lips pursed, as if for a kiss, right into the overseer's ear, so that no syllable might be lost, 'because I couldn't find any food I liked. If I had found any, believe me, I should have made no bones about it and stuffed myself like you or anyone else.' These were his last words, but in his dimming eyes remained the firm though no longer proud persuasion that he was still continuing to fast.

'Well, clear this out now!' said the overseer, and they buried the fasting showman, straw and all. Into the cage they put a young panther. Even the most insensitive felt it refreshing to see this wild creature leaping around the cage that had so long been dreary. The panther was all right. The food he liked was brought him without hesitation by the attendants; he seemed not even to miss his freedom; his noble body, furnished almost to bursting point with all that it needed, seemed to carry freedom around with it too; somewhere in his jaws it seemed to lurk; and the joy of life streamed with such ardent passion from his throat that for the onlookers it was not easy to stand the shock of it. But they braced themselves, crowded round the cage, and did not want ever to move away.

James Joyce born 1882 in Dublin, Ireland. *The eldest of ten children, Joyce was educated at school and university in Dublin. He left Ireland for Paris at the age of twenty, but returned when his mother was dying in 1903. After teaching in a school for a short time he eloped with his wife-to-be to Switzerland, then moved to Trieste, where he taught languages in the Berlitz School. Although he returned only once for a brief period to his homeland, for which he harboured contradictory feelings of attraction and repulsion, all Joyce's stories and novels are firmly set in Ireland. He died in Switzerland in 1941. Often unconventional in behaviour, Joyce brought a refreshing spirit of experiment to prose writing, particularly in his three outstanding though difficult novels,* A PORTRAIT OF THE ARTIST AS A YOUNG MAN, ULYSSES, *and* FINNEGANS WAKE.

Throughout his work, the experiences of insignificant city dwellers are given prominence. Although signs of an early interest in people's psychological processes are apparent in DUBLINERS (*the collection from which* 'CLAY' *is taken*), *Joyce's 'stream of consciousness' techniques are more fully developed in the novels. Nevertheless, a story like* 'CLAY' *is deceptively simple. It is noticeable how, for instance, the almost child-like prose simulates Maria's simple, uneducated thinking, with which we are therefore better able to sympathise. The reader has to work too, in searching for the meaning of Maria's life and for the significance of the story's title. Here is a writer who expects an effort on the part of his reader.*

Suggested further reading: 'THE SISTERS', 'A PAINFUL CASE', 'THE DEAD', *in* DUBLINERS, *1914.*

CLAY

James Joyce

THE MATRON HAD GIVEN HER LEAVE TO GO OUT AS SOON AS THE WOMEN'S tea was over, and Maria looked forward to her evening out. The kitchen was spick and span: the cook said you could see yourself in the big copper boilers. The fire was nice and bright and on one of the side-tables were four very big barmbracks. These barmbracks seemed uncut; but if you went closer you would see that they had been cut into long thick even slices and were ready to be handed round at tea. Maria had cut them herself.

Maria was a very, very small person indeed, but she had a very long nose and a very long chin. She talked a little through her nose, always soothingly: 'Yes, my dear,' and 'No, my dear.' She was always sent for when the women quarrelled over their tubs and always succeeded in making peace. One day the matron had said to her:

'Maria, you are a veritable peace-maker!'

And the sub-matron and two of the Board ladies had heard the compliment. And Ginger Mooney was always saying what she wouldn't do to the dummy who had charge of the irons if it wasn't for Maria. Everyone was so fond of Maria.

The women would have their tea at six o'clock and she would be able to get away before seven. From Ballsbridge to the Pillar, twenty minutes; from the Pillar to Drumcondra, twenty minutes; and twenty minutes to buy the things. She would be there before eight. She took out her purse with the silver clasps and read again the words *A Present from Belfast*. She was very fond of that purse because Joe had brought it to her five years before when he and Alphy had gone to Belfast on a Whit-Monday trip. In the purse were two half-crowns and some coppers. She would have five shillings clear after paying tram fare. What a nice evening they would have, all the children singing! Only she hoped that Joe wouldn't come in drunk. He was so different when he took any drink.

Often he had wanted her to go and live with them; but she would have felt herself in the way (though Joe's wife was ever so nice with her) and she had become accustomed to the life of the laundry. Joe was a good fellow. She had nursed him and Alphy too; and Joe used often to say:

'Mamma is mamma, but Maria is my proper mother.'

After the break-up at home the boys had got her that position in the *Dublin by Lamplight* laundry, and she liked it. She used to have such a bad opinion of Protestants, but now she thought they were very nice people, a little quiet and serious, but still very nice people to live with. Then she had her plants in the conservatory and she liked looking after them. She had lovely ferns and wax-plants and, whenever anyone came to visit her, she always gave the visitor one or two slips from her conservatory. There was one thing she didn't like and that was the tracts on the walls; but the matron was such a nice person to deal with, so genteel.

When the cook told her everything was ready she went into the women's room and began to pull the big bell. In a few minutes the women began to come in by twos and threes, wiping their steaming hands in their petticoats and pulling down the sleeves of their blouses over their red steaming arms. They settled down before their huge mugs which the cook and the dummy filled up with hot tea, already mixed with milk and sugar in huge tin cans. Maria superintended the distribution of the barmbrack and saw that every woman got her four slices. There was a great deal of laughing and joking during the meal. Lizzie Fleming said Maria was sure to get the ring and, though Fleming had said that for so many Hallow Eves, Maria had to laugh and say she didn't want any ring or man either; and when she laughed her grey-green eyes sparkled with disappointed shyness and the tip of her nose nearly met the tip of her chin. Then Ginger Mooney lifted up her mug of tea and proposed Maria's health, while all the other women clattered with their mugs on the table, and said she was sorry she hadn't a sup of porter to drink it in. And Maria laughed again till the tip of her nose nearly met the tip of her chin and till her minute body nearly shook itself asunder, because she knew that Mooney meant well, though of course she had the notions of a common woman.

But wasn't Maria glad when the women had finished their tea and the cook and the dummy had begun to clear away the tea-things! She went into her little bedroom and, remembering that the next morning was a mass morning, changed the hand of the alarm from seven to six. Then she took off her working skirt and her house-boots and laid her best skirt out on the bed and her tiny dress-boots beside the foot of the bed. She changed her blouse too and, as she stood before the mirror, she thought of how she used to dress for mass on Sunday morning when she was a young girl; and she looked with quaint affection at the diminutive body which she had so often adorned. In spite of its years she found it a nice tidy little body.

When she got outside the streets were shining with rain and she was glad of her old brown waterproof. The tram was full and she had to sit on the little stool at the end of the car, facing all the people, with her toes barely touching the floor. She arranged in her mind all she was going to do, and thought how much better it was to be independent and to have your own money in your pocket. She hoped they would have a nice evening. She was sure they would, but she could not help thinking what a pity it was Alphy and Joe were not speaking. They were always falling out now, but when they were boys together they used to be the best of friends; but such was life.

She got out of her tram at the Pillar and ferreted her way quickly among the crowds. She went into Downes's cake-shop but the shop was so full of people that it was a long time before she could get herself attended to. She bought a dozen of mixed penny cakes, and at last came out of the shop laden with a big bag. Then she thought what else would she buy: she wanted to buy something really nice. They would be sure to have plenty of apples and nuts. It was hard to know what to buy and all she could think of was cake. She decided to buy some plumcake, but Downes's plumcake had not enough almond icing on top of it, so she went over to a shop in Henry Street. Here she was a long time in suiting herself, and the stylish young lady behind the counter, who was evidently a little annoyed by her, asked her was it wedding-cake she wanted to buy. That made Maria blush and smile at the young lady; but the young lady took it all very seriously and finally cut a thick slice of plumcake, parcelled it up and said:

'Two-and-four, please.'

She thought she would have to stand in the Drumcondra tram because none of the young men seemed to notice her, but an elderly gentleman made room for her. He was a stout gentleman and he wore a brown hard hat; he had a square red face and a greyish moustache. Maria thought he was a colonel-looking gentleman and she reflected how much more polite he was than the young men who simply stared straight before them. The gentleman began to chat with her about Hallow Eve and the rainy weather. He supposed the bag was full of good things for the little ones and said it was only right that the youngestrs should enjoy themselves while they were young. Maria agreed with him and favoured him with demure nods and hems. He was very nice with her, and when she was getting out at the Canal Bridge she thanked him and bowed, and he bowed to her and raised his hat and smiled agreeably; and while she was going up along the terrace, bending her tiny head under the rain, she thought how easy it was to know a gentleman even when he has a drop taken.

Everybody said: 'O, *here's Maria!*' when she came to Joe's house. Joe was there, having come home from business, and all the children had their Sunday dresses on. There were two big girls in from next door and games were going on. Maria gave the bag of cakes to the eldest boy, Alphy, to divide, and Mrs Donnelly said it was too good of her to bring such a big bag of cakes, and made all the children say:

'Thanks, Maria.'

But Maria said she had brought something special for papa and mamma, something they would be sure to like, and she began to look for her plumcake. She tried in Downes's bag and then in the pockets of her waterproof and then on the hallstand, but nowhere could she find it. Then she asked all the children had any of them eaten it—by mistake, of course—but the children all said no and looked as if they did not like to eat cakes if they were to be accused of stealing. Everybody had a solution for the mystery and Mrs Donnelly said it was plain that Maria had left it behind her in the tram. Maria, remembering how confused the gentleman with the greyish moustache had made her, coloured with shame and vexation and disappointment. At the thought of the failure of her little surprise and of the two and fourpence she had thrown away for nothing she nearly cried outright.

But Joe said it didn't matter and made her sit down by the fire. He was very nice with her. He told her all that went on in his office, repeating for her a smart answer which he had made to the manager. Maria did not understand why Joe laughed so much over the answer he had made, but she said that the manager must have been a very overbearing person to deal with. Joe said he wasn't so bad when you knew how to take him, that he was a decent sort so long as you didn't rub him the wrong way. Mrs Donnelly played the piano for the children and they danced and sang. Then the two next-door girls handed round the nuts. Nobody could find the nutcrackers, and Joe was nearly getting cross over it and asked how did they expect Maria to crack nuts without a nutcracker. But Maria said she didn't like nuts and that they weren't to bother about her. Then Joe asked would she take a bottle of stout, and Mrs Donnelly said there was port wine too in the house if she would prefer that. Maria said she would rather they didn't ask her to take anything: but Joe insisted.

So Maria let him have his way and they sat by the fire talking over old times and Maria thought she would put in a good word for Alphy. But Joe cried that God might strike him stone dead if ever he spoke a word to his brother again and Maria said she was sorry she had mentioned the matter. Mrs Donnelly told her husband it was a great shame for him to speak that way of his own flesh and blood, but Joe said that Alphy was no brother of his and there was nearly being a row on the head of it. But Joe said he would not lose his temper on account of the night it was, and asked his wife to open some more stout. The two next-door girls had arranged some Hallow Eve games and soon everything was merry again. Maria was delighted to see the children so merry and Joe and his wife in such good spirits. The next-door girls put some saucers on the table and then led the children up to the table, blindfold. One got the prayer-book and the other three got the water; and when one of the next-door girls got the ring Mrs Donnelly shook her finger at the blushing girl as much as to say: *O, I know all about it!* They insisted then on blindfolding Maria and leading her up to the table to see what she would get; and, while they were putting on the bandage, Maria laughed and laughed again till the tip of her nose nearly met the tip of her chin.

They led her up to the table amid laughing and joking, and she put her hand out in the air, as she was told to do. She moved her hand about here and there in the air and descended on one of the saucers. She felt a soft wet substance with her fingers and was surprised that nobody spoke or took off her bandage. There was a pause for a few seconds; and then a great deal of scuffling and whispering. Somebody said something about the garden, and at last Mrs Donnelly said something very cross to one of the next-door girls and told her to throw it out at once: that was no play. Maria understood that it was wrong that time and so she had to do it over again: and this time she got the prayer-book.

After that Mrs Donnelly played Miss McCloud's Reel for the children, and Joe made Maria take a glass of wine. Soon they were all quite merry again, and Mrs Donnelly said Maria would enter a convent before the year was out because she had got the prayer-book. Maria had never seen Joe so nice to her as he was that night, so full of pleasant talk and reminiscences. She said they were all very good to her.

At last the children grew tired and sleepy and Joe asked Maria would she not sing some little song before she went, one of the old songs. Mrs Donnelly said 'Do please, Maria!' and so Maria had to get up and stand beside the piano. Mrs Donnelly bade the children be quiet and listen to Maria's song. Then she played the prelude and said 'Now, Maria!' and Maria, blushing very much, began to sing in a tiny quavering voice. She sang 'I Dreamt that I Dwelt', and when she came to the second verse she sang again:

> *I dreamt that I dwelt in marble halls*
> *With vassals and serfs at my side,*
> *And of all who assembled within those walls*
> *That I was the hope and the pride.*

> *I had riches too great to count, could boast*
> *Of a high ancestral name,*
> *But I also dreamt, which pleased me most,*
> *That you loved me still the same.*

But no one tried to show her her mistake; and when she had ended her song Joe was very much moved. He said that there was no time like the long ago and no music for him like poor old Balfe, whatever other people might say; and his eyes filled up so much with tears that he could not find what he was looking for and in the end he had to ask his wife to tell him where the corkscrew was.

Thomas Wolfe born 1900 in Asheville, North Carolina. He studied at the University of North Carolina from 1916 to 1920, and took a master's degree at Harvard in 1922. He travelled abroad, and from 1924 to 1930 taught English at Washington College of New York University. In 1930 he resigned to write and travel abroad on a Guggenheim fellowship. His first novel, LOOK HOMEWARD ANGEL, in 1929, appeared to be close to his early youth and his family and home town. His novels were long, and all much reduced from his original manuscripts. His editor, Maxwell Perkins cut more than fifty thousand words from OF TIME AND THE RIVER. His love of detail, and his tendency to over-write was obvious in the novels, and their final form owed much to his editor. Wolfe is less well known for his stories, his style and method being much more suited to the novel. Apart from the novels above, he wrote THE WEB AND THE ROCK, published in 1939, and stories and sketches in FROM DEATH TO MORNING, 1935.

Wolfe died in 1938.

THE FAR AND THE NEAR

Thomas Wolfe

ON THE OUTSKIRTS OF A LITTLE TOWN UPON A RISE OF LAND THAT SWEPT back from the railway there was a tidy little cottage of white boards, trimmed vividly with green blinds. To one side of the house there was a garden neatly patterned with plots of growing vegetables, and an arbor for the grapes which ripened late in August. Before the house there were three mighty oaks which sheltered it in their clean and massive shade in summer, and to the other side there was a border of gay flowers. The whole place had an air of tidiness, thrift, and modest comfort.

Every day, a few minutes after two o'clock in the afternoon, the limited express between two cities passed this spot. At that moment the great train, having halted for a breathing-space at the town near by, was beginning to lengthen evenly into its stroke, but it had not yet reached the full drive of its terrific speed. It swung into view deliberately, swept past with a powerful swaying motion of the engine, a low smooth rumble of its heavy cars upon pressed steel, and then it vanished in the cut. For a moment the progress of the engine could be marked by heavy bellowing puffs of smoke that burst at spaced intervals above the edges of the meadow grass, and finally nothing could be heard but the solid clacking tempo of the wheels receding into the drowsy stillness of the afternoon.

Every day for more than twenty years, as the train had approached this house, the engineer had blown on the whistle, and every day, as soon as she heard this signal, a woman had appeared on the back porch of the little house and waved to him. At first she had a small child clinging to her skirts, and now this child had grown to full womanhood, and every day she, too, came with her mother to the porch and waved.

The engineer had grown old and gray in service. He had driven his great train, loaded with its weight of lives, across the land ten thousand times. His own children had grown up and married, and four times he had seen before him on the tracks the ghastly dot of tragedy converging like a cannon-ball to its eclipse of horror at the boiler heat—a light spring-wagon filled with children, with its clustered row of small stunned faces; a cheap automobile stalled upon the tracks, set with the wooden figures of people paralyzed with fear; a battered hobo walking by the rail, too deaf and old to hear the whistle's warning; and a form flung past his window with a scream—all this the man had seen and known. He had known all the grief, the joy, the peril and the labor such a man could know; he had grown seamed and weathered in his loyal service, and now, schooled by the qualities of faith and courage and humbleness that attended his labor, he had grown old, and had the grandeur and the wisdom these men have.

But no matter what peril or tragedy he had known, the vision of the little house and the women waving to him with a brave free motion of the arm had become fixed in the mind of the engineer as something beautiful and enduring, something beyond all change and ruin, and something that would always be the same, no matter what mishap, grief or error might break the iron schedule of his days.

The sight of the little house and of these two women gave him the most extraordinary happiness he had ever known. He had seen them in a thousand lights, a hundred weathers. He had seen them through the harsh bare light of wintry gray across the brown and frosted stubble of the earth, and he had seen them again in the green luring sorcery of April.

He felt for them and for the little house in which they lived such tenderness as a man might feel for his own children, and at length the picture of their lives was carved so sharply in his heart that he felt that he knew their lives completely, to every hour and moment of the day, and he resolved that one day, when his years of service should be ended, he would go and find these people and speak at last with them whose lives had been so wrought into his own.

That day came. At last the engineer stepped from a train onto the station platform of the town where these two women lived. His years upon the rail had ended. He was a pensioned servant of his company, with no more work to do. The engineer walked slowly through the station and out into the streets of the town. Everything was as strange to him as if he had never seen this town before. As he walked on, his sense of bewilderment and confusion grew. Could this be the town he had passed ten thousand times? Were these the same houses he had seen so often from the high windows of his cab? It was all as unfamiliar, as disquieting as a city in a dream, and the perplexity of his spirit increased as he went on.

Presently the houses thinned into the straggling outposts of the town, and the street faded into a country road—the one on which the women lived. And the man plodded on slowly in the heat and dust. At length he stood before the house he sought. He knew at once that he had found the proper place. He saw the lordly oaks before the house, the flower beds, the garden and the arbor, and farther off, the glint of rails.

Yes, this was the house he sought, the place he had passed so many times, the destination he had longed for with such happiness. But now that he had found it, now that he was here, why did his hand falter on the gate; why had the town, the road, the earth, the very entrance to this place he loved turned unfamiliar as the landscape of some ugly dreams? Why did he now feel this sense of confusion, doubt, and hopelessness?

At length he entered by the gate, walked slowly up the path and in a moment more had mounted three short steps that led up to the porch and was knocking at the door. Presently he heard steps in the hall, the door was opened, and a woman stood facing him.

And instantly, with a sense of bitter loss and grief, he was sorry he had come. He knew at once that the woman who stood there looking at him with a mistrustful eye was the same woman who had waved to him so many thousand times. But her face was harsh and pinched and meager; the flesh sagged wearily in sallow folds, and the small eyes peered at him with timid suspicion and uneasy doubt. All the brave freedom, the warmth and the affection that he had read into her gesture, vanished in the moment that he saw her and heard her unfriendly tongue.

And now his own voice sounded unreal and ghastly to him as he tried to explain his presence, to tell her who he was and the reason he had come. But he faltered on, fighting stubbornly against the horror of regret, confusion, disbelief that surged up in his spirit, drowning all his former joy and making his act of hope and tenderness seem shameful to him.

At length the woman invited him almost unwillingly into the house, and called her daughter in a harsh shrill voice. Then, for a brief agony of time, the man sat in an ugly little parlor, and he tried to talk while the two women stared at him with a dull, bewildered hostility, a sullen, timorous restraint.

And finally, stammering a crude farewell, he departed. He walked away down the path and then along the road toward town, and suddenly he knew that he was an old man. His heart, which had been brave and confident when it looked along the familiar vista of the rails, was now sick with doubt and horror as it saw the strange and unsuspected visage of an earth which had always been within a stone's throw of him, and which he had never seen or known. And he knew that all the magic of that bright lost way, the vista of that shining line, the imagined corner of that small good universe of hope's desire, was gone forever, could never be got back again.

James Thurber *born in Columbus, Ohio, in 1894, and educated at Ohio University. He lost the sight in one eye when young, and became totally blind in later life. He explained that this dictated the form of his line drawings, as he had only partial cognisance of the shape and area of the objects he was drawing. He worked as a code clerk with the United States State Department, and as a journalist for the Columbus* DISPATCH, *and then the Chicago* TRIBUNE. *In 1926 he joined the* EVENING POST, *and became a regular contributor of line drawings and witty stories to* THE NEW YORKER, *in which most of his best work appeared. He collaborated with Elliott Nugent in writing* 'THE MALE ANIMAL' *which, like* 'THE SECRET LIFE OF WALTER MITTY', *was later made into a film.*

'To me', he once wrote, 'humour is a kind of emotional chaos told about calmly and quietly in retrospect.' His stories employ the natural, vernacular tradition established by Mark Twain. His more symbolic, imaginative stories, like 'IN THE MAZE', *include an element of irony characteristic of more recent American writers dealing with folk characters and situations. Yet in both his stories and his line drawings, he is an admirable technician, who achieves a highly personal idiom. The fantasies of his small, sad men are at once hilarious and evocative of pathos. His parodies are both incisively critical and sympathetic.*

Probably the best collection of his work is to be found in THE CREAM OF THURBER, *1939.*

He died in 1961.

THE CATBIRD SEAT

James Thurber

MR MARTIN BOUGHT THE PACK OF CAMELS ON MONDAY NIGHT IN THE MOST crowded cigar store on Broadway. It was theatre time and seven or eight men were buying cigarettes. The clerk didn't even glance at Mr Martin, who put the pack in his overcoat pocket and went out. If any of the staff at F & S had seen him buy the cigarettes, they would have been astonished, for it was generally known that Mr Martin did not smoke, and never had. No one saw him.

It was just a week to the day since Mr Martin had decided to rub out Mrs Ulgine Barrows. The term 'rub out' pleased him because it suggested nothing more than the correction of an error—in this case an error of Mr Fitweiler. Mr Martin had spent each night of the past week working out his plan and examining it. As he walked home now he went over it again. For the hundredth time he resented the element of imprecision, the margin of guesswork that entered into the business. The project as he had worked it out was casual and bold, the risks were considerable. Something might go wrong anywhere along the line. And therein lay the cunning of his scheme. No one would ever see in it the cautious, painstaking hand of Erwin Martin, head of the filing department at F & S, of whom Mr Fitweiler had once said, 'Man is fallible but Martin isn't.' No one would see his hand, that is, unless it were caught in the act.

Sitting in his apartment, drinking a glass of milk, Mr Martin reviewed his case against Mrs Ulgine Barrows, as he had every night for seven nights. He began at the beginning. Her quacking voice and braying laugh had first profaned the halls of F & S on March 7, 1941 (Mr Martin had a head for dates). Old Roberts, the personnel chief, had introduced her as the newly appointed special adviser to the president of the firm, Mr Fitweiler. The woman had appalled Mr Martin instantly, but he hadn't shown it. He had given her his dry hand, a look of studious concentration, and a faint smile. 'Well,' she had said, looking at the papers on his desk, 'are you lifting the oxcart out of the ditch?' As Mr Martin recalled that moment, over his milk, he squirmed slightly. He must keep his mind on her crimes as a special adviser, not on her peccadillos as a personality. This he found difficult to do, in spite of entering an objection and sustaining it. The faults of the woman as a woman kept chattering on in his mind like an unruly witness. She had, for almost two years now, baited him. In the halls, in the elevator, even in his own office, into which she romped now and then like a circus horse, she was constantly shouting these silly questions at him. 'Are you lifting the oxcart out of the ditch? Are you tearing up the pea patch? Are you hollering down the rain barrel?

Are you scraping around the bottom of the pickle barrel? Are you sitting
in the catbird seat?'

It was Joey Hart, one of Mr Martin's two assistants, who had explained
what the gibberish meant. 'She must be a Dodger fan,' he had said.
'Red Barber announces the Dodger games over the radio and he uses
those expressions—picked 'em up down South.' Joey had gone on to
explain one or two. 'Tearing up the pea patch' meant going on a ram-
page; 'Sitting in the catbird seat' meant sitting pretty, like a batter with
three balls and no strikes on him. Mr Martin dismissed all this with an
effort. It had been annoying, it had driven him near to distraction, but
he was too solid a man to be moved to murder by anything so childish.
It was fortunate, he reflected as he passed on to the important charges
against Mrs Burrows, that he had stood up under it so well. He had main-
tained always an outward appearance of polite tolerance. 'Why, I even
believe you like the woman,' Miss Paird, his other assistant, had once
said to him. He had simply smiled.

A gavel rapped in Mr Martin's mind and the case proper was resumed.
Mrs Ulgine Barrows stood charged with willful, blatant, and persistent
attempts to destroy the efficiency and system of F & S. It was competent,
material, and relevant to review her advent and rise to power. Mr Martin
had got the story from Miss Paird, who seemed always able to find
things out. According to her, Mrs Barrows had met Mr Fitweiler at a
party, where she had rescued him from the embraces of a powerfully
built drunken man who had mistaken the president of F & S for a famous
retired Middle Western football coach. She had led him to a sofa and
somehow worked upon him a monstrous magic. The aging gentleman
had jumped to the conclusion there and then that this was a woman of
singular attainments, equipped to bring out the best in him and in the
firm. A week later he had introduced her into F & S as his special adviser.
On that day confusion got its foot in the door. After Miss Tyson, Mr
Brundage, and Mr Bartlett had been fired and Mr Munson had taken his
hat and stalked out, mailing in his resignation later, old Roberts had
been emboldened to speak to Mr Fitweiler. He mentioned that Mr
Munson's department had been 'a little disrupted' and hadn't they
perhaps better resume the old system there? Mr Fitweiler had said
certainly not. He had the greatest faith in Mrs Barrows' ideas. 'They
require a little seasoning, a little seasoning, is all,' he had added. Mr
Roberts had given it up. Mr Martin reviewed in detail all the changes
wrought by Mrs Barrows. She had begun chipping at the cornices of
the firm's edifice and now she was swinging at the foundation stones
with a pickaxe.

Mr Martin came now, in his summing up, to the afternoon of Monday,
November 2, 1942—just one week ago. On that day, at 3 P.M., Mrs

Barrows had bounced into his office. 'Boo!' she had yelled. 'Are you scraping around the bottom of the pickle barrel?' Mr Martin had looked at her from under his green eyeshade, saying nothing. She had begun to wander about the office, taking it in with her great, popping eyes. 'Do you really need *all* these filing cabinets?' she had demanded suddenly. Mr Martin's heart had jumped. 'Each of these files,' he had said, keeping his voice even, 'plays an indispensable part in the system of F & S.' She had brayed at him, 'Well, don't tear up the pea patch!' and gone to the door. From there she had bawled, 'But you sure have got a lot of fine scrap in here!' Mr Martin could no longer doubt that the finger was on his beloved department. Her pickaxe was on the upswing, poised for the first blow. It had not come yet; he had received no blue memo from the enchanted Mr Fitweiler bearing nonsensical instructions deriving from the obscene woman. But there was no doubt in Mr Martin's mind that one would be forthcoming. He must act quickly. Already a precious week had gone by. Mr Martin stood up in his living room, still holding his milk glass. 'Gentlemen of the jury,' he said to himself, 'I demand the death penalty for this horrible person.'

The next day Mr Martin followed his routine, as usual. He polished his glasses more often and once sharpened an already sharp pencil, but not even Miss Paird noticed. Only once did he catch sight of his victim; she swept past him in the hall with a patronizing 'Hi!' At five-thirty he walked home, as usual, and had a glass of milk, as usual. He had never drunk anything stronger in his life—unless you could count ginger ale. The late Sam Schlosser, the S of F & S, had praised Mr Martin at a staff meeting several years before for his temperate habits. 'Our most efficient worker neither drinks nor smokes,' he had said. 'The results speak for themselves.' Mr Fitweiler had sat by, nodding approval.

Mr Martin was still thinking about that red-letter day as he walked over to the Schrafft's on Fifth Avenue near Forty-sixth Street. He got there, as he always did, at eight o'clock. He finished his dinner and the financial page of the *Sun* at a quarter to nine, as he always did. It was his custom after dinner to take a walk. This time he walked down Fifth Avenue at a casual pace. His gloved hands felt moist and warm, his forehead cold. He transferred the Camels from his overcoat to a jacket pocket. He wondered, as he did so, if they did not represent an unnecessary note of strain. Mrs Barrows smoked only Luckies. It was his idea to puff a few puffs on a Camel (after the rubbing-out), stub it out in the ashtray holding her lipstick-stained Luckies, and thus drag a small red herring across the trail. Perhaps it was not a good idea. It would take time. He might even choke, too loudly.

Mr Martin had never seen the house on West Twelfth Street where Mrs Barrows lived, but he had a clear enough picture of it. Fortunately, she had bragged to everybody about her ducky first-floor apartment in the perfectly darling three-storey red-brick. There would be no doorman or other attendants; just the tenants of the second and third floors. As he walked along, Mr Martin realized that he would get there before nine-thirty. He had considered walking north on Fifth Avenue from Schrafft's to a point from which it would take him until ten o'clock to reach the house. At that hour people were less likely to be coming in or going out. But the procedure would have made an awkward loop in the straight thread of his casualness, and he had abandoned it. It was impossible to figure when people would be entering or leaving the house, anyway. There was a great risk at any hour. If he ran into anybody, he would simply have to place the rubbing-out of Ulgine Barrows in the inactive file forever. The same thing would hold true if there were someone in her apartment. In that case he would just say that he had been passing by, recognized her charming house, and thought to drop in.

It was eighteen minutes after nine when Mr Martin turned into Twelfth Street. A man passed him, and a man and a woman, talking. There was no one within fifty paces when he came to the house, halfway down the block. He was up the steps and in the small vestibule in no time, pressing the bell under the card that said 'Mrs Ulgine Barrows'. When the clicking in the lock started, he jumped forward against the door. He got inside fast, closing the door behind him. A bulb in a lantern hung from the hall ceiling on a chain seemed to give a monstrously bright light. There was nobody on the stair, which went up ahead of him along the left wall. A door opened down the hall in the wall on the right. He went toward it swiftly, on tiptoe.

'Well, for God's sake, look who's here!' bawled Mrs Barrows, and her braying laugh rang out like the report of a shotgun. He rushed past her like a football tackle, bumping her. 'Hey, quit shoving!' she said, closing the door behind them. They were in her living room, which seemed to Mr Martin to be lighted by a hundred lamps. 'What's after you?' she said. 'You're as jumpy as a goat.' He found he was unable to speak. His heart was wheezing in his throat. 'I—yes,' he finally brought out. She was jabbering and laughing as she started to help him off with his coat. 'No, no,' he said. 'I'll put it here.' He took it off and put it on a chair near the door. 'Your hat and gloves, too,' she said. 'You're in a lady's house.' He put his hat on top of the coat. Mrs Barrows seemed larger than he had thought. He kept his gloves on. 'I was passing by,' he said. 'I recognized—is there anyone here?' She laughed louder than ever. 'No,' she said, 'we're all alone. You're as white as a sheet, you funny man. Whatever *has* come over you? I'll mix you a toddy.' She started toward a door across the room. 'Scotch-and-soda be all right?

But say, you don't drink, do you?' She turned and gave him her amused look. Mr Martin pulled himself together. 'Scotch-and-soda will be all right,' he heard himself say. He could hear her laughing in the kitchen.

Mr Martin looked quickly around the living room for the weapon. He had counted on finding one there. There were andirons and a poker and something in a corner that looked like an Indian club. None of them would do. It couldn't be that way. He began to pace around. He came to a desk. On it lay a metal paper knife with an ornate handle. Would it be sharp enough? He reached for it and knocked over a small brass jar. Stamps spilled out of it and it fell to the floor with a clatter. 'Hey,' Mrs Barrows yelled from the kitchen, 'are you tearing up the pea patch?' Mr Martin gave a strange laugh. Picking up the knife, he tried its point against his left wrist. It was blunt. It wouldn't do.

When Mrs Barrows reappeared, carrying two highballs, Mr Martin, standing there with his gloves on, became acutely conscious of the fantasy he had wrought. Cigarettes in his pocket, a drink prepared for him—it was all too grossly improbable. It was more than that; it was impossible. Somewhere in the back of his mind a vague idea stirred, sprouted. 'For heaven's sake, take off those gloves,' said Mrs Barrows. 'I always wear them in the house,' said Mr Martin. The idea began to bloom, strange and wonderful. She put the glasses on a coffee table in front of a sofa and sat on the sofa. 'Come over here, you odd little man,' she said. Mr Martin went over and sat beside her. It was difficult getting a cigarette out of the pack of Camels, but he managed it. She held a match for him, laughing. 'Well,' she said, handing him his drink, 'this is perfectly marvellous. You with a drink and a cigarette.'

Mr Martin puffed, not too awkwardly, and took a gulp of the high-ball. 'I drink and smoke all the time,' he said. He clinked his glass against hers. 'Here's nuts to that old wind-bag, Fitweiler,' he said, and gulped again. The stuff tasted awful, but he made no grimace. 'Really, Mr Martin,' she said, her voice and posture changing, 'you are insulting our employer.' Mrs Barrows was now all special adviser to the president. 'I am preparing a bomb,' said Mr Martin, 'which will blow the old goat higher than hell.' He had only had a little of the drink, which was not strong. It couldn't be that. 'Do you take dope or something?' Mrs Barrows asked coldly. 'Heroin,' said Mr Martin. 'I'll be coked to the gills when I bump that old buzzard off.' 'Mr Martin!' she shouted, getting to her feet. 'That will be all of that. You must go at once.' Mr Martin took another swallow of his drink. He tapped his cigarette out in the ashtray and put the pack of Camels on the coffee table. Then he got up. She stood glaring at him. He walked over and put on his hat and coat. 'Not a word about this,' he said, and laid an index finger against his lips.

All Mrs Barrows could bring out was 'Really!' Mr Martin put his hand on the doorknob. 'I'm sitting in the catbird seat,' he said. He stuck his tongue out at her and left. Nobody saw him go.

Mr Martin got to his apartment, walking, well before eleven. No one saw him go in. He had two glasses of milk after brushing his teeth, and he felt elated. It wasn't tipsiness, because he hadn't been tipsy. Anyway, the walk had worn off all effects of the whiskey. He got in bed and read a magazine for a while. He was asleep before midnight.

Mr Martin got to the office at eight-thirty the next morning, as usual. At a quarter to nine, Ulgine Barrows, who had never before arrived at work before ten, swept into his office. 'I'm reporting to Mr Fitweiler now!' she shouted. 'If he turns you over to the police, it's no more than you deserve!' Mr Martin gave her a look of shocked surprise. 'I beg your pardon?' he said. Mrs Barrows snorted and bounced out of the room, leaving Miss Paird and Joey Hart staring after her. 'What's the matter with that old devil now?' asked Miss Paird. 'I have no idea,' said Mr Martin, resuming his work. The other two looked at him and then at each other. Miss Paird got up and went out. She walked slowly past the closed door of Mr Fitweiler's office. Mrs Barrows was yelling inside, but she was not braying. Miss Paird could not hear what the woman was saying. She went back to her desk.

Forty-five minutes later, Mrs Barrows left the president's office and went into her own, shutting the door. It wasn't until half an hour later that Mr Fitweiler sent for Mr Martin. The head of the filing department, neat, quiet, attentive, stood in front of the old man's desk. Mr Fitweiler was pale and nervous. He took his glasses off and twiddled them. He made a small, bruffing sound in his throat. 'Martin,' he said, 'you have been with us more than twenty years.' 'Twenty-two, sir,' said Mr Martin. 'In that time,' pursued the president, 'your work and your—uh—manner have been exemplary.' 'I trust so, sir,' said Mr Martin. 'I have understood, Martin,' said Mr Fitweiler, 'that you have never taken a drink or smoked.' 'That is correct, sir,' said Mr Martin. 'Ah, yes.' Mr Fitweiler polished his glasses. 'You may describe what you did after leaving the office yesterday, Martin,' he said. Mr Martin allowed less than a second for his bewildered pause. 'Certainly, sir,' he said. 'I walked home. Then I went to Schrafft's for dinner. Afterward I walked home again. I went to bed early, sir, and read a magazine for a while. I was asleep before eleven.' 'Ah, yes,' said Mr Fitweiler again. He was silent for a moment, searching for the proper words to say to the head of the filing department. 'Mrs Barrows,' he said finally, 'Mrs Barrows has worked hard, Martin, very hard. It grieves me to report that she has suffered a severe breakdown. It has taken the form of a persecution complex accompanied by distressing hallucinations.' 'I am very sorry, sir,' said Mr Martin. 'Mrs Barrows is under the delusion,' continued Mr Fitweiler, 'that you visited her last evening and behaved yourself in an—uh—unseemly manner.' He raised his hand to silence Mr Martin's little pained outcry. 'It is the nature of these psychological diseases,' Mr Fitweiler said, 'to fix upon the least likely and most innocent party as the—uh—source of persecution. These matters are not for the lay mind to grasp, Martin. I've just had my psychiatrist, Dr Fitch, on the phone. He would not, of course, commit himself, but he made enough generalizations to substantiate my suspicions. I suggested to Mrs Barrows, when she had completed her—uh—story to me this morning, that she visit Dr Fitch, for I suspected a condition at once. She flew, I regret to say, into a rage, and demanded—uh—requested that I call you on the carpet. You may not know, Martin, but Mrs Barrows had planned a reorganization of your department—subject to my approval, of course, subject to my approval. This brought you, rather than anyone else, to her mind—but again that is a phenomenon for Dr Fitch and not for us. So, Martin, I am afraid Mrs Barrows' usefulness here is at an end.' 'I am dreadfully sorry, sir,' said Mr Martin.

It was at this point that the door to the office blew open with the suddenness of a gas-main explosion and Mrs Barrows catapulted through it. 'Is the little rat denying it?' she screamed. 'He can't get away with that!' Mr Martin got up and moved discreetly to a point beside Mr Fitweiler's chair. 'You drank and smoked at my apartment,' she bawled at Mr Martin, 'and you know it! You called Mr Fitweiler an old windbag and said you were going to blow him up when you got coked to the gills on your heroin!' She stopped yelling to catch her breath and a new glint came into her popping eyes. 'If you weren't such a drab, ordinary little man,' she said, 'I'd think you'd planned it all. Sticking your tongue out, saying you were sitting in the catbird seat, because you thought no one would believe me when I told it! My God, it's really too perfect!' She brayed loudly and hysterically, and the fury was on her again. She glared at Mr Fitweiler. 'Can't you see how he has tricked us, you old fool? Can't you see his little game?' But Mr Fitweiler had been surreptitiously pressing all the buttons under the top of his desk and employees of F & S began pouring into the room. 'Stockton,' said Mr Fitweiler, 'you and Fishbein will take Mrs Burrows to her home. Mrs Powell, you will go with them.' Stockton, who had played a little football in high school, blocked Mrs Barrows as she made for Mr Martin. It took him and Fishbein together to force her out of the door into the hall, crowded with stenographers and office boys. She was still screaming imprecations at Mr Martin, tangled and contradictory imprecations. The hubbub finally died out down the corridor.

'I regret that this has happened,' said Mr Fitweiler. 'I shall ask you to dismiss it from your mind, Martin.' 'Yes, sir,' said Mr Martin, anticipating his chief's 'That will be all' by moving to the door. 'I will dismiss it.' He went out and shut the door, and his step was light and quick in the hall. When he entered his department he had slowed down to his customary gait, and he walked quietly across the room to the W20 file, wearing a look of studious concentration.

Katherine Anne Porter born 1894 Indian Creek, Texas. She *has travelled widely, and worked at reviewing and editing. Though she has published one novel* THE SHIP OF FOOLS, *1962, her main work has been in the short story.*

Short stories: FLOWERING JUDAS, *1930,* HACIENDA, *1934,* NOON WINE, *1931,* PALE HORSE, PALE RIDER, *1939.*

ROPE

Katherine Anne Porter

ON THE THIRD DAY AFTER THEY MOVED TO THE COUNTRY HE CAME WALKING back from the village carrying a basket of groceries and a twenty-four-yard coil of rope. She came out to meet him, wiping her hands on her green smock. Her hair was tumbled, her nose was scarlet with sunburn; he told her that already she looked like a born country woman. His gray flannel shirt stuck to him, his heavy shoes were dusty. She assured him he looked like a rural character in a play.

Had he brought the coffee? She had been waiting all day long for coffee. They had forgot it when they ordered at the store the first day.

Gosh, no, he hadn't. Lord, now he'd have to go back. Yes, he would if it killed him. He thought, though, he had everything else. She reminded him it was only because he didn't drink coffee himself. If he did he would remember it quick enough. Suppose they ran out of cigarettes? Then she saw the rope. What was that for? Well, he thought it might do to hang clothes on, or something. Naturally she asked him if he thought they were going to run a laundry? They already had a fifty-foot line hanging right before his eyes? Why, hadn't he noticed it, really? It was a blot on the landscape to her.

He thought there were a lot of things a rope might come in handy for. She wanted to know what, for instance. He thought a few seconds, but nothing occurred. They could wait and see, couldn't they? You need all sorts of strange odds and ends around a place in the country. She said, yes, that was so; but she thought just at that time when every penny counted, it seemed funny to buy more rope. That was all. She hadn't meant anything else. She hadn't just seen, not at first, why he felt it was necessary.

Well, thunder, he had brought it because he wanted to, and that was all there was to it. She thought that was reason enough, and couldn't understand why he hadn't said so, at first. Undoubtedly it would be useful, twenty-four yards of rope, there were hundreds of things, she couldn't think of any at the moment, but it would come in. Of course. As he had said, things always did in the country.

But she was a little disappointed about the coffee, and oh, look, look, look at the eggs! Oh, my, they're all running! What had he put on top of them? Hadn't he known eggs mustn't be squeezed? Squeezed, who had squeezed them, he wanted to know. What a silly thing to say. He had simply brought them along in the basket with the other things. If they got broke it was the grocer's fault. He should know better than to put heavy things on top of eggs.

She believed it was the rope. That was the heaviest thing in the pack, she saw him plainly when he came in from the road, the rope was a big package on top of everything. He desired the whole wide world to witness that this was not a fact. He had carried the rope in one hand and the basket in the other, and what was the use of her having eyes if that was the best they could do for her?

Well, anyhow, she could see one thing plain: no eggs for breakfast. They'd have to scramble them now, for supper. It was too damned bad. She had planned to have steak for supper. No ice, meat wouldn't keep. He wanted to know why she couldn't finish breaking the eggs in a bowl and set them in a cool place.

Cool place! If he could find one for her, she'd be glad to set them there. Well, then, it seemed to him they might very well cook the meat at the same time they cooked the eggs and then warm up the meat for tomorrow. The idea simply choked her. Warmed-over meat, when they might as well have had it fresh. Second best and scraps and makeshifts, even to the meat! He rubbed her shoulder a little. It doesn't really matter so much, does it, darling? Sometimes when they were playful, he would rub her shoulder and she would arch and purr. This time she hissed and almost clawed. He was getting ready to say that they could surely manage somehow when she turned on him and said, if he told her they could manage somehow she would certainly slap his face.

He swallowed the words red hot, his face burned. He picked up the rope and started to put it on the top shelf. She would not have it on the top shelf, the jars and tins belonged there; positively she would not have the top shelf cluttered up with a lot of rope. She had borne all the clutter she meant to bear in the flat in town, there was space here at least and she meant to keep things in order.

Well, in that case, he wanted to know what the hammer and nails were doing up there? And why had she put them there when she knew very well he needed that hammer and those nails upstairs to fix the window sashes? She simply slowed down everything and made double work on the place with her insane habit of changing things around and hiding them.

She was sure she begged his pardon, and if she had had any reason to believe he was going to fix the sashes this summer she would have left the hammer and nails right where he put them; in the middle of the bedroom floor where they could step on them in the dark. And now if he didn't clear the whole mess out of there she would throw them down the well.

Oh, all right, all right—could he put them in the closet? Naturally not, there were brooms and mops and dustpans in the closet, and why couldn't he find a place for his rope outside her kitchen? Had he stopped to consider there were seven God-forsaken rooms in the house, and only one kitchen?

He wanted to know what of it? And did she realize she was making a complete fool of herself? And what did she take him for, a three-year-old idiot? The whole trouble with her was she needed something weaker than she was to heckle and tyrannize over. He wished to God now they had a couple of children she could take it out on. Maybe he'd get some rest.

Her face changed at this, she reminded him that he had forgot the coffee and had bought a worthless piece of rope. And when she thought of all the things they actually needed to make the place even decently fit to live in, well, she could cry, that was all. She looked so forlorn, so lost and despairing he couldn't believe it was only a piece of rope that was causing all the racket. What *was* the matter, for God's sake?

Oh, would he please hush and go away, and *stay* away, if he could, for five minutes? By all means, yes, he would. He'd stay away indefinitely if she wished. Lord, yes, there was nothing he'd like better than to clear out and never come back. She couldn't for the life of her see what was holding him, then. It was a swell time. Here she was, stuck, miles from a railroad, with a half-empty house on her hands, and not a penny in her pocket, and everything on earth to do; it seemed the God-sent moment for him to get out from under. She was surprised he hadn't stayed in town as it was until she had come out and done the work and got things straightened out. It was his usual trick.

It appeared to him that this was going a little far. Just a touch out of bounds, if she didn't mind his saying so. Why the hell had he stayed in town the summer before? To do a half-dozen extra jobs to get the money he had sent her. That was it. She knew perfectly well they couldn't have done it otherwise. She had agreed with him at the time. And that was the only time so help him he had ever left her to do anything by herself.

Oh, he could tell that to his great grandmother. She had her notion of what had kept him in town. Considerably more than a notion, if he wanted to know. So, she was going to bring all that up again, was she? Well, she could just think what she pleased. He was tired of explaining. It may have looked funny but he had simply got hooked in, and what could he do? It was impossible to believe that she was going to take it seriously. Yes, yes, she knew how it was with a man: if he was left by himself a minute, some woman was certain to kidnap him. And naturally he couldn't hurt her feelings by refusing!

Well, what was she raving about? Did she forget she had told him those two weeks alone in the country were the happiest she had known for four years? And how long had they been married when she said that? All right, shut up! If she thought that hadn't stuck in his craw.

She hadn't meant she was happy because she was away from him. She meant she was happy getting the devilish house nice and ready for him. That was what she had meant, and now look! Bringing up something she had said a year ago simply to justify himself for forgetting her coffee and breaking the eggs and buying a wretched piece of rope they couldn't afford. She really thought it was time to drop the subject, and now she wanted only two things in the world. She wanted him to get that rope from underfoot, and go back to the village and get her coffee, and if he could remember it, he might bring a metal mitt for the skillets, and two more curtain rods, and if there were any rubber gloves in the village, her hands were simply raw, and a bottle of milk of magnesia from the drugstore.

He looked out at the dark blue afternoon sweltering on the slopes, and mopped his forehead and sighed heavily and said, if only she could wait a minute for *anything*, he was going back. He had said so, hadn't he, the very instant they found he had overlooked it?

Oh, yes, well . . . run along. She was going to wash windows. The country was so beautiful! She doubted they'd have a moment to enjoy it. He meant to go, but he could not until he had said that if she wasn't such a hopeless melancholiac she might see that this was only for a few days. Couldn't she remember anything pleasant about the other summers? Hadn't they ever had any fun? She hadn't time to talk about it, and now would he please not leave that rope lying around for her to trip on? He picked it up, somehow it had toppled off the table, and walked out with it under his arm.

Was he going this minute? He certainly was. She thought so. Sometimes it seemed to her he had second sight about the precisely perfect moment to leave her ditched. She had meant to put the mattresses out to sun, if they put them out this minute they would get at least three hours, he must have heard her say that morning she meant to put them out. So of course he would walk off and leave her to it. She supposed he thought the exercise would do her good.

Well, he was merely going to get her coffee. A four-mile walk for two pounds of coffee was ridiculous, but he was perfectly willing to do it. The habit was making a wreck of her, but if she wanted to wreck herself there was nothing he could do about it. If he thought it was coffee that was making a wreck of her, she congratulated him: he must have a damned easy conscience.

Conscience or no conscience, he didn't see why the mattresses couldn't very well wait until tomorrow. And anyhow, for God's sake, were they living *in* the house, or were they going to let the house ride them to death? She paled at this, her face grew livid about the mouth, she looked quite dangerous, and reminded him that housekeeping was no more her work than it was his: she had other work to do as well, and when did he think she was going to find time to do it at this rate?

Was she going to start on that again? She knew as well as he did that his work brought in the regular money, hers was only occasional, if they depended on what *she* made—and she might as well get straight on this question once for all!

That was positively not the point. The question was, when both of them were working on their own time, was there going to be a division of the housework, or wasn't there? She merely wanted to know, she had to make her plans. Why, he thought that was all arranged. It was understood that he was to help. Hadn't he always, in summers?

Hadn't he, though? Oh, just hadn't he? And when, and where, and doing what? Lord, what an uproarious joke!

It was such a very uproarious joke that her face turned slightly purple, and she screamed with laughter. She laughed so hard she had to sit down, and finally a rush of tears spurted from her eyes and poured down into the lifted corners of her mouth. He dashed towards her and dragged her up to her feet and tried to pour water on her head. The dipper hung by a string on a nail and he broke it loose. Then he tried to pump water with one hand while she struggled in the other. So he gave it up and shook her instead.

She wrenched away, crying out for him to take his rope and go to hell, she had simply given him up: and ran. He heard her high-heeled bedroom slippers clattering and stumbling on the stairs.

He went out around the house and into the lane; he suddenly realized he had a blister on his heel and his shirt felt as if it were on fire. Things broke so suddenly you didn't know where you were. She could work herself into a fury about simply nothing. She was terrible, damn it: not an ounce of reason. You might as well talk to a sieve as that woman when she got going. Damned if he'd spend his life humoring her? Well, what to do now? He would take back the rope and exchange it for something else. Things accumulated, things were mountainous, you couldn't move them or sort them out or get rid of them. They just lay and rotted around. He'd take it back. Hell, why should he? He wanted it. What was it anyhow? A piece of rope. Imagine anybody caring more about a piece of rope than about a man's feelings. What earthly right had she to say a word about it? He remembered all the useless, meaningless things she bought for herself: Why? because I wanted it, that's why! He stopped and selected a large stone by the road. He would put the rope behind it. He would put it in the tool-box when he got back. He'd heard enough about it to last him a life-time.

When he came back she was leaning against the post box beside the road waiting. It was pretty late, the smell of broiled steak floated nose high in the cooling air. Her face was young and smooth and fresh-looking. Her unmanageable funny black hair was all on end. She waved to him from a distance, and he speeded up. She called out that supper was ready and waiting, was he starved?

You bet he was starved. Here was the coffee. He waved it at her. She looked at his other hand. What was that he had there?

Well, it was the rope again. He stopped short. He had meant to exchange it but forgot. She wanted to know why he should exchange it, if it was something he really wanted. Wasn't the air sweet now, and wasn't it fine to be here?

She walked beside him with one hand hooked into his leather belt. She pulled and jostled him a little as he walked, and leaned against him. He put his arm clear around her and patted her stomach. They exchanged wary smiles. Coffee, coffee for the Ootsum-Wootsums! He felt as if he were bringing her a beautiful present.

He was a love, she firmly believed, and if she had had her coffee in the morning, she wouldn't have behaved so funny . . . There was a whippoorwill still coming back, imagine, clear out of season, sitting in the crab-apple tree calling all by himself. Maybe his girl stood him up. Maybe she did. She hoped to hear him once more, she loved whippoorwills . . . He knew how she was, didn't he?

Sure, he knew how she was.

Eudora Welty born 1909 Jackson, Mississippi. Studied at the University of Wisconsin, and at Columbia, New York. Her work has a background of her own Southern States, but her stories are varied in subject and mood, ranging from sharp satire in stories like 'THE PETRIFIED MAN', to the difficult kind of story where imagination and memory and fact are mingled to suggest different kinds of reality, as 'THE DEATH OF A TRAVELLING SALESMAN' is able to do. She has claimed that the beauty of a story is often in what the author holds back. Hence her work makes imaginative demands on the reader. And in this, most contemporary writers of short stories would agree with her.

Short stories: A CURTAIN OF GREEN, *1941*, THE WIDE NET, *1943*. Novels: THE ROBBER BRIDEGROOM, DELTA WEDDING, THE GOLDEN APPLES.

DEATH OF A TRAVELLING SALESMAN

Eudora Welty

R. J. BOWMAN, WHO FOR FOURTEEN YEARS HAD TRAVELLED FOR A SHOE company through Mississippi, drove his Ford along a rutted dirt path. It was a long day! The time did not seem to clear the noon hurdle and settle into soft afternoon. The sun, keeping its strength here even in winter, stayed at the top of the sky, and every time Bowman stuck his head out of the dusty car to stare up the road, it seemed to reach a long arm down and push against the top of his head, right through his hat—like the practical joke of an old drummer, long on the road. It made him feel all the more angry and helpless. He was feverish, and he was not quite sure of the way.

This was his first day back on the road after a long siege of influenza. He had had very high fever, and dreams, and had become weakened and pale, enough to tell the difference in the mirror, and he could not think clearly. . . . All afternoon, in the midst of his anger, and for no reason, he had thought of his dead grandmother. She had been a comfortable soul. Once more Bowman wished he could fall into the big feather bed that had been in her room. . . . Then he forgot her again.

This desolate hill country! And he seemed to be going the wrong way—it was as if he were going back, far back. There was not a house in sight. . . . There was no use wishing he were back in bed, though. By paying the hotel doctor his bill he had proved his recovery. He had not even been sorry when the pretty trained nurse said good-bye. He did not like illness, he distrusted it, as he distrusted the road without signposts. It angered him. He had given the nurse a really expensive bracelet, just because she was packing up her bag and leaving.

But now—what if in fourteen years on the road he had never been ill before and never had an accident? His record was broken, and he had even begun almost to question it. . . . He had gradually put up at better hotels, in the bigger towns, but weren't they all, eternally, stuffy in summer and draughty in winter? Women? He could only remember little rooms within little rooms, like a nest of Chinese paper boxes, and if he thought of one woman he saw the worn loneliness that the furniture of that room seemed built of. And he himself—he was a man who always wore rather wide-brimmed black hats, and in the wavy hotel mirrors had looked something like a bull-fighter, as he paused for that inevitable instant on the landing, walking downstairs to supper. . . . He leaned out of the car again, and once more the sun pushed at his head.

Bowman had wanted to reach Beulah by dark, to go to bed and

sleep off his fatigue. As he remembered, Beulah was fifty miles away from the last town, on a gravelled road. This was only a cow trail. How had he ever come to such a place? One hand wiped the sweat from his face, and he drove on.

He had made the Beulah trip before. But he had never seen this hill or this petering-out path before—or that cloud, he thought shyly, looking up and then down quickly—any more than he had seen this day before. Why did he not admit he was simply lost and had been for miles? . . . He was not in the habit of asking the way of strangers, and these people never knew where the very roads they lived on went to; but then he had not even been close enough to anyone to call out. People standing in the fields now and then, or on top of the haystacks, had been too far away, looking like leaning sticks or weeds, turning a little at the solitary rattle of his car across their countryside, watching the pale sobered winter dust where it chunked out behind like big squashes down the road. The stares of these distant people had followed him solidly like a wall, impenetrable, behind which they turned back after he had passed.

The cloud floated there to one side like the bolster on his grandmother's bed. It went over a cabin on the edge of a hill, where two bare chinaberry trees clutched at the sky. He drove through a heap of dead oak leaves, his wheels stirring their weightless sides to make a silvery melancholy whistle as the car passed through their bed. No car had been along this way ahead of him. Then he saw that he was on the edge of a ravine that fell away, a red erosion, and that this was indeed the road's end.

He pulled the brake. But it did not hold, though he put all his strength into it. The car, tipped toward the edge, rolled a little. Without doubt, it was going over the bank.

He got out quietly, as though some mischief had been done him and he had his dignity to remember. He lifted his bag and sample case out, set them down, and stood back and watched the car roll over the edge. He heard something—not the crash he was listening for, but a slow un-uproarious crackle. Rather distastefully he went to look over, and he saw that his car had fallen into a tangle of immense grape vines as thick as his arm, which caught it and held it, rocked it like a grotesque child in a dark cradle, and then, as he watched, concerned somehow that he was not still inside it, released it gently to the ground.

He sighed.

Where am I? he wondered with a shock. Why didn't I do something? All his anger seemed to have drifted away from him. There was the house, back on the hill. He took a bag in each hand and with almost childlike willingness went toward it. But his breathing came with difficulty, and he had to stop to rest.

It was a shotgun house, two rooms and an open passage between, perched on the hill. The whole cabin slanted a little under the heavy heaped-up vine that covered the roof, light and green, as though forgotten from summer. A woman stood in the passage.

He stopped still. Then all of a sudden his heart began to behave strangely. Like a rocket set off, it began to leap and expand into uneven patterns of beats which showered into his brain, and he could not think. But in scattering and falling it made no noise. It shot up with great power, almost elation, and fell gently, like acrobats into nets. It began to pound profoundly, then waited irresponsibly, hitting in some sort of inward mockery first at his ribs, then against his eyes, then under his shoulder blades, and against the roof of his mouth when he tried to say, "Good afternoon, madam." But he could not hear his heart—it was as quiet as ashes falling. This was rather comforting; still, it was shocking to Bowman to feel his heart beating at all.

Stockstill in his confusion, he dropped his bags, which seemed to drift in slow bulks gracefully through the air and to cushion themselves on the grey prostrate grass near the doorstep.

As for the woman standing there, he saw at once that she was old. Since she could not possibly hear his heart, he ignored the pounding and now looked at her carefully, and yet in his distraction dreamily, with his mouth open.

She had been cleaning the lamp, and held it, half blackened, half clear, in front of her. He saw her with the dark passage behind her. She was a big woman with a weather-beaten but unwrinkled face; her lips were held tightly together, and her eyes looked with a curious dulled brightness into his. He looked at her shoes, which were like bundles. If it were summer she would be barefoot. . . . Bowman who automatically judged a woman's age on sight, set her age at fifty. She wore a formless garment of some grey coarse material, rough-dried from a washing, from which her arms appeared pink and unexpectedly round. When she never said a word, and sustained her quiet pose of holding the lamp, he was convinced of the strength in her body.

"Good afternoon, madam," he said.

She stared on, whether at him or at the air around him he could not tell, but after a moment she lowered her eyes to show that she would listen to whatever he had to say.

"I wonder if you would be interested—" He tried once more. "An accident—my car . . ."

Her voice emerged low and remote, like a sound across a lake. "Sonny he ain't here."

"Sonny?"

"Sonny ain't here now."

77

Her son—a fellow able to bring my car up, he decided in blurred relief. He pointed down the hill. "My car's in the bottom of the ditch. I'll need help."

"Sonny ain't here, but he'll be here."

She was becoming clearer to him and her voice stronger, and Bowman saw that she was stupid.

He was hardly surprised at the deepening postponement and tedium of his journey. He took a breath, and heard his voice speaking over the silent blows of his heart. "I was sick. I am not strong yet. . . . May I come in?"

He stooped and laid his big black hat over the handle on his bag. It was a humble motion, almost a bow, that instantly struck him as absurd and betraying of all his weakness. He looked up at the woman, the wind blowing his hair. He might have continued for a long time in this unfamiliar attitude; he had never been a patient man, but when he was sick he had learned to sink submissively into the pillows, to wait for his medicine. He waited on the woman.

Then she, looking at him with blue eyes, turned and held open the door, and after a moment Bowman, as if convinced in his action, stood erect and followed her in.

Inside, the darkness of the house touched him like a professional hand, the doctor's. The woman set the half-cleaned lamp on a table in the centre of the room and pointed, also like a professional person, a guide, to a chair with a yellow cowhide seat. She herself crouched on the hearth, drawing her knees up under the shapeless dress.

At first he felt hopefully secure. His heart was quieter. The room was enclosed in the gloom of yellow pine boards. He could see the other room, with the foot of an iron bed showing, across the passage. The bed had been made up with a red-and-yellow pieced quilt that looked like a map or a picture, a little like his grandmother's girlhood painting of Rome burning.

He had ached for coolness, but in this room it was cold. He stared at the hearth with dead coals lying on it and iron pots in the corners. The hearth and smoked chimney were of the stone he had seen ribbing the hills, mostly slate. Why is there no fire? he wondered.

And it was so still. The silence of the fields seemed to enter and move familiarly through the house. The wind used the open hall. He felt that he was in a mysterious, quiet, cool danger. It was necessary to do what? . . . To talk.

"I have a nice line of women's low-priced shoes . . ." he said.

But the woman answered, "Sonny'll be here. He's strong. Sonny'll move your car."

"Where is he now?"

"Farms for Mr. Redmond."

Mr. Redmond. Mr. Redmond. That was someone he would never have to encounter, 'and he was glad. Somehow the name did not appeal to him. . . . In a flare of touchiness and anxiety, Bowman wished to avoid even mention of unknown men and their unknown farms.

"Do you two live here alone?" He was surprised to hear his old voice, chatty, confidential, inflected for selling shoes, asking a question like that—a thing he did not even want to know.

"Yes. We are alone."

He was surprised at the way she answered. She had taken a long time to say that. She had nodded her head in a deep way too. Had she wished to affect him with some sort of premonition? he wondered unhappily. Or was it only that she would not help him, after all, by talking with him? For he was not strong enough to receive the impact of unfamiliar things without a little talk to break their fall. He had lived a month in which nothing had happened except in his head and his body—an almost inaudible life of heartbeats and dreams that came back, a life of fever and privacy, a delicate life which had left him weak to the point of—what? Of begging. The pulse in his palm leapt like a trout in a brook.

He wondered over and over why the woman did not go ahead with cleaning the lamp. What prompted her to stay there across the room, silently bestowing her presence upon him? He saw that with her it was not a time for doing little tasks. Her face was grave; she was feeling how right she was. Perhaps it was only politeness. In docility he held his eyes stiffly wide; they fixed themselves on the woman's clasped hands as though she held the cord they were strung on.

Then, "Sonny's coming," she said.

He himself had not heard anything, but there came a man passing the window and then plunging in at the door, with two hounds beside him. Sonny was a big enough man, with his belt slung low about his hips. He looked at least thirty. He had a hot, red face that was yet full of silence. He wore muddy blue pants and an old military coat stained and patched. World War? Bowman wondered. Great God, it was a Confederate coat. On the back of his light hair he had a wide filthy black hat which seemed to insult Bowman's own. He pushed down the dogs from his chest. He was strong with dignity and heaviness in his way of moving. . . . There was the resemblance to his mother.

They stood side by side. . . . He must account again for his presence here.

"Sonny, this man, he had his car to run off over the prec'pice an' wants to know if you will git it out for him," the woman said after a few minutes.

Bowman could not even state his case.

Sonny's eyes lay upon him.

He knew he should offer explanations and show money—at least appear either penitent or authoritative. But all he could do was to shrug slightly.

Sonny brushed by him going to the window, followed by the eager dogs, and looked out. There was effort even in the way he was looking, as if he could throw his sight out like a rope. Without turning Bowman felt that his own eyes could have seen nothing: it was too far.

"Got me a mule out there an' got me a block an' tackle," said Sonny meaningfully. "I *could* catch me my mule an' git me my ropes, an' before long I'd git your car out the ravine."

He looked completely round the room, as if in meditation, his eyes roving in their own distance. Then he pressed his lips firmly and yet shyly together, and with the dogs ahead of him this time, he lowered his head and strode out. The hard earth sounded, cupping to his powerful way of walking—almost a stagger.

Mischievously, at the suggestion of those sounds, Bowman's heart leapt again. It seemed to walk about inside him.

"Sonny's goin' to do it," the woman said. She said it again, singing it almost, like a song. She was sitting in her place by the hearth.

Without looking out, he heard some shouts and the dogs barking and the pounding of hoofs in short runs on the hill. In a few minutes Sonny passed under the window with a rope, and there was a brown mule with quivering, shining, purple-looking ears. The mule actually looked in the window. Under its eyelashes it turned target-like eyes into his. Bowman averted his head and saw the woman looking serenely back at the mule, with only satisfaction in her face.

She sang a little more, under her breath. It occurred to him, and it seemed quite marvellous, that she was not really talking to him, but rather following the thing that came about with words that were unconscious and part of her looking.

So he said nothing, and this time when he did not reply he felt a curious and strong emotion, not fear, rise up in him.

This time, when his heart leapt, something—his soul—seemed to leap too, like a little colt invited out of a pen. He stared at the woman while the frantic nimbleness of his feeling made his head sway. He could not move; there was nothing he could do, unless perhaps he might embrace this woman who sat there growing old and shapeless before him.

But he wanted to leap up, to say to her, I have been sick and I found out then, only then, how lonely I am. Is it too late? My heart puts up a struggle inside me, and you may have heard it, protesting against emptiness. . . . It should be full, he would rush on to tell her, thinking of his heart now as a deep lake, it should be holding love like other hearts. It should be flooded with love. There would be a warm spring day . . . Come and stand in my heart, whoever you are, and a whole river would cover your feet and rise higher and take your knees in whirlpools, and draw you down to itself, your whole body, your heart too.

But he moved a trembling hand across his eyes, and looked at the placid crouching woman across the room. She was still as a statue. He felt ashamed and exhausted by the thought that he might, in one more moment, have tried by simple words and embraces to communicate some strange thing—something which seemed always to have just escaped him . . . .

Sunlight touched the farthest pot on the hearth. It was late afternoon. This time to-morrow he would be somewhere on a good gravelled road, driving his car past things that happened to people, quicker than their happening. Seeing ahead to the next day, he was glad, and knew that this was no time to embrace an old woman. He could feel in his pounding temples the readying of his blood for motion and for hurrying away.

"Sonny's hitched up your car by now," said the woman. "He'll git it out the ravine right shortly."

"Fine!" he cried with his customary enthusiasm.

Yet it seemed a long time that they waited. It began to get dark. Bowman was cramped in his chair. Any man should know enough to get up and walk around while he waited. There was something like guilt in such stillness and silence.

But instead of getting up, he listened. . . . His breathing restrained, his eyes powerless in the growing dark, he listened uneasily for a warning sound, forgetting in wariness what it would be. Before long he heard something—soft, continuous, insinuating.

"What's the noise?" he asked, his voice jumping into the dark. Then wildly he was afraid it would be his heart beating so plainly in the quiet room, and she would tell him so.

"You might hear the stream," she said grudgingly.

Her voice was closer. She was standing by the table. He wondered why she did not light the lamp. She stood there in the dark and did not light it.

Bowman would never speak to her now, for the time was past. I'll sleep in the dark, he thought, in his bewilderment pitying himself.

Heavily she moved on to the window. Her arm, vaguely white, rose straight from her full side and she pointed out into the darkness.

"That white speck's Sonny," she said, talking to herself.

He turned unwillingly and peered over her shoulder; he hesitated to rise and stand beside her. His eyes searched the dusky air. The white speck floated smoothly toward her finger, like a leaf on a river, growing whiter in the dark. It was as if she had shown him something secret, part of her life, but had offered no explanation. He looked away. He was moved almost to tears, feeling for no reason that she had made a silent declaration equivalent to his own. His hand waited upon his chest.

Then a step shook the house, and Sonny was in the room. Bowman felt how the woman left him there and went to the other man's side.

"I done got your car out, mister," said Sonny's voice in the dark. "She's settin' a-waitin' in the road, turned to go back where she come from."

"Fine!" said Bowman, projecting his own voice to loudness. "I'm surely much obliged—I could never have done it myself—I was sick. . . ."

"I could do it easy," said Sonny.

Bowman could feel them both waiting in the dark, and he could hear the dogs panting out in the yard, waiting to bark when he should go. He felt strangely helpless and resentful. Now that he could go, he longed to stay. From what was he being deprived? His chest was rudely shaken by the violence of his heart. These people cherished something here that he could not see, they withheld some ancient promise of food and warmth and light. Between them they had a conspiracy. He thought of the way she had moved away from him and gone to Sonny, she had flowed toward him. He was shaking with cold, he was tired, and it was not fair. Humbly and yet angrily he stuck his hand into his pocket.

"Of course I'm going to pay you for everything—"

"We don't take money for such," said Sonny's voice belligerently.

"I want to pay. But do something more . . . Let me stay—to-night. . . ." He took another step toward them. If only they could see him, they would know his sincerity, his real need! His voice went on, "I'm not very strong yet, I'm not able to walk far, even back to my car, maybe, I don't know—I don't know exactly where I am—"

He stopped. He felt as if he might burst into tears. What would they think of him!

Sonny came over and put his hands on him. Bowman felt them pass (they were professional too) across his chest, over his hips. He could feel Sonny's eyes upon him in the dark.

"You ain't no revenuer come sneakin' here, mister, ain't got no gun?"

To this end of nowhere! And yet *he* had come. He made a grave answer. "No."

"You can stay."

"Sonny," said the woman, "you'll have to borry some fire."

"I'll go git from Redmond's," said Sonny.

"What?" Bowman strained to hear their words to each other.

"Our fire, it's out, and Sonny's got to borry some, because it's dark an' cold," she said.

"But matches—I have matches—"

"We don't have no need for 'em," she said proudly. "Sonny's goin' after his own fire."

"I'm goin' to Redmond's," said Sonny with an air of importance, and he went out.

After they had waited a while, Bowman looked out the window and saw a light moving over the hill. It spread itself out like a little fan. It zigzagged along the field, darting and swift, not like Sonny at all.... Soon enough, Sonny staggered in, holding a burning stick behind him in tongs, fire flowing in his wake, blazing light into the corners of the room.

"We'll make a fire now," the woman said, taking the brand.

When that was done she lit the lamp. It showed its dark and light. The whole room turned golden-yellow like some sort of flower, and the walls smelled of it and seemed to tremble with the quiet rushing of the fire and the waving of the burning lampwick in its funnel of light.

The woman moved among the iron pots. With the tongs she dropped hot coals on top of the iron lids. They made a set of soft vibrations, like the sound of a bell far away.

She looked up and over at Bowman, but he could not answer. He was trembling....

"Have a drink, mister?" Sonny asked. He had brought in a chair from the other room and sat astride it with his folded arms across the back. Now we are all visible, to one another, Bowman thought, and cried, "Yes sir, you bet, thanks!"

"Come after me and do just what I do," said Sonny.

It was another excursion into the dark. They went through the hall, out to the back of the house, past a shed and a hooded well. They came to a wilderness of thicket.

"Down on your knees," said Sonny.

"What?" Sweat broke out on his forehead.

He understood when Sonny began to crawl through a sort of tunnel that the bushes made over the ground. He followed, startled in spite of himself when a twig or a thorn touched him gently without making a sound, clinging to him and finally letting him go.

Sonny stopped crawling and, crouched on his knees, began to dig with both his hands into the dirt. Bowman shyly struck matches and made a light. In a few minutes Sonny pulled up a jug. He poured out some of the whisky into a bottle from his coat pocket, and buried the jug again. "You never know who's liable to knock at your door," he said, and laughed. "Start back," he said, almost formally. "Ain't no need for us to drink outdoors, like hogs."

At the table by the fire, sitting opposite each other in their chairs,

Sonny and Bowman took drinks out of the bottle, passing it across. The dogs slept; one of them was having a dream.

"This is good," said Bowman. "That is what I needed." It was just as though he were drinking the fire off the hearth.

"He makes it," said the woman with quiet pride.

She was pushing the coals off the pots, and the smells of corn bread and coffee circled the room. She set everything on the table before the men, with a bone-handled knife stuck into one of the potatoes, splitting out its golden fibre. Then she stood for a minute looking at them, tall and full above them where they sat. She leaned a little toward them.

"You-all can eat now," she said, and suddenly smiled.

Bowman had just happened to be looking at her. He set his cup back on the table in unbelieving protest. A pain pressed at his eyes. He saw that she was not an old woman. She was young, still young. He could think of no number of years for her. She was the same age as Sonny, and she belonged to him. She stood with the deep dark corner of the room behind her, the shifting yellow light scattering over her head and her grey formless dress, trembling over her tall body when it bent over them in its sudden communication. She was young. Her teeth were shining and her eyes glowed. She turned and walked slowly and heavily out of the room, and he heard her sit down on the cot and then lie down. The pattern on the quilt moved.

"She goin' to have a baby," said Sonny, popping a bite into his mouth.

Bowman could not speak. He was shocked with knowing what was really in this house. A marriage, a fruitful marriage. That simple thing. Anyone could have had that.

Somehow he felt unable to be indignant or protest, although some sort of joke had certainly been played upon him. There was nothing remote or mysterious here—only something private. The only secret was the ancient communication between two people. But the memory of the woman's waiting silently by the cold hearth, of the man's stubborn journey a mile away to get fire, and how they finally brought out their food and drink and filled the room proudly with all they had to show, was suddenly too clear and too enormous within him for response. . . .

"You ain't as hungry as you look," said Sonny.

The woman came out of the bedroom as soon as the men had finished, and ate her supper while her husband stared peacefully into the fire.

Then they put the dogs out, with the food that was left.

"I think I'd better sleep here by the fire, on the floor," said Bowman.

He felt that he had been cheated, and that he could afford now to be generous. Ill though he was, he was not going to ask them for their bed. He was through with asking favours in this house, now that he understood what was there.

"Sure, mister."

But he had not known yet how slowly he understood. They had not meant to give him their bed. After a little interval they both rose and looking at him gravely went into the other room.

He lay stretched by the fire until it grew low and dying. He watched every tongue of blaze lick out and vanish. "There will be special reduced prices on all footwear during the month of January," he found himself repeating quietly, and then he lay with his lips tight shut.

How many noises the night had! He heard the stream running, the fire dying, and he was now sure that he heard his heart beating, too, the sound it made under his ribs. He heard breathing, round and deep, of the man and his wife in the room across the passage. And that was all. But emotion swelled patiently within him, and he wished that the child were his.

He must get back to where he had been before. He stood weakly before the red coals, and put on his overcoat. It felt too heavy on his shoulders. As he started out he looked and saw that the woman had never got through with cleaning the lamp. On some impulse he put all the money from his billfold under its fluted glass base, almost ostentatiously.

Ashamed, shrugging a little, and then shivering, he took his bags and went out. The cold of the air seemed to lift him bodily. The moon was in the sky.

On the slope he began to run, he could not help it. Just as he reached the road, where his car seemed to sit in the moonlight like a boat, his heart began to give off tremendous explosions like a rifle, bang bang bang.

He sank in fright on to the road, his bags falling about him. He felt as if all this had happened before. He covered his heart with both hands to keep anyone from hearing the noise it made.

But nobody heard it.

William Carlos Williams born in *New Jersey, in 1883.*
He studied medicine and became a physician and paediatrician, practising in the
area surrounding Rutherford, New Jersey, where he spent most of his life. A
prolific writer of poetry and prose, Williams had thirty eight volumes of his
writings published during his lifetime. 'THE USE OF FORCE' *is typical of the fine*
stories in LIFE ALONG THE PASSAIC RIVER. *Outwardly a simple, first person*
anecdote, it reveals through the dialogue which takes up most of the story,
and which is not distinguished from the narrator's comments by the normal
convention of punctuation, a subtle and intelligent insight into the nature of
conflict and tension.

Williams died in 1963.

THE USE OF FORCE

William Carlos Williams

THEY WERE NEW PATIENTS TO ME, ALL I HAD WAS THE NAME, OLSON. PLEASE come down as soon as you can, my daughter is very sick.

When I arrived I was met by the mother, a big startled looking woman, very clean and apologetic who merely said, Is this the doctor? and let me in. In the back, she added. You must excuse us, doctor, we have her in the kitchen where it is warm. It is very damp here sometimes.

The child was fully dressed and sitting on her father's lap near the kitchen table. He tried to get up, but I motioned for him not to bother, took off my overcoat and started to look things over. I could see that they were all very nervous, eyeing me up and down distrustfully. As often, in such cases, they weren't telling me more than they had to, it was up to me to tell them; that's why they were spending three dollars on me.

The child was fairly eating me up with her cold, steady eyes, and no expression to her face whatever. She did not move and seemed, inwardly, quiet; an unusually attractive little thing, and as strong as a heifer in appearance. But her face was flushed, she was breathing rapidly, and I realized that she had a high fever. She had magnificent blonde hair, in profusion. One of those picture children often reproduced in advertising leaflets and the photogravure sections of the Sunday papers.

She's had a fever for three days, began the father and we don't know what it comes from. My wife has given her things, you know, like people do, but it don't do no good. And there's been a lot of sickness around. So we tho't you'd better look her over and tell us what is the matter.

As doctors often do I took a trial shot at it as a point of departure. Had she had a sore throat?

Both parents answered me together, No . . . No, she says her throat don't hurt her.

Does your throat hurt you? added the mother to the child. But the little girl's expression didn't change nor did she move her eyes from my face.

Have you looked?

I tried to, said the mother, but I couldn't see.

As it happens we had been having a number of cases of diphtheria in the school to which this child went during that month and we were all, quite apparently, thinking of that, though no one had as yet spoken of the thing.

Well, I said, suppose we take a look at the throat first. I smiled in my best professional manner and asking for the child's first name I said, come on, Mathilda, open your mouth and let's take a look at your throat.

Nothing doing.

Aw, come on, I coaxed, just open your mouth wide and let me take a look. Look, I said opening both hands wide, I haven't anything in my hands. Just open up and let me see.

Such a nice man, put in the mother. Look how kind he is to you. Come on, do what he tells you to. He won't hurt you.

At that I ground my teeth in disgust. If only they wouldn't use the word 'hurt' I might be able to get somewhere. But I did not allow myself to be hurried or disturbed but speaking quietly and slowly I approached the child again.

As I moved my chair a little nearer suddenly with one cat-like movement both her hands clawed instinctively for my eyes and she almost reached them too. In fact she knocked my glasses flying and they fell, though unbroken, several feet away from me on the kitchen floor.

Both the mother and father almost turned themselves inside out in embarrassment and apology. You bad girl, said the mother, taking her and shaking her by one arm. Look what you've done. The nice man . . .

For heaven's sake, I broke in. Don't call me a nice man to her. I'm here to look at her throat on the chance that she might have diphtheria and possibly die of it. But that's nothing to her. Look here, I said to the child, we're going to look at your throat. You're old enough to understand what I'm saying. Will you open it now by yourself or shall we have to open it for you?

Not a move. Even her expression hadn't changed. Her breaths however were coming faster and faster. Then the battle began. I had to do it. I had to have a throat culture for her own protection. But first I told the parents that it was entirely up to them. I explained the danger but said that I would not insist on a throat examination so long as they would take the responsibility.

If you don't do what the doctor says you'll have to go to the hospital, the mother admonished her severely.

Oh yeah? I had to smile to myself. After all, I had already fallen in love with the savage brat, the parents were contemptible to me. In the ensuing struggle they grew more and more abject, crushed, exhausted while she surely rose to magnificent heights of insane fury of effort bred of her terror of me.

The father tried his best, and he was a big man but the fact that she was his daughter, his shame at her behaviour and his dread of hurting her made him release her just at the critical moment several times when I had almost achieved success, till I wanted to kill him. But his dread also that she might have diphtheria made him tell me to go on, go on though he himself was almost fainting, while the mother moved back and forth behind us raising and lowering her hands in an agony of apprehension.

Put her in front of you on your lap, I ordered, and held both her wrists.

But as soon as he did the child let out a scream. Don't, you're hurting me. Let go of my hands. Let them go I tell you. Then she shrieked terrifyingly, hysterically. Stop it! Stop it! You're killing me!

Do you think she can stand it, doctor! said the mother.

You get out, said the husband to his wife. Do you want her to die of diphtheria?

Come on now, hold her, I said.

Then I grasped the child's head with my left hand and tried to get the wooden tongue depressor between her teeth. She fought, with clenched teeth, desperately! But now I also had grown furious—at a child. I tried to hold myself down but I couldn't. I know how to expose a throat for inspection. And I did my best. When finally I got the wooden spatula behind the last teeth and just the point of it into the mouth cavity, she opened up for an instant but before I could see anything she came down again and gripping the wooden blade between her molars she reduced it to splinters before I could get it out again.

Aren't you ashamed, the mother yelled at her. Aren't you ashamed to act like that in front of the doctor?

Get me a smooth-handled spoon of some sort, I told the mother. We're going through with this. The child's mouth was already bleeding. Her tongue was cut and she was screaming in wild hysterical shrieks. Perhaps I should have desisted and come back in an hour or more. No doubt it would have been better. But I have seen at least two children lying dead in bed of neglect in such cases, and feeling that I must get a diagnosis now or never I went at it again. But the worst of it was that I too had got beyond reason. I could have torn the child apart in my own fury and enjoyed it. It was a pleasure to attack her. My face was burning with it.

The damned little brat must be protected against her own idiocy, one says to one's self at such times. Others must be protected against her. It is a social necessity. And all these things are true. But a blind fury, a feeling of adult shame, bred of a longing for muscular release are the operatives. One goes on to the end.

In a final unreasoning assault I overpowered the child's neck and jaws. I forced the heavy silver spoon back of her teeth and down her throat till she gagged. And there it was—both tonsils covered with membrane. She had fought valiantly to keep me from knowing her secret. She had been hiding that sore throat for three days at least and lying to her parents in order to escape just such an outcome as this.

Now truly she *was* furious. She had been on the defensive before but now she attacked. Tried to get off her father's lap and fly at me while tears of defeat blinded her eyes.

Ernest Hemingway born *1899 at Oak Park, Illinois. Before joining a voluntary ambulance unit in France during the First World War Hemingway worked as a reporter in Kansas City. During the latter part of this war he joined the Italian Infantry and served on the Italian front, where he was wounded. After the war he was a foreign correspondent for* THE TORONTO STAR *and for the Hearst newspapers. He was a correspondent in the Spanish Civil War and in the Second World War. His experiences in Spain provided the background for the story* 'OLD MAN AT THE BRIDGE'.

His influence on his contemporaries and on later writers has been considerable, his style aimed at bare prose from which he stripped all the unnecessary adjectives and literary embellishments. His prose is direct, forceful, and capable of great power of feeling. Like Sherwood Anderson he used brief sentences, a colloquial diction, and the repetition of key words and phrases, though he used this to greater effect than Anderson. His prose reveals intense selection of detail, a strict relevance of what is described. His method of using conversation to condense a story, to carry on plot or situation, and to express character, may be seen in even such a short piece as 'OLD MAN AT THE BRIDGE'.

His novels include A FAREWELL TO ARMS, *a story of the First World War,* FOR WHOM THE BELL TOLLS, *set in Spain during the Spanish Revolution, and his short stories are collected in* THE FIRST FORTY-NINE STORIES, *and in the* ESSENTIAL HEMINGWAY *in Penguin edition.*

Hemingway died in 1961.

OLD MAN AT THE BRIDGE

Ernest Hemingway

AN OLD MAN WITH STEEL RIMMED SPECTACLES AND VERY DUSTY CLOTHES sat by the side of the road. There was a pontoon bridge across the river and carts, trucks, and men, women and children were crossing it. The mule-drawn carts staggered up the steep bank from the bridge with soldiers helping push against the spokes of the wheels. The trucks ground up and away heading out of it all and the peasants plodded along in the ankle deep dust. But the old man sat there without moving. He was too tired to go any farther.

It was my business to cross the bridge, explore the bridgehead beyond and find out to what point the enemy had advanced. I did this and returned over the bridge. There were not so many carts now and very few people on foot, but the old man was still there.

"Where do you come from?" I asked him.

"From San Carlos," he said, and smiled.

That was his native town and so it gave him pleasure to mention it and he smiled.

"I was taking care of animals," he explained.

"Oh," I said, not quite understanding.

"Yes," he said, "I stayed, you see, taking care of animals. I was the last one to leave the town of San Carlos."

He did not look like a shepherd nor a herdsman and I looked at his black dusty clothes and his gray dusty face and his steel rimmed spectacles and said, "What animals were they?"

"Various animals," he said, and shook his head. "I had to leave them."

I was watching the bridge and the African looking country of the Ebro Delta and wondering how long now it would be before we would see the enemy, and listening all the while for the first noises that would signal that ever mysterious event called contact, and the old man still sat there.

"What animals were they?" I asked.

"There were three animals altogether," he explained. "There were two goats and a cat and then there were four pairs of pigeons."

"And you had to leave them?" I asked.

"Yes. Because of the artillery. The captain told me to go because of the artillery."

"And you have no family?" I asked, watching the far end of the bridge where a few last carts were hurrying down the slope of the bank.

"No," he said, "only the animals I stated. The cat, of course, will be all right. A cat can look out for itself, but I cannot think what will become of the others."

"What politics have you?" I asked.

"I am without politics," he said. "I am seventy-six years old. I have come twelve kilometers now and I think now I can go no further."

"This is not a good place to stop," I said. "If you can make it, there are trucks up the road where it forks for Tortosa."

"I will wait a while," he said, "and then I will go. Where do the trucks go?"

"Towards Barcelona," I told him.

"I know no one in that direction," he said, "but thank you very much. Thank you again very much."

He looked at me very blankly and tiredly, then said, having to share his worry with some one, "The cat will be all right, I am sure. There is no need to be unquiet about the cat. But the others. Now what do you think about the others?"

"Why they'll probably come through it all right."

"You think so?"

"Why not," I said, watching the far bank where now there were no carts.

"But what will they do under the artillery when I was told to leave because of the artillery?"

"Did you leave the dove cage unlocked?" I asked.

"Yes."

"Then they'll fly."

"Yes, certainly they'll fly. But the others. It's better not to think about the others," he said.

"If you are rested I would go," I urged. "Get up and try to walk now."

"Thank you," he said and got to his feet, swayed from side to side and then sat down backwards in the dust.

"I was taking care of animals," he said dully, but no longer to me. "I was only taking care of animals."

There was nothing to do about him. It was Easter Sunday and the Fascists were advancing toward the Ebro. It was a gray overcast day with a low ceiling so their planes were not up. That and the fact that cats know how to look after themselves was all the good luck that old man would ever have.

Douglas Stewart born in Eltham, New Zealand, in 1913 and educated at Victoria University College. At the Age of 20 Stewart went to Australia, where he worked as a freelance journalist. Two years later he worked his passage by ship to England. In 1938 he returned to join the staff of THE BULLETIN in Sydney and has lived there ever since. Although he is better known for his poetry and plays than for his fiction, a collection of Stewart's short stories under the title A GIRL WITH RED HAIR was published in 1944. Several of these stories draw on his early New Zealand experience and show an interest in country life and the Maori people. His COLLECTED POEMS, 1967, comprehend a considerable range of topics and styles, including some fine nature lyrics of the Australian countryside. Stewart's verse plays, NED KELLY and THE FIRE ON THE SNOW are powerful dramatizations of the character and exploits of two 'hero' figures, the Australian bushranger, Ned Kelly, and Captain Scott of the Antarctic.

In 'THE THREE JOLLY FOXES', two married couples are satirically portrayed. They are unromantic and distinctly unheroic, but through their exploits the author makes a witty though serious point about aspects of human nature.

THE THREE JOLLY FOXES

Douglas Stewart

AT THE HOUR OF SEVEN ON A FINE JUNE MORNING, TWO HANDSOME GLOSSY foxes are hurrying towards the store and teashop on Fat Chow Creek. The one who is closest is carrying no rabbit in his mouth; and that is a pity, for the great red fellow, trotting from the tea-tree to the golden rushes by the creek, ears up, plumy brush waving—a rabbit in his mouth would make him the perfect picture of a fox on the hunt in the morning.

As for Mr Hardcastle, his big, knuckly hands gripping the steering wheel of his shiny red car—he's got his rabbit all right, and you can almost see her in his mouth; the new Mrs Hardcastle—brand-new; only last night—snuggling beside him in her cony-seal coat. The tip of her small nose twitches.

'You're cold!' shouts Mr Hardcastle. You can tell he's a fox by the bark of his laughter. 'You're cold.' (Bark! Bark! Bark!)

'Oh, no,' she says, archly, sarcastically. She laughs, too, very loud and shrill and high, like a tremendous and surprising bell; the pealing of wedding bells.

'Hey, yes you are, you're cold. It's too early in the morning for you. Ha, we'll make a man of you yet.'

'You wouldn't want to do that.'

'Ha, that's right!' Mr Hardcastle barks and barks. 'But you *are* cold. I'll warm you up. I'll stop the car and warm you up.'

'You'd better drive on. Besides, I'm not a bit cold. Really I'm not. I love this south coast in the morning. The mountains with the sun on them; and the sea that delicate, delicate blue; and the foam. It's a wonderful place—for a honeymoon.'

'Honeymoon! Ha!' The big fox barks. His hair is silver, there is a bald patch on top, his eyes are grey and small; the character of his face is in his large, fleshy nose and his mouth, which sets firmly, even savagely, as he steers the big car round a bend. He makes it lurch round the corners.

'Just to be driving along,' says the rabbit. She smiles up at him, so that her frizzy hair and her horn-rimmed glasses seem to disappear, and all he can see are her red, red lips and her enormous false teeth. 'And a whole week of it,' she says. 'A whole week to Melbourne.'

'If I can find that Middleton scoundrel in Melbourne I'll prosecute the brute,' he says. 'He took us down. Deliberately. We supply him with the goods—two years ago—and that's the last we hear of him. I'll get him and I'll send him to jail.' Mr. Hardcastle has a factory.

'Oh,' says the new Mrs Hardcastle, 'don't let us think about business. This is too heavenly.'

But the fox—the other red fox in the rushes—is certainly thinking about business.

He knows it is heavenly, all right. The sun is warm on his back; the creek before him glitters; he can smell the salt sea, the tidal mud, the crabs; he can see a black-and-white bird, a pee-wee, that runs along the path between the rushes. But he cannot catch that pee-wee. And if he could it would not be much for a fox's breakfast. To run from dawn to seven o'clock, to hunt from dawn to seven o'clock, to hunt and sniff and hunt and sniff all the way from the rocky bush to within sight of Joe Packet's store and teashop by the bridge on Fat Chow Creek, to watch the mist lift and the dew dry and the seagulls go over in a clear, shiny light, to have the scent of shellfish and birds and vegetation in your nostrils—all this is to make hunger grow immense, a madness.

And if it is a madness to sneak right to the edge of the rushes where, along the line of his withered corn, Joe Packet has set his rabbit-traps—then let it be madness. But nobody sings or shouts in Joe Packet's store and tearooms, no smoke yet curls from the chimney. Joe Packet and Mrs Packet lie snug abed while the fox is at their rabbit-traps.

Yet it might, indeed, be a mad fox who thinks he can catch Joe Packet asleep. Joe is like a fox, too; he lies snug with his vixen in the warm burrow of the bed, but all night long he leaves his mouth out in the paddock to catch the rabbits; his spare mouth, his dozen spare mouths, all gaping, waiting, with sharp steel teeth. Joe Packet has caught two rabbits while he sleeps. Broken, they lie in his spare steel mouths—fast shut these mouths are. How warm, how appetizing they smell! How inviting is the thought of pink flesh under that soft grey fur! The red fox lolls his tongue. He whines with pleasure.

He takes a little run round the rabbits, partly for joy, partly to make sure Joe Packet is not about. Not a sign of him; only, on the steel mouths, a little rank smell of Joe Packet where he has touched them last night; to cover a yawn, it might be.

Fox, fox, Joe Packet never yawns. Look out, red fox!

Yes, yelp! But yelp too late, you mad red dog of the mountains. Joe Packet is a lucky man, he has caught a fox in his trap.

Joe Packet stirs in his bed. Time for a cup of tea. And the store and the tearooms to open. Someone might be coming along the road. A fine day for business.

And then, too, a fine day to take a little walk round the traps while the wife lights the fire and cooks the breakfast. A black woman in the mornings! But a blue day outside. Joe Packet in his blue dungarees, his hard, big belly rolling over the narrow black belt; his open grey shirt showing the dark hair on his chest; dark hair turning grey.

The square head of Joe Packet, usually hunched forward, now thrown back as he snuffs the salty air. The feet of Joe Packet, in the unlaced, torn, dirty, comfortable, rubber-soled sandshoes, travelling lightly over Fat Chow bridge. Grunt as he climbs through the fence. Stealthily along the corn, as if the dead rabbits could run away out of his mouths. Ho! And a high, whinnying laugh.

A fox, a fox in the trap! Before he can bite his leg off. A stick, a stick, a cudgel. The red fox spins and dances.

Joe Packet, a heavy man, light on his feet, darting about the cornfield and the rushes, hunting for a cudgel—he hardly notices the big red car crossing the bridge.

Burly man, tall skinny girl, Mr and Mrs Hardcastle alight from the car at the tearooms. Ah, Joe Packet sees them.

Thud goes the stick on the fox. 'Tourists!' says Joe. 'My lucky day to-day!'

Mr Hardcastle is as hungry as the fox was, but nobody is going to hit him on the head with a cudgel. Not if he knows it.

'Come on now. Quick, quick, quick!' he says to Joe Packet's wife. 'A cup of tea before we start. Then bacon and eggs for two.'

'Oh,' says Mrs Hardcastle. 'Just a piece of toast. Just a *wafer*.'

'Bacon and eggs for two!' shouts Mr Hardcastle. 'Now, quick about it, old dear.'

'Certainly,' says Joe Packet's wife.

The honeymoon couple are alone. They are among fragile cane chairs, and glass-topped tables and vases of paper roses. A wall of windows shows between creamy curtains the distant blue of the sea and a section of the white-painted railing of the bridge. Shafts of sunlight enter. Almost, a faint, subsiding rattle is heard as Mr Hardcastle's jollity ceases to crash about the glassy room. The floor quakes as Joe Packet's wife goes about her business.

'They'd do pretty well here,' says Mr Hardcastle confidentially. 'Cheap. No rent. Grow your own vegetables. Pluck your own fowls. Pluck the tourists.'

'Really?' says Mrs Hardcastle. 'So far from anywhere—I wouldn't have thought. But of course you'd know.'

Is she mocking him when she flatters, or does she really respect it so much—his business ability? Mr Hardcastle's eyes narrow. His mouth takes on that savage, down-curving line that shows when he is heaving the car round a bend. 'Of course they'd do well!' he shouts.

'A peculiar woman, isn't she?' says Mrs Hardcastle. 'So dark and slinking. She gives me a creepy feeling. That long, snooping nose, those jet-black eyes. She's the sort of woman who'd have lain in wait for travellers in the old days—an innkeeper's wife—and murdered them in their beds.' Mrs Hardcastle's large eyes blink behind the horn-rimmed glasses. She thrusts her hands into her frizzy hair and drags forward a black curl of it, as if she is the villain in a melodrama throwing his cloak over his features. 'Like some cold, slinking animal. I'm sure she'd like to murder us.'

'Stuff!' roars Mr Hardcastle. He has noticed his wife's tendency to romanticize. It might become worse.

Joe Packet's wife brings in tea and toast. She points her long nose at the tourists. 'Joe's caught a fox. He's out there now with the skin.'

'Now, what's that worth?' says Mr Hardcastle quickly.

'A fox. The skin of a fox. Oh, I must see it!' cries Mrs Hardcastle. 'Where is it? Can I see it? Where?'

'On the garage door,' says Mrs Packet. 'He's nailing it up to dry.'

'To think,' says Mrs Hardcastle dramatically, pausing in the doorway, 'to think that at this very hour I would have been arriving at the office and taking the cover off my typewriter; and here—down the south coast —on the way to Melbourne—and the lovely skin of a fox!' She rushes out.

'She's excited, isn't she?' says Joe Packet's lean dark wife. 'Just like a girl.'

'My dear lady,' says Mr. Hardcastle very winningly, 'how much you could excite me by bringing me my bacon and eggs.' He pushes a whole finger of toast into his mouth, and the butter runs down his fingers. He sucks them. 'Ah!'

'Just like a girl, eh?' he thinks as Joe Packet's wife retires to the kitchen. 'Ha! Last night!' (He barks.) Yes, like a girl. And not as if—well, she'd been his secretary for ten years. Secretary, you could call it. And still like a girl; kittenish, excited; rolling her big eyes behind the glasses, twitching her nose, smiling with her huge white teeth. A girl, a kitten, a rabbit.

Mr Hardcastle's rabbit is forty years old. Why marry her, then? And after ten years. Well, we grow old. Time, loneliness and—the dark thing. A widower in a dark house. And then, she wanted it so much. On the shelf; spinsterish; really, a little bit dotty; damn' nearly, anyhow. Why not please her? A house, money, a cony-seal coat, a car, a wedding, a honeymoon on the south coast; and a man—ha, yes, a man!—how much he could give his little rabbit.

Joe Packet's dark-eyed wife brings him his bacon and eggs. 'I'll keep the lady's warm for her,' she said. 'Are you sure she really wants it?'

'Of course she wants it,' says Mr Hardcastle roughly. 'Fill her out. Do her good. A leaf of lettuce in a back room in Darlinghurst, that's what these girls live on.'

Mrs Hardcastle's knees are too bony, he thinks, Ah. well, she shall eat. Not really a girl, not trim and tight and bouncy; but there you are.

'How would I look with a girl?' he asks Joe Packet's wife. 'An old codger like me!'

'I'm sure you'd look very well with a girl, sir,' says the sallow-faced woman diplomatically.

'Ha!' he says scornfully. 'Run you down into the grave and then make off with your money. You don't catch me like that.'

Mrs Hardcastle comes flying in.

'Oh!' she cries, 'it's horrible. He's got it all pegged out on the wall, crucified. The inside of the skin showing. Ugh, slimy. And the head's lolling forward, it looks alive. And it's grinning. There on the wall, grinning.' Her frizzy hair seems to be springing up and down with alarm.

'Ha!' says Mr Hardcastle. 'I must have a look at that.' He rises from the table.

'Oh,' says his wife, 'let's go. We've miles to go to-day. Let's drive on now.'

Mr Hardcastle pushes the brand-new Mrs Hardcastle into her chair. 'You sit down and eat your breakfast,' he says.

'I couldn't.'

'Eat it. It's ordered. We'll have to pay for it—*you'll* have to pay, because you're the housekeeper—so eat it up and be done with it.' He goes out.

Joe Packet's wife looks sympathetically at Mrs Hardcastle. 'You must have been up very early,' she says, 'if you came from Sydney this morning.'

'Oh, yes,' says Mrs Hardcastle airily. 'Mr Hardcastle likes to make an early start when he's travelling. Even—well, even this morning.'

'A special morning, my dear?' asks the sympathetic wife of Joe Packet.

'Oh, no,' says Mrs Hardcastle. 'Oh, nothing special.' *Is* it, she wonders. *Is* it? What have I done? He's so rough, he's so burly; blundering through life like a footballer.

'I wonder,' says the sympathetic lady, leaning towards her and dangling a little trumpery necklace of bright flowers made from dough, 'I wonder if you'd like to help me with my good work. These are for the Red Cross.'

Joe Packet's wife does not look like a lady who sells things for the Red Cross. She has a long, ominous nose, which is piercing Mrs Hardcastle in the bosom; she has a cold, glittering black eye which Mrs Hardcastle would prefer to see fixed on someone else; she has a stealthy, cat-like tread, which Mrs Hardcastle wishes would transport her out of the room. But Joe Packet's wife does not move away from the breakfast-table. She stands there still and ominous.

'Oh,' says Mrs Hardcastle, 'you sell them, do you?'

'For the Red Cross, my dear. Ten shillings.'

Ten shillings. But Mr Hardcastle, strong, protective Mr Hardcastle, is not to be seen on the left of Joe Packet's wife's nose, nor on the right of her nose. If only she will go away.

Mrs Hardcastle fumbles in her purse.

'Thank you, my dear,' says the woman. 'Now would you like another little necklace? Pretty, aren't they? Or some earrings? For the Red Cross.'

'I think,' says Mrs Hardcastle desperately, 'that will be enough for just now. Perhaps some other time. When we come back. I *think*,' says Mrs Hardcastle bravely, 'I'll just pay for the breakfasts now and then we can be on the road.'

'Another ten shillings, my dear,' says the lean wife of Joe Packet.

Ten shillings for bacon and eggs! But Mrs Hardcastle pays it. Shall she face the fox again? She must find Mr Hardcastle and go.

But Mr Hardcastle is not outside by the garage door, where the red fox grins at his wife. Joe Packet has him in the store.

'Packet's my name,' says Joe Packet, 'and Packet's my nature. Ham, Mr Hardcastle, eh? You'll want it for the trip. I'll pack it.' Swift and light in his movements, swift and fluent in his speech.

'Ha!' roars Mr Hardcastle happily, 'you want to pack me the whole blasted shop.'

'The old red fox, he's dead, eh?' says Joe Packet. 'He's finished, that one. But you and I, we live. Hey, Mr Hardcastle, we live—and while we live we eat.'

'You got any salmon?' asks Mr Hardcastle. 'Put it in.'

'Three tins,' says Joe, chuckling. 'Four tins. We'll make it four. The old red salmon, he swims in the sea no more.' He's a hard case, is Joe; his face all wrinkled with laughter, and his upper lip lifted at the corner in a permanent grin that shows a yellow fang.

'What the hell will I ever do with four tins of salmon?' Mr Hardcastle joyously bellows.

'You're going to Melbourne. With a lady. You take a week for the journey. You eat by the roadside. Plenty, to keep your strength up.'

'Put 'em in then, put 'em in,' says Mr Hardcastle. 'To keep my strength up.' (Bark.)

Joe laughs. Square head lifted off his chest again, thrown back, and the high whinnying laugh shooting up, it seems, at the tins of biscuits on the top shelf. His hands hold his belly in.

'Right!' says Joe. 'Now then. Fruit, chocolates, cigarettes, what else does the lady like? Biscuits! Gingernuts, wafers—no, chocolate fingers.' He climbs a ladder to the top shelf. Force of habit alone prevents his blue dungarees from slipping off.

Mrs Hardcastle is astounded. The pile of foodstuffs and groceries. Simply squandering money. And him, of all people! What would he say if he knew about the ten shillings for the necklace and the other ten shillings for breakfast?

Why, at the moment, he, Mr Hardcastle, shrewd, tough, tightfisted managing director of a factory, he would say nothing at all. How curious; curious. What have he and Joe Packet been saying to each other while they stared at the old dead dog-fox? What male jokes have they cracked? She knows. She knows. The three jolly foxes together.

But here comes that woman behind her; the long, sharp nose is making a hole in her spine. 'Oh, come,' says Mrs Hardcastle to her husband. 'We must go.'

Joe Packet slithers down the ladder.

'Yes,' says Mr Hardcastle. 'In a minute.'

'I'm sure you'll have a lovely journey,' says the wife of Joe.

'I think,' says Mrs Hardcastle to her husband, 'I'll sit in the car and wait for you. Don't be long.' She looks down, over the tops of her horn-rimmed glasses, at Mrs Packet, who is not now some sliding, sinister animal, but, because Mrs Hardcastle is departing, merely the avaricious wife of a storekeeper. 'Good-bye,' trills Mrs Hardcastle sarcastically as she goes out the door, 'I do hope you bring lots of success to the Red Cross.'

Mrs Packet smiles, her long flickering upper lip, with its faint black moustache, disclosing very small white teeth, like a fish's. Such a repellent-looking woman.

'Quick, then,' says Joe. 'Three at one-and-two is three-and-nine, the biscuits two-and-sevenpence, salmon, pears, three tins of peaches, chocolates, say two shillings, no half a crown, ham, chicken-paste, loaf of bread sevenpence, then there's the cigarettes; look here, Mr Hardcastle, I'll throw in a packet of matches; now that's two-pounds-ten the lot. And no charge at all for looking at the old red fox.'

'Ha!' laughs Mr Hardcastle. 'I know who's the old red fox. Two-pounds-ten!'

'But isn't it worth it?' said Joe. 'Life is worth it! Picnics by the road are worth it. You and me, we know, Mr Hardcastle. You're only old once.' His whinnying laughter.

'Two-pounds-ten, then,' says Mr Hardcastle, a little sadly, for, after all, money is money.

'And ten shillings for the breakfasts, don't forget,' says Mrs Packet, her long nose entering the conversation.

'Three quid,' says Joe. 'Three jolly old quid the lot.'

Mr Hardcastle pays him. 'I'll tell you what,' he says, 'that damned old fox-skin won't be worth a cracker to you, anyhow. You saw the holes where the ticks had got into it.'

'Never mind about that,' says Joe. 'We'll find a use for him somehow. He was a good fox in his day. Good-bye, Mr Hardcastle.'

As Mr Hardcastle drives off Joe Packet waves, and the red fox, on the garage door, is grinning.

'I thought we'd never get away,' says Mrs Hardcastle, looking back from a bend in the road at the store by Fat Chow Creek. 'Those awful people. They robbed us.'

'I told you they'd do pretty well there,' Mr Hardcastle answers. 'Three quid they got out of me. Well, it was worth it.'

'*What* was?' asks the brand-new Mrs Hardcastle. 'Three pounds just for that box of groceries.'

'Ten bob of it was for the breakfasts,' says Mr Hardcastle.

'But I paid them for the breakfasts!'

'Damn it, I did!'

'We both paid!' Mrs Hardcastle is aghast. 'We've paid them twice for it. Oh!'

'Ha!' laughs Mr Hardcastle, placing his hand on her knee as, doubtless in error for the gear-lever, he so often does. 'Diddled us, diddled us properly.'

'We'll put the police on to them!' says Mrs Hardcastle.

'No,' her big husband scorns her. 'I can afford it. Let 'em go.'

'I think you should drive straight back to that shop and demand your money back. You must have gone absolutely mad to take it so calmly. Laughing.'

'I like to see it!' Mr Hardcastle shouts with his bark of laughter. 'The old fox and the vixen! They'll do all right, that pair. They'll make money. I'd like to have that old fox on my sales staff.'

'You're a bit of a fox yourself,' says Mrs Hardcastle softly. She looks at him archly, over the rims of her glasses. 'But you want to look out, you know. More than one old fox has put his foot right into a rabbit-trap. And that was the end of him.' Her wedding-bells peal and peal.

Mr Hardcastle begins to laugh, then does not. He stares at his brand-new wife. There is something strangely steel-like in Mrs Hardcastle's appearance. Bones, wires, those horn-rimmed glasses, that frizz of springs on her head, those enormous teeth. And the old fox in a trap. He stamps his foot on the accelerator.

Peter Cowan born *1914, Perth, Western Australia. Teaches in the* English Department of the University of W.A.

Short stories: DRIFT, *1944,* THE UNPLOUGHED LAND, *1958,* THE EMPTY STREET, *1965. Novels:* SUMMER, *1964,* SEED, *1966.*

THE RED-BACKED SPIDERS

Peter Cowan

IT HAD BEGUN THAT MORNING AT BREAKFAST, ONE OF THE INTERMINABLE disputes that arose from nothing, yet became suddenly sharp and fierce, exploding into the violence of words or force. At first I had thought the force was worse, but it burnt out in a kind of shock, whereas the words stayed bitterly so that even I, as an outsider, felt their pain. He had hit the girl abruptly with the flat of his hand, jerking her head back, and her eyes dark with misery, she had gone from the room.

As he had done himself. Almost before I realized it had happened, the incident had jarred sharply to a focal point, and was past. For the woman, rising quickly, had said: 'No, please—it's not his fault. . . .'

Nor was it perhaps anyone else's business. And I did not want it mine. I had known when I first saw the house, standing on the bare ground of the hillside, that this was no place where one would stay, and the time I had spent there had not changed that feeling.

I was going across after the meal from my room by the sheds to harness the horse when I saw the boy. The track passed the old jarrah by the fence of the house-yard. The twisted trunk held a scarred hollow reaching up from the base, mark of a fire; the tree itself had been useless for timber or for sleepers even before it had been burnt. It was the only one in the yard, though out in the paddocks numbers of them still stood.

Scattered across the ground between the fence and the tree, and about the base of the trunk, the rubbish of an old dump lay. The boy was playing in it. He was picking out the old jam-tins and the tinned-meat cans, spacing them in a kind of design; the jam-tins going one way and the short fat meat-cans spaced out at an angle to them. The dump held bits of old machinery, old tyres, rusty kero. tins, and the tins and bottles from the house. Near the tree lay an old stove and some rusted cream-cans. From among it all the boy was picking out the small jam- and meat-tins, digging among the rest of the junk for them, and making his design on the ground.

I could see him as I crossed the yard, but he gave no sign; it was as though he had not noticed me. I went over to the dump and stood by the tree, looking down at him.

'What are you making?' I asked.

He did not look up. He had one of the jam-tins in his hand, the top partly covered by his fingers.

'You'll rustle a snake out of there one day. And it'll be too bad if you both make for the house at the same time.'

'There's not,' the boy said. 'Not in here.'

'Well, you never know. And your father doesn't like you playing here.

How about finding somewhere else for a while, eh?'

The boy made no move, but his hand shifted down away from the top of the tin so that he was grasping the round rusted surface of the can. I could see into the tin.

'You'd better chuck that one away,' I said. 'Look, there's a red-back in it. They won't hurt you unless you interfere with them, but that one's not going to like what you're doing to his tin. Throw it away.'

I moved my hand to take the tin, but the boy held it tightly. I heard the door of the house slam and looked across the yard. It was too late then.

'Here's your father. He's not going to be too pleased finding you here. To say nothing of me not having the horse harnessed up. You come down the shed with me and we'll harness up.'

The boy might not have heard. He was sitting quite still, the rusty tin in his hand.

'Well, I'm going to get the horse in.'

I began to walk towards the sheds.

The boy's father was coming across the yard to the dump.

'I told you to keep out of that,' he said. His voice was raised, but not as though suddenly, rather as if in a kind of constant irritability that was part of his make-up, like his features, or his quick jerky walk.

'You get messing about in there and you'll find one of those red spiders bite you. I told you to keep away.'

He grabbed the boy's arm and pulled him to his feet.

'One bite from those spiders and they'll kill you. I told you that. Get out of the dump, keep over round the house. I catch you here again I'll stop you wanting to come over here properly.'

He pushed him so that the boy ran a few paces to keep his balance, and then began to walk over towards the house. He had not said anything. Round the house the ground was bare and dusty, swept clean and hard about the back door and the veranda near the door. His father came on across the yard to the sheds.

'All right?' he asked.

'Just about,' I said.

'We want to be back by lunchtime.'

It wouldn't be my fault if we weren't, but there was no need to tell him that. We drove out towards the back paddock where we were to pick up the load of wood, and cut a couple of saplings for rails. The horse went along slowly, the man jerking the reins impatiently until it broke into an awkward trot. The animal was not over fond of work, and it gave an impression of the smallest action requiring an immense and pitiful labour. I looked at the man sitting forward in the cart, staring ahead, his hands jerking the reins. But I was thinking of the boy rather than of him. And the way the boy had looked. He had had that queer kind of expression as though he did not understand. It was not that he didn't know when he was doing something that was forbidden, but his face could take on a blankness as though he tried to keep the expression from it. And he was too young to do that deliberately, or so you would have thought. It was not the things round him, what he could and could not do, that he did not understand and that bewildered him so that he was forced in on himself, but rather the people about him, the way they acted. He was trying to look into an adult world that simply did not hold meaning for him.

Looking at the man driving the cart, his face set with a kind of nervous tension, a tension that you could see in his quick jerky walk and raised voice, I thought the boy had reason enough for his lack of understanding. When I first came to the place there had been enough that I had not understood. And they were not things the boy would know, perhaps not things he would ever know. There seemed no bridge for him into that other world he stood at the edge of.

The woman and the girls left the man alone, retreating in a knowledge that had been gained in bitterness and perhaps defeat. But the boy wanted his father, and his world was plainly incomplete without him. He would still go up to his father to talk to him, sometimes for the affection that seemed now inevitably denied, that perhaps had never been there, sometimes to ask the questions that his mind was filled with and that were reduced quickly to the man's ridicule. So that he had become now too quiet and solitary for a boy of his age.

And yet quite soon I had begun to feel sorry for the man. He had a kind of hatred that had turned against those who were around him, and against this place with its indifferent soil and slow yields, its quiet and total involvement that was imprisonment; but it was a hate that had also turned in against himself.

There was no point in trying to apportion blame. In time one might have come close to understanding it all, and yet that same time would see one's own involvement. I was going when the digging season for the potatoes started, and I wanted only to be able to keep out of it. But the situation could break out suddenly into something I would be forced to interfere in, uselessly, because nothing would be achieved, and I would have to go, and it would all go on afterwards, just the same, perhaps worse for my interference.

It was in my mind as we worked in the back paddock during the morning. I was loading the cart while the man went off to look for the saplings. There was not much of the fallen wood that needed cutting, so I had little to do but load it.

We came in again at midday and took the load off. He went over to the house while I took the horse out and gave it its feed. Then I went

109

across towards the veranda. The yard was hot and without shade. I took the basin from the staging of the tank at the edge of the veranda and had a wash. I was drying myself slowly, standing in the sun, and looking along the veranda without seeing anything in particular, just feeling the heat of the sun and rubbing my neck and head with the towel. The veranda was partly shaded from the sun, and had two beds pulled lengthways along the wall, where the man and the boy slept. But I suddenly noticed two of the rusty jam-tins on the floor under the boy's bed. I knew they hadn't been there at breakfast-time, so the boy must have been over to the dump again and brought them back. Strange that boys should seem to want things so much.

After lunch the boy came out with us as we left the house. He usually came out to see us off, but the man would not let him work with us, even if we were to be near the house. He seemed to get on his father's nerves and it was a hell of a time for us all. I thought of the tins as we came out, but the boy did not look towards the beds; they might have gone completely from his mind. His father saw the tins on the veranda. He bent down and pulled them out from under the bed.

'I told you about those tins.' His voice rose shrilly. 'D'you want these spiders getting in your bed—how can you see them when you get in there in the dark—haven't you got any sense at all? You just can't learn.'

He threw the tins out towards the dump and went across the yard. The boy stayed by the veranda looking down at the hard, swept earth that was hot under his bare feet.

We had yarded the cows the next afternoon for the milking and I was going over to the separator shed for the cans when I saw the boy playing in the dump. The shade from the old jarrah was drawn thinly across the ground that was still hot from the day. I looked at the boy playing with the rusty tins and the pieces of old iron. You do not know what things take possession of boys' minds and what they seem to have to do. I suppose it's too far back to that time in one's own life, too distant to such compulsions that held their own validity.

It was as if the boy had never been told not to play there. Looking at him I was going to go over and warn him when I saw that the man had seen him too. He was striding quickly towards the dump. The boy did not hear him, he seemed totally absorbed in what he was doing among the tins and bits of iron. His face went suddenly white with fear and shock when the man pulled him up and he twisted round, looking up at his father. I saw with a strange, irrelevant clarity that the boy had made a castle of the tins, a splendid thing, the high mass of the central building, the turrets and the walls. You no longer saw the parts, the rusty discarded tins, but only the whole that he had built, the compulsion that had been in his mind so that he had had to create its likeness.

The tins rattled from the man's foot out towards the dump, scattered, incongruous. He hit the boy across the head so that he stumbled, and then kicked him. I knew then there was no help for it, and this was what I had been afraid of all along. I had seen him try to treat the elder girl like this. She had some chance to look after herself and could get away. In this mood the man was beyond reason or thinking. If an animal went like this you would shoot it. I started towards the dump, beginning to run. Then, suddenly, the man stopped and turned away and went off towards the sheds with his quick jerky walk. He was talking and moving his hands as though making gestures to someone.

It was getting dark and I had washed the milk buckets and finished in the dairy. In the window of the house the light had begun to take on distinctness. At first I thought one of the calves had got into the yard and had been rummaging round the dump and made off as it heard me coming. Then I saw the small upright shape of the boy walking across towards the veranda and there was something in his hands. It was too dark to see clearly, but I had no doubt then that it was the boy and that he was carrying something. The rest were inside busy with the tea and they did not miss him. He came in for his tea. I thought I would see if the tin had been left on the veranda when I came out afterwards, and shift it if it had, to save any more trouble. And yet, inside, in the lighted kitchen, I did not really believe it could have been the boy, that he would have gone over there again. So that when, afterwards, in the darkness, I could find nothing on the veranda I thought I had imagined seeing the boy—in the dark of the yard I could have been mistaken. Inside I could hear the man saying something, his voice raised as though in argument, and I did not stay.

Someone knocking suddenly on the door of the small room where I slept woke me. For a moment I wondered if I had overslept, and I imagined the man's voice, querulous, sarcastic. Then I knew it was not that, and I could hear the girl saying something. I pushed the door open, looking out. The girl said something confused about her father being sick. I pulled my coat and trousers on and went across to the house with her. She told me they did not know what was the matter with the man; they thought at first he had been bitten by a snake. It was not that, but they must get him into town.

The woman and the other girl were in the kitchen. The man was sitting on one of the plain, hard chairs, his head and shoulders slumped across the table. I took him across to the truck, and the woman got up in the cab beside him. We drove down the track, in the darkness, to the road. I took the truck along fast, watching the road that wound and was hard to see in the darkness, all my attention concentrated so that I was scarcely aware of the others. On the straight portion, near the town, I could look across at the man and I saw that the woman had put his head down against her shoulder, and that he was lying against her, quite still. And it was like something I should not have seen.

The woman stayed in town and I drove back by myself to the farm. It was beginning to get light, the sky becoming pale and the bands of long, thin, cloud streamers close above the horizon taking on colour, changing from dull grey to long, crimson bands, the yellow of the light behind them. And driving I thought of the difference from the way we had come in, with the hurry and urgency, and I thought of the strange, fatalistic fear of the woman, as though she knew it had all concentrated here, drawn in to this, and knew the briefness of what was ahead, like a contrast to the resignation that was perhaps indifference in the man. It was an indifference that made him a stranger, the constant edge of temper gone, the querulousness, the seeking for something to make discord from. And as I watched the road in the gaining light I thought that perhaps that was what he had been, a stranger, and as much to those he had lived with as to one outside, like myself. Because we had accepted that exterior of irritability and harshness. It seemed all there was. And soon one did not look for anything else. So that it was with a sense of shock and uneasiness you realized it had not always been like that, as I had realized when I saw them in the cab of the truck as we drove in, as though the two of them had been alone there and I had no existence. Perhaps some of that other time had come back for them then, deep buried though it must have been, with the kind of angry aloofness and separation of the man gone.

His health had never been anything but poor, and it seemed he had been bitten more than once, from what I gathered briefly before I left the hospital; but I thought his state of health must have been partly to blame, because I had never really believed any of those spiders had a fatal bite, despite the stories you always heard. But I could not forget the change in the man, the way he seemed to have let go, as though he no longer cared about anything. He had not wanted to be taken in to hospital, and he would not wake the boy. He seemed afraid we would make a noise and wake him.

And then suddenly it seemed to come together in my mind, and I realized how it must have come to the man, how he must have seen it all then with a sudden clearness; how this had happened, and beyond this, to the way it had all become set so that there was no changing anything. And he had had no strength and knew it was no use to go on. That was only a guess; no one will know. And I thought how the man could not have seen the boy, as I had, just before tea as the darkness came about the house and yards and the dump. And, as I turned the truck off the road along the track towards the house, now, in the growing light, that seemed unreal again, too, as though I had imagined it.

Angelica Gibbs Her short story, 'THE TEST', *was first printed in* THE NEW YORKER, *and again in the first collection of the best stories written in* THE NEW YORKER *during its first fifteen years, 1925–40. It is an excellent example of the compression which a short story can achieve, and the richness of meaning it can offer. The story is extremely brief, and told almost entirely in dialogue. The characters reveal themselves, and reveal the problems which the story wants to raise, through the dialogue. The author never intrudes, the story relies on only a very few points of action, and almost no exposition. It is a story which offers a considerable insight through the carefully controlled speech of its characters, and which is content to work through implication rather than explanation.*

THE TEST

Angelica Gibbs

ON THE AFTERNOON MARIAN TOOK HER SECOND DRIVER'S TEST, MRS. ERICSON
went with her. 'It's probably better to have someone a little older with
you,' Mrs. Ericson said as Marian slipped into the driver's seat beside her.
'Perhaps the last time your Cousin Bill made you nervous, talking too
much on the way.'

'Yes, Ma'am,' Marian said in her soft unaccented voice. 'They probably
do like it better if a white person shows up with you.'

'Oh, I don't think it's *that*,' Mrs. Ericson began, and subsided after a
glance at the girl's set profile. Marian drove the car slowly through the
shady suburban streets. It was one of the first hot days in June, and when
they reached the boulevard they found it crowded with cars headed
for the beaches.

'Do you want me to drive?' Mrs. Ericson asked. 'I'll be glad to if you're
feeling jumpy.' Marian shook her head. Mrs. Ericson watched her dark,
competent hands and wondered for the thousandth time how the house
had ever managed to get along without her, or how she had lived through
those earlier years when her household had been presided over by a series
of slatternly white girls who had considered housework demeaning and
the care of children an added insult. 'You drive beautifully, Marian,' she
said. 'Now, don't think of the last time. Anybody would slide on a steep
hill on a wet day like that.'

'It takes four mistakes to flunk you,' Marian said. 'I don't remember
doing all the things the inspector marked down on my blank.'

'People say that they only want you to slip them a little something,'
Mrs. Ericson said doubtfully.

'*No*,' Marian said. 'That would only make it worse, Mrs. Ericson,
I know.'

The car turned right, at a traffic signal, into a side road and slid up to the
curb at the rear of a short line of parked cars. The inspectors had not
arrived yet.

'You have the papers?' Mrs. Ericson asked. Marian took them out of
her bag: her learner's permit, the car registration, and her birth certificate.
They settled down to the dreary business of waiting.

'It will be marvellous to have someone dependable to drive the children
to school every day,' Mrs. Ericson said.

Marian looked up from the list of driving requirements she had been
studying. 'It'll make things simpler at the house, won't it?' she said.

'Oh, Marian,' Mrs. Ericson exclaimed, 'if I could only pay you half of
what you're worth!'

115

'Now, Mrs. Ericson,' Marian said firmly. They looked at each other and smiled with affection.

Two cars with official insignia on their doors stopped across the street. The inspectors leaped out, very brisk and military in their neat uniforms. Marian's hands tightened on the wheel. 'There's the one who flunked me last time,' she whispered, pointing to a stocky, self-important man who had begun to shout directions at the driver at the head of the line. 'Oh, Mrs. Ericson.'

'Now, Marian,' Mrs. Ericson said. They smiled at each other again, rather weakly.

The inspector who finally reached their car was not the stocky one but a genial, middle-aged man who grinned broadly as he thumbed over their papers. Mrs. Ericson started to get out of the car. 'Don't you want to come along?' the inspector asked. 'Mandy and I don't mind company.'

Mrs. Ericson was bewildered for a moment. 'No,' she said, and stepped to the curb. 'I might make Marian self-conscious. She's a fine driver, Inspector.'

'Sure thing,' the inspector said, winking at Mrs. Ericson. He slid into the seat beside Marian. 'Turn right at the corner, Mandy-Lou.'

From the curb, Mrs. Ericson watched the car move smoothly up the street.

The inspector made notations in a small black book. 'Age?' he inquired presently, as they drove along.

'Twenty-seven.'

He looked at Marian out of the corner of his eye. 'Old enough to have quite a flock of pickaninnies, eh?'

Marian did not answer.

'Left at this corner,' the inspector said, 'and park between that truck and the green Buick.'

The two cars were very close together, but Marian squeezed in between them without too much manoeuvering. 'Driven before, Mandy-Lou?' the inspector asked.

'Yes, sir. I had a license for three years in Pennsylvania.'

'Why do you want to drive a car?'

'My employer needs me to take her children to and from school.'

'Sure you don't really want to sneak out nights to meet some young blood?' the inspector asked. He laughed as Marian shook her head.

'Let's see you take a left at the corner and then turn around in the middle of the next block, the inspector said. He began to whistle 'Swanee River.' 'Make you homesick?' he asked.

Marian put out her hand, swung around neatly in the street, and headed back in the direction from which they had come. 'No,' she said. 'I was born in Scranton, Pennsylvania.'

The inspector feigned astonishment. 'You-all ain't Southern?' he said. 'Well, dog my cats if I didn't think you-all came from down yondah.'

'No, sir,' Marian said.

'Turn onto Main Street and let's see how you-all does in heavier traffic.'

They followed a line of cars along Main Street for several blocks until they came in sight of a concrete bridge which arched high over the railroad tracks.

'Read that sign at the end of the bridge,' the inspector said.

' "Proceed with caution. Dangerous in slippery weather," ' Marian said.

'You-all sho can read fine,' the inspector exclaimed. 'Where d'you learn to do that, Mandy?'

'I got my college degree last year,' Marian said. Her voice was not quite steady.

As the car crept up the slope of the bridge the inspector burst out laughing. He laughed so hard he could scarcely give his next direction. 'Stop here,' he said, wiping his eyes, 'then start 'er up again. Mandy got her degree, did she? Dog my cats!'

Marian pulled up beside the curb. She put the car in neutral, pulled on the emergency, waited a moment, and then put the car into gear again. Her face was set. As she released the brake her foot slipped off the clutch pedal and the engine stalled.

'Now, Mistress Mandy,' the inspector said, 'remember your degree.'

'*Damn* you!' Marian cried. She started the car with a jerk.

The inspector lost his joviality in an instant. 'Return to the starting place, please,' he said, and made four very black crosses at random in the squares on Marian's application blank.

Mrs. Ericson was waiting at the curb where they had left her. As Marian stopped the car, the inspector jumped out and brushed past her, his face purple. 'What happened?' Mrs. Ericson asked, looking after him with alarm.

Marian stared down at the wheel and her lip trembled.

'Oh, Marian, *again?*' Mrs. Ericson said.

Marian nodded. 'In a sort of different way,' she said, and slid over to the right-hand side of the car.

Shirley Jackson born *in San Francisco, in 1916, and educated at Syracuse University. A prolific writer of essays, short stories, and novels, she was married to folk-lorist Edgar Hyman, whose influence may be detected in her frequent use of ideas and attitudes drawn from the study of anthropology. Her best stories, many of which are collected in* THE LOTTERY, 1948, *are characterized by a tension between the normal and the abnormal, the obvious and the latent. Apparently trivial social activities are often seen as a fragile veneer over repressed, disruptive emotions. Among her many works are* LIFE AMONG THE SAVAGES, THE ROOM THROUGH THE WALL, THE WITCHCRAFT OF SALEM, *and* WE HAVE ALWAYS LIVED IN THE CASTLE.
She died in 1965.

AFTER YOU, MY DEAR ALPHONSE

Shirley Jackson

MRS. WILSON WAS JUST TAKING THE GINGERBREAD OUT OF THE OVEN WHEN she heard Johnny outside talking to someone.

'Johnny,' she called, 'you're late. Come in and get your lunch.'

'Just a minute, Mother,' Johnny said. 'After you, my dear Alphonse.'

'After *you*, my dear Alphonse,' another voice said.

'No, after *you*, my dear Alphonse,' Johnny said.

Mrs. Wilson opened the door. 'Johnny,' she said, 'you come in this minute and get your lunch. You can play after you've eaten.'

Johnny came in after her, slowly. 'Mother,' he said, 'I brought Boyd home for lunch with me.'

'Boyd?' Mrs. Wilson thought for a moment. 'I don't believe I've met Boyd. Bring him in, dear, since you've invited him. Lunch is ready.'

'Boyd!' Johnny yelled. 'Hey, Boyd, come on in!'

'I'm coming. Just got to unload this stuff.'

'Well, hurry, or my mother'll be sore.'

'Johnny, that's not very polite to either your friend or your mother,' Mrs. Wilson said. 'Come sit down, Boyd.'

As she turned to show Boyd where to sit, she saw he was a Negro boy, smaller than Johnny but about the same age. His arms were loaded with split kindling wood. 'Where'll I put this stuff, Johnny?' he asked.

Mrs. Wilson turned to Johnny. 'Johnny,' she said, 'what did you make Boyd do? What is that wood?'

'Dead Japanese,' Johnny said mildly. 'We stand them in the ground and run over them with tanks.'

'How do you do, Mrs. Wilson?' Boyd said.

'How do you do, Boyd? You shouldn't let Johnny make you carry all that wood. Sit down now and eat lunch, both of you.'

'Why shouldn't he carry the wood, Mother? It's his wood. We got it at his place.'

'Johnny,' Mrs. Wilson said, 'go on and eat your lunch.'

'Sure,' Johnny said. He held out the dish of scrambled eggs to Boyd. 'After you, my dear Alphonse.'

'After *you*, my dear Alphonse,' Boyd said.

'After *you*, my dear Alphonse,' Johnny said. They began to giggle.

'Are you hungry, Boyd?' Mrs. Wilson asked.

'Yes, Mrs. Wilson.'

'Well, don't let Johnny stop you. He always fusses about eating, so you just see that you get a good lunch. There's plenty of food here for you to have all you want.'

'Thank you, Mrs. Wilson.'

'Come on, Alphonse,' Johnny said. He pushed half the scrambled eggs on to Boyd's plate. Boyd watched while Mrs. Wilson put a dish of stewed tomatoes beside his plate.

'Boyd don't eat tomatoes, do you, Boyd?' Johnny said.

'*Doesn't* eat tomatoes, Johnny. And just because you don't like them, don't say that about Boyd. Boyd will eat *anything*.'

'Bet he won't,' Johnny said, attacking his scrambled eggs.

'Boyd wants to grow up and be a big strong man so he can work hard,' Mrs. Wilson said. 'I'll bet Boyd's father eats stewed tomatoes.'

'My father eats anything he wants to,' Boyd said.

'So does mine,' Johnny said. 'Sometimes he doesn't eat hardly anything. He's a little guy, though. Wouldn't hurt a flea.'

'Mine's a little guy, too,' Boyd said.

'I'll bet he's strong, though,' Mrs. Wilson said. She hesitated. 'Does he . . . work?'

'Sure,' Johnny said. 'Boyd's father works in a factory.'

'There, you see?' Mrs. Wilson said. 'And he certainly has to be strong to do that—all that lifting and carrying at a factory.'

'Boyd's father doesn't have to,' Johnny said. 'He's a foreman.'

Mrs. Wilson felt defeated. 'What does your mother do, Boyd?'

'My mother?' Boyd was surprised. 'She takes care of us kids.'

'Oh. She doesn't work, then?'

'Why should she?' Johnny said through a mouthful of eggs. 'You don't work.'

'You really don't want any stewed tomatoes, Boyd?'

'No, thank you, Mrs. Wilson,' Boyd said.

'No, thank you, Mrs. Wilson, no, thank you, Mrs. Wilson, no thank you, Mrs. Wilson,' Johnny said. 'Boyd's sister's going to work, though. She's going to be a teacher.'

'That's a very fine attitude for her to have, Boyd.' Mrs. Wilson restrained an impulse to pat Boyd on the head. 'I imagine you're all very proud of her?'

'I guess so,' Boyd said.

'What about all your other brothers and sisters? I guess all of you want to make just as much of yourselves as you can.'

'There's only me and Jean,' Boyd said. 'I don't know yet what I want to be when I grow up.'

'We're going to be tank drivers, Boyd and me,' Johnny said. 'Zoom.' Mrs. Wilson caught Boyd's glass of milk as Johnny's napkin ring, suddenly transformed into a tank, plowed heavily across the table.

'Look, Johnny,' Boyd said. 'Here's a foxhole. I'm shooting at you.'

Mrs. Wilson, with the speed born of long experience, took the ginger-bread off the shelf and placed it carefully between the tank and the foxhole.

'Now eat as much as you want to, Boyd,' she said. 'I want to see you get filled up.'

'Boyd eats a lot, but not as much as I do,' Johnny said. 'I'm bigger than he is.'

'You're not much bigger,' Boyd said. 'I can beat you running.'

Mrs. Wilson took a deep breath. 'Boyd,' she said. Both boys turned to her. 'Boyd, Johnny has some suits that are a little too small for him, and a winter coat. It's not new, of course, but there's lots of wear in it still. And I have a few dresses that your mother or sister could probably use. Your mother can make them into lots of things for all of you, and I'd be very happy to give them to you. Suppose before you leave I make up a big bundle and then you and Johnny can take it over to your mother right away . . .' Her voice trailed off as she saw Boyd's puzzled expression.

'But I have plenty of clothes, thank you,' he said. 'And I don't think my mother knows how to sew very well, and anyway I guess we buy about everything we need. Thank you very much, though.'

'We don't have time to carry that old stuff around, Mother,' Johnny said. 'We got to play tanks with the kids today.'

Mrs. Wilson lifted the plate of gingerbread off the table as Boyd was about to take another piece. 'There are many little boys like you, Boyd, who would be very grateful for the clothes someone was kind enough to give them.'

'Boyd will take them if you want him to, Mother,' Johnny said.

'I didn't mean to make you mad, Mrs. Wilson,' Boyd said.

'Don't think I'm angry, Boyd. I'm just disappointed in you, that's all. Now let's not say anything more about it.'

She began clearing the plates off the table, and Johnny took Boyd's hand and pulled him to the door. ' 'Bye, Mother,' Johnny said. Boyd stood for a minute, staring at Mrs. Wilson's back.

'After you, my dear Alphonse,' Johnny said, holding the door open.

'Is your mother still mad?' Mrs. Wilson heard Boyd ask in a low voice.

'I don't know,' Johnny said. 'She's screwy sometimes.'

'So's mine,' Boyd said. He hesitated. 'After *you*, my dear Alphonse.'

Ray Bradbury born Waukegan, Illinois, in 1920, educated at Los Angeles High School. Between 1941 and 1944 many of his stories appeared in leading American magazines, and in the annual collections of BEST AMERICAN SHORT STORIES. 'THE PEDESTRIAN' is one of twenty short stories in a collection called THE GOLDEN APPLES OF THE SUN, published in 1953. Among the most successful of his other works are THE SILVER LOCUSTS (published in the United States as THE MARTIAN CHRONICLES) and the novels, DANDELION WINE and FAHRENHEIT 451.

Bradbury's short stories and novels show a deep concern with the effects of a technological revolution on human society. This concern is dramatised in situations where individuals try, often vainly, to assert their humanity in the face of uncontrollable, impersonal but man-made forces.

The horror of a situation like that in THE PEDESTRIAN is emphasized by the neutral tone and precise, matter-of-fact narration.

THE PEDESTRIAN

Ray Bradbury

TO ENTER OUT INTO THAT SILENCE THAT WAS THE CITY AT EIGHT O'CLOCK of a misty evening in November, to put your feet upon that buckling concrete walk, to step over grassy seams and make your way, hands in pockets, through the silences, that was what Mr Leonard Mead most dearly loved to do. He would stand upon the corner of an intersection and peer down long moonlit avenues of side-walk in four directions, deciding which way to go, but it really made no difference; he was alone in this world of A.D. 2052, or as good as alone, and with a final decision made, a path selected, he would stride off, sending patterns of frosty air before him like the smoke of a cigar.

Sometimes he would walk for hours and miles and return only at midnight to his house. And on his way he would see the cottages and homes with their dark windows, and it was not unlike walking through a graveyard where only the faintest glimmers of firefly light appeared in flickers behind the windows. Sudden grey phantoms seemed to manifest upon inner room walls where a curtain was still undrawn against the night, or there were whisperings and murmurs where a window in a tomb-like building was still open.

Mr Leonard Mead would pause, cock his head, listen, look, and march on, his feet making no noise on the lumpy walk. For long ago he had wisely changed to sneakers when strolling at night, because the dogs in intermittent squads would parallel his journey with barkings if he wore hard heels, and lights might click on and faces appear and an entire street would be startled by the passing of a lone figure, himself, in the early November evening.

On this particular evening he began his journey in a westerly direction, towards the hidden sea. There was a good crystal frost in the air; it cut the nose and made the lungs blaze like a Christmas tree inside; you could feel the cold light going on and off, all the branches filled with invisible snow. He listened to the faint push of his soft shoes through autumn leaves with satisfaction, and whistled a cold quiet whistle between his teeth, occasionally picking up a leaf as he passed, examining its skeletal pattern in the infrequent lamp-lights as he went on, smelling its rusty smell.

'Hello, in there,' he whispered to every house on every side as he moved. 'What's up to-night on Channel 4, Channel 7, Channel 9? Where are the cowboys rushing, and do I see the United States Cavalry over the next hill to the rescue?'

The street was silent and long and empty, with only his shadow moving like the shadow of a hawk in mid-country. If he closed his eyes and stood very still, frozen, he could imagine himself upon the centre of a plain, a wintry, windless Arizona desert with no house in a thousand miles, and only dry river beds, the streets, for company.

'What is it now?' he asked the houses, noticing his wrist watch. 'Eight-thirty p.m.? Time for a dozen assorted murders? A quiz? A revue? A comedian falling off the stage?'

Was that a murmur of laughter from within a moon-white house? He hesitated, but went on when nothing more happened. He stumbled over a particularly uneven section of side-walk. The cement was vanishing under flowers and grass. In ten years of walking by night or day, for thousands of miles, he had never met another person walking, not one in all that time.

He came to a cloverleaf intersection which stood silent where two main highways crossed the town. During the day it was a thunderous surge of cars, the gas stations open, a great insect rustling and a ceaseless jockeying for position as the scarab-beetles, a faint incense puttering from their exhausts, skimmed homeward to the far directions. But now these high-ways, too, were like streams in a dry season, all stone and bed and moon radiance.

He turned back on a side street, circling around towards his home. He was within a block of his destination when the lone car turned a corner quite suddenly and flashed a fierce white cone of light upon him. He stood entranced, not unlike a night moth, stunned by the illumination, and then drawn towards it.

A metallic voice called to him:

'Stand still. Stay where you are! Don't move!'

He halted.

'Put up your hands!'

'But——' he said.

'Your hands up! Or we'll shoot!'

The police, of course, but what a rare, incredible thing; in a city of three million, there was only *one* police car left, wasn't that correct? Ever since a year ago, 2051, the election year, the force had been cut down from three cars to one. Crime was ebbing; there was no need now for the police, save for this one lone car wandering and wandering the empty streets.

'Your name?' said the police car in a metallic whisper. He couldn't see the men in it for the bright light in his eyes.

'Leonard Mead,' he said.

'Speak up!'

'Leonard Mead!'

'Business or profession?'

'I guess you'd call me a writer.'

'No profession,' said the police car, as if talking to itself. The light held him fixed, like a museum specimen, needle thrust through chest.

'You might say that,' said Mr Mead. He hadn't written in years.

Magazines and books didn't sell any more. Everything went on in the tomblike houses at night now, he thought, continuing his fancy. The tombs, ill-lit by television light, where the people sat like the dead, the grey or multicoloured lights touching their faces, but never really touching *them*.

'No profession,' said the phonograph voice, hissing. 'What are you doing out?'

'Walking,' said Leonard Mead.

'Walking!'

'Just walking,' he said simply, but his face felt cold.

'Walking, just walking, walking?'

'Yes, sir.'

'Walking where? For what?'

'Walking for air. Walking to *see*.'

'Your address!'

'Eleven South Saint James Street.'

'And there is air *in* your house, you have an air *conditioner*, Mr Mead?'

'Yes.'

'And you have a viewing screen in your house to see with?'

'No.'

'No?' There was a crackling quiet that in itself was an accusation.

'Are you married, Mr Mead?'

'No.'

'Not married,' said the police voice behind the fiery beam. The moon was high and clear among the stars and the houses were grey and silent.

'Nobody wanted me,' said Leonard Mead with a smile.

'Don't speak unless you're spoken to!'

Leonard Mead waited in the cold night.

'Just *walking*, Mr Mead?'

'Yes.'

'But you haven't explained for what purpose.'

'I explained; for air, and to see, and just to walk.'

'Have you done this often?'

'Every night for years.'

The police car sat in the centre of the street with its radio throat faintly humming.

'Well, Mr Mead,' it said.

'Is that all?' he asked politely.

'Yes,' said the voice. 'Here.' There was a sigh, a pop. The back door of the police car sprang wide. 'Get in.'

'Wait a minute, I haven't done anything!'

'Get in.'

'I protest!'

'Mr Mead.'

He walked like a man suddenly drunk. As he passed the front window of the car he looked in. As he had expected, there was no one in the front seat, no one in the car at all.

'Get in.'

He put his hand to the door and peered into the back seat, which was a little cell, a little black jail with bars. It smelled of riveted steel. It smelled of harsh antiseptic; it smelled too clear and hard and metallic. There was nothing soft there.

'Now if you had a wife to give you an alibi,' said the voice. 'But——'

'Where are you taking me?'

The car hesitated, or rather gave a faint whirring click, as if information, somewhere, was dripping card by punch-slotted card under electric eyes. 'To the Psychiatric Centre for Research on Regressive Tendencies.'

He got in. The door shut with a soft thud. The police car rolled through the night avenues, flashing its dim lights ahead.

They passed one house on one street a moment later, one house in an entire city of houses that were dark, but this one particular house had all of its electric lights brightly lit, every window a loud yellow illumination, square and warm in the cool darkness.

'That's *my* house,' said Leonard Mead.

No one answered him.

The car moved down the empty river-bed streets and off away, leaving the empty streets with the empty sidewalks, and no sound and no motion all the rest of the chill November night.

Philip K. Dick born 1928 in Chicago. He has spent most of his life in the Bay section of Los Angeles, California, and attended the University of California, but did not complete a degree. A prolific writer of science fiction short stories and novels, he won the Hugo award for the best science fiction novel written in 1963 with THE MAN IN THE HIGH CASTLE. Although some of his work, such as EYE IN THE SKY is written in the traditional science fiction mode of sheer fantasy, 'THE IMPOSTOR' and 'ALL WE MARSMEN' characterise the present emphasis in science fiction writing upon human problems. Although the characteristic setting of science fiction writing is retained, its importance in the story is diminished. The action of the story is explained through analysis of the states of mind of the main characters.

THE MAN IN THE HIGH CASTLE and TIME OUT OF JOINT, both available in Penguin books, are suggested for further reading.

IMPOSTOR

Philip K. Dick

'ONE OF THESE DAYS I'M GOING TO TAKE TIME OFF,' SPENCE OLHAM SAID AT first-meal. He looked around at his wife. 'I think I've earned a rest. Ten years is a long time.'

'And the Project?'

'The war will be won without me. This ball of clay of ours isn't really in much danger.' Olham sat down at the table and lit a cigarette. 'The news machines alter dispatches to make it appear the Outspacers are right on top of us. You know what I'd like to do on my vacation? I'd like to take a camping trip in those mountains outside of town, where we went that time. Remember? I got poison oak and you almost stepped on a gopher snake.'

'Sutton Wood?' Mary began to clear away the food dishes. 'The Wood was burned a few weeks ago. I thought you knew. Some kind of a flash fire.'

Olham sagged, 'Didn't they even try to find the cause?' His lips twisted. 'No one cares any more. All they can think of is the war.' He clamped his jaws together, the whole picture coming up in his mind, the Outspacers, the war, the needle ships.

'How can we think about anything else?'

Olham nodded. She was right, of course. The dark little ships out of Alpha Centauri had by-passed the Earth cruisers easily, leaving them like helpless turtles. It had been one-way fights, all the way back to Terra.

All the way, until the protec-bubble was demonstrated at Westinghouse Labs. Thrown around the major Earth cities and finally the planet itself, the bubble was the first real defence, the first legitimate answer to the Outspacers—as the news machines labelled them.

But to win the war, that was another thing. Every lab, every project was working night and day, endlessly, to find something more: a weapon for positive combat. His own project, for example. All day long, year after year.

Olham stood up, putting out his cigarette. 'Like the Sword of Damocles. Always hanging over us. I'm getting tired. All I want to do is take a long rest. But I guess everybody feels that way.'

He got his jacket from the closet and went out on the front porch. The shoot would be along any moment, the fast little bug that would carry him to the Project.

'I hope Nelson isn't late.' He looked at his watch. 'It's almost seven.'

'Here the bug comes,' Mary said, gazing between the rows of houses. The sun glittered behind the roofs, reflecting against the heavy lead plates. The settlement was quiet; only a few people were stirring. 'I'll see you later. Try not to work beyond your shift, Spence.'

Olham opened the car door and slid inside, leaning back against the seat with a sigh. There was an older man with Nelson.

'Well?' Olham said, as the bug shot ahead. 'Heard any interesting news?'

'The usual,' Nelson said. 'A few Outspace ships hit, another asteroid abandoned for strategic reasons.'

'It'll be good when we get the Project into final stage. Maybe it's just the propaganda from the news machines, but in the last month I've got weary of all this. Everything seems so grim and serious, no colour to life.'

'Do you think the war is in vain?' the older man said suddenly. 'You are an integral part of it, yourself.'

'This is Major Peters,' Nelson said. Olham and Peters shook hands. Olham studied the older man.

'What brings you along so early?' he said, 'I don't remember seeing you at the Project before.'

'No, I'm not with the Project,' Peters said, 'but I know something about what you're doing. My own work is altogether different.'

A look passed between him and Nelson. Olham noticed it and he frowned. The bug was gaining speed, flashing across the barren, lifeless ground toward the distant rim of the Project buildings.

'What is your business?' Olham said. 'Or aren't you permitted to talk about it?'

'I'm with the government,' Peters said. 'With FSA, the Security Organ.'

'Oh?' Olham raised an eyebrow. 'Is there any enemy infiltration in this region?'

'As a matter of fact I'm here to see you, Mr. Olham.'

Olham was puzzled. He considered Peters' words, but he could make nothing of them. 'To see me? Why?'

'I'm here to arrest you as an Outspace spy. That's why I'm up so early this morning. *Grab him, Nelson*—'

The gun drove into Olham's ribs. Nelson's hands were shaking, trembling with released emotion, his face pale. He took a deep breath and let it out again.

'Shall we kill him now?' he whispered to Peters. 'I think we should kill him now. We can't wait.'

Olham stared into his friend's face. He opened his mouth to speak, but no words came. Both men were staring at him steadily, rigid and grim with fright. Olham felt dizzy. His head ached and spun.

'I don't understand,' he murmured.

At that moment the shoot car left the ground and rushed up, heading into space. Below them the Project fell away, smaller and smaller, disappearing. Olham shut his mouth.

'We can wait a little,' Peters said. 'I want to ask him some questions first.'

Olham gazed dully ahead as the bug rushed through space.

'The arrest was made all right,' Peters said into the vidscreen. On the screen the features of the Security chief showed. 'It should be a load off everyone's mind.'

'Any complications?'

'None. He entered the bug without suspicion. He didn't seem to think my presence was too unusual.'

'Where are you now?'

'On our way out, just inside the protec-bubble. We're moving at maximum speed. You can assume that the critical period is past. I'm glad the take-off jets in this craft were in good working order. If there had been any failure at that point—'

'Let me see him,' the Security chief said. He gazed directly at Olham where he sat, his hands in his lap, staring ahead.

'So that's the man.' He looked at Olham for a time. Olham said nothing. At last the chief nodded to Peters. 'All right. That's enough.' A faint trace of disgust wrinkled his features. 'I've seen all I want. You've done something that will be remembered for a long time. They're preparing some sort of citation for both of you.'

'That's not necessary,' Peters said.

'How much danger is there now? Is there still much chance that—'

'There is some chance, but not too much. According to my understanding, it requires a verbal key phrase. In any case we'll have to take the risk.'

'I'll have the Moon base notified you're coming.'

'No,' Peters shook his head. 'I'll land the ship outside, beyond the base. I don't want it in jeopardy.'

'Just as you like.' The chief's eyes flickered as he glanced again at Olham. Then his image faded. The screen blanked.

Olham shifted his gaze to the window. The ship was already through the protec-bubble, rushing with greater and greater speed all the time. Peters was in a hurry; below him, rumbling under the floor, the jets were wide open. They were afraid, hurrying frantically, because of him.

Next to him on the seat, Nelson shifted uneasily. 'I think we should do it now,' he said. 'I'd give anything if we could get it over with.'

'Take it easy,' Peters said. 'I want you to guide the ship for a while so I can talk to him.'

He slid over beside Olham, looking into his face. Presently he reached out and touched him gingerly, on the arm and then on the cheek.

Olham said nothing, *If I could let Mary know*, he thought again. *If I could find some way of letting her know.* He looked around the ship. How? The vidscreen? Nelson was sitting by the board, holding the gun. There was nothing he could do. He was caught, trapped.

But why?

'Listen,' Peters said. 'I want to ask you some questions. You know where we're going. We're moving Moonward. In an hour we'll land on the far side, on the desolate side. After we land you'll be turned over immediately to a team of men waiting there. Your body will be destroyed at once. Do you understand that?' He looked at his watch. 'Within two hours your parts will be strewn over the landscape. There won't be anything left of you.'

Olham struggled out of his lethargy. 'Can't you tell me—'

'Certainly, I'll tell you.' Peters nodded. 'Two days ago we received a report that an Outspace ship had penetrated the protec-bubble. The ship let off a spy in the form of a humanoid robot. The robot was to destroy a particular human being and take his place.'

Peters looked calmly at Olham.

'Inside the robot was a U-bomb. Our agent did not know how the bomb was to be detonated. but he conjectured that it might be by a particular spoken phrase, a certain group of words. The robot would live the life of the person he killed, entering into his usual activities, his job, his social life. He had been constructed to resemble that person. No one would know the difference.'

Olham's face went sickly chalk.

'The person whom the robot was to impersonate was Spence Olham, a high-ranking official at one of the Research projects. Because this particular project was approaching crucial stage, the presence of an animate bomb, moving toward the centre of the Project—'

Olham stared down at his hands. *'But I'm Olham!'*

'Once the robot had located and killed Olham, it was a simple matter to take over his life. The robot was probably released from the ship eight days ago. The substitution was probably accomplished over the last week end, when Olham went for a short walk in the hills.'

'But I'm Olham.' He turned to Nelson, sitting at the controls. 'Don't you recognize me? You've known me for twenty years. Don't you remember how we went to college together?' He stood up. 'You and I were at the University. We had the same room.' He went toward Nelson.

'Stay away from me!' Nelson snarled.

'Listen. Remember our second year? Remember that girl. What was her name—' He rubbed his forehead. 'The one with the dark hair. The one we met over at Ted's place.'

'Stop!' Nelson waved the gun frantically. 'I don't want to hear any more. You killed him! You . . . machine.'

Olham looked at Nelson. 'You're wrong. I don't know what happened, but the robot never reached me. Something must have gone wrong. maybe the ship crashed.' He turned to Peters. 'I'm Olham. I know it. No transfer was made. I'm the same as I've always been.'

He touched himself, running his hands over his body. 'There must be some way to prove it. Take me back to Earth. An X-ray examination, a neurological study, anything like that will show you. Or maybe we can find the crashed ship.'

Neither Peters nor Nelson spoke.

'I am Olham,' he said again. 'I know I am. But I can't prove it.'

'The robot,' Peters said, 'would be unaware that he was not the real Spence Olham. He would become Olham in mind as well as in body. He was given an artificial memory system, false recall. He would look like him, have his memories, his thoughts and interests, perform his job.

'But there would be one difference. Inside the robot is a U-bomb, ready to explode at the trigger phrase.' Peters moved a little away. 'That's the one difference. That's why we're taking you to the Moon. They'll disassemble you and remove the bomb. Maybe it will explode, but it won't matter, not there.'

Olham sat down slowly.

'We'll be there soon,' Nelson said.

He lay back, thinking frantically, as the ship dropped slowly down. Under them was the pitted surface of the Moon, the endless expanse of ruin. What could he do? What would save him?

'Get ready,' Peters said.

In a few minutes he would be dead. Down below he could see a tiny dot, a building of some kind. There were men in the building, the demolition team, waiting to tear him to bits. They would rip him open, pull off his arms and legs, break him apart. When they found no bomb they would be surprised; they would know, but it would be too late.

Olham looked around the small cabin. Nelson was still holding the gun. There was no chance there. If he could get to a doctor, have an examination made—that was the only way. Mary could help him. He thought frantically, his mind racing. Only a few minutes, just a little time left. If he could contact her, get word to her some way.

'Easy,' Peters said. The ship came down slowly, bumping on the rough ground. There was silence.

'Listen,' Olham said thickly. 'I can prove I'm Spence Olham. Get a doctor. Bring him here—'

'There's the squad.' Nelson pointed. 'They're coming.' He glanced nervously at Olham. 'I hope nothing happens.'

'We'll be gone before they start work,' Peters said. 'We'll be out of here in a moment.' He put on his pressure suit. When he had finished he took the gun from Nelson. 'I'll watch him for a moment.'

Nelson put on his pressure suit, hurrying awkwardly. 'How about him?' He indicated Olham. 'Will he need one?'

'No,' Peters shook his head. 'Robots probably don't require oxygen.'

The group of men were almost to the ship. They halted, waiting.

Peters signalled to them.

'Come on!' He waved his hand and the men approached warily; stiff, grotesque figures in their inflated suits.

'If you open the door,' Olham said, 'it means my death. It will be murder.'

'Open the door,' Nelson said. He reached for the handle.

Olham watched him. He saw the man's hand tighten around the metal rod. In a moment the door would swing back, the air in the ship would rush out. He would die, and presently they would realize their mistake. Perhaps at some other time, when there was no war, men might not act this way, hurrying an individual to his death because they were afraid. Everyone was frightened, everyone was willing to sacrifice the individual because of the group fear.

He was being killed because they could not wait to be sure of his guilt. There was not enough time.

He looked at Nelson. Nelson had been his friend for years. They had gone to school together. He had been best man at his wedding. Now Nelson was going to kill him. But Nelson was not wicked; it was not his fault. It was the times. Perhaps it had been the same way during the plagues. When men had shown a spot they probably had been killed, too, without a moment's hesitation, without proof, on suspicion alone. In times of danger there was no other way.

He did not blame them. But he had to live. His life was too precious to be sacrificed. Olham thought quickly. What could he do? Was there anything? He looked around.

'Here goes,' Nelson said.

'You're right,' Olham said. The sound of his own voice surprised him. It was the strength of desperation. 'I have no need of air. Open the door.'

They paused, looking at him in curious alarm.

'Go ahead. Open it. It makes no difference.' Olham's hand disappeared inside his jacket. 'I wonder how far you two can run.'

'Run?'

'You have fifteen seconds to live.' Inside his jacket his fingers twisted, his arm suddenly rigid. He relaxed, smiling a little. 'You were wrong about the trigger phrase. In that respect you were mistaken. Fourteen seconds, now.'

Two shocked faces stared at him from the pressure suits. Then they were struggling, running, tearing the door open. The air shrieked out, spilling into the void. Peters and Nelson bolted out of the ship. Olham came after them. He grasped the door and dragged it shut. The automatic pressure system chugged furiously, restoring the air. Olham let his breath out with a shudder.

One more second—

Beyond the window the two men had joined the group. The group scattered, running in all directions. One by one they threw themselves down, prone on the ground. Olham seated himself at the control board. He moved the dials into place. As the ship rose up into the air the men below scrambled to their feet and stared up, their mouths open.

'Sorry,' Olham murmured, 'but I've got to get back to Earth.'

He headed the ship back the way it had come.

It was night. All around the ship crickets chirped, disturbing the chill darkness. Olham bent over the vidscreen. Gradually the image formed; the call had gone through without trouble. He breathed a sigh of relief.

'Mary,' he said. The woman stared at him. She gasped.

'Spence! Where are you? What's happened?'

'I can't tell you. Listen, I have to talk fast. They may break this call off any minute. Go to the Project grounds and get Dr Chamberlain. If he isn't there, get any doctor. Bring him to the house and have him stay there. Have him bring equipment, X-ray, fluoroscope, everything.'

'But— '

'Do as I say. Hurry. Have him get it ready in an hour.' Olham leaned toward the screen. 'Is everything all right? Are you alone?'

'Alone?'

'Is anyone with you? Has . . . has Nelson or anyone contacted you?'

'No, Spence, I don't understand.'

'All right. I'll see you at the house in an hour. And don't tell anyone anything. Get Chamberlain there on any pretext. Say you're very ill.'

He broke the connection and looked at his watch. A moment later he left the ship, stepping down into the darkness. He had a half-mile to go.

He began to walk.

One light showed in the window, the study light. He watched it, kneeling against the fence. There was no sound, no movement of any kind. He held his watch up and read it by starlight. Almost an hour had passed.

Along the street a shoot bug came. It went on.

Olham looked toward the house. The doctor should have already come. He should be inside, waiting with Mary. A thought struck him. Had she been able to leave the house? Perhaps they had intercepted her. Maybe he was moving into a trap.

But what else could he do?

With a doctor's records, photographs and reports, there was a chance, a chance of proof. If he could be examined, if he could remain alive long enough for them to study him——

He could prove it that way. It was probably the only way. His one hope lay inside the house. Dr Chamberlain was a respected man. He was the staff doctor for the Project. He would know; his word on the matter would have meaning. He could overcome their hysteria, their madness, with facts.

Madness—That was what it was. If only they could wait, act slowly, take their time. But they could not wait. He had to die, die at once, without proof, without any kind of trial or examination. The simplest test would tell, but they had not time for the simplest test. They could think only of the danger. Danger, and nothing more.

He stood up and moved toward the house. He came up on the porch. At the door he paused, listening. Still no sound. The house was absolutely still.

Too still.

Olham stood on the porch, unmoving. They were trying to be silent inside. Why? It was a small house; only a few feet away, beyond the door, Mary and Dr Chamberlain should be standing. Yet he could hear nothing, no sound of voices, nothing at all. He looked at the door. It was a door he had opened and closed a thousand times, every morning and every night.

He put his hand on the knob. Then, all at once, he reached out and touched the bell instead. The bell pealed, off some place in the back of the house. Olham smiled. He could hear movement.

Mary opened the door. As soon as he saw her face he knew.

He ran, throwing himself into the bushes. A Security officer shoved Mary out of the way, firing past her. The bushes burst apart. Olham wriggled around the side of the house. He leaped up and ran, racing frantically into the darkness. A searchlight snapped on, a beam of light circling past him.

He crossed the road and squeezed over a fence. He jumped down and made his way across a backyard. Behind him men were coming. Security officers, shouting to each other as they came. Olham gasped for breath, his chest rising and falling.

Her face—He had known at once. The set lips, the terrified, wretched eyes. Suppose he had gone ahead, pushed open the door and entered! They had tapped the call and come at once, as soon as he had broken off. Probably she believed their account. No doubt she thought he was the robot, too.

Olham ran on and on. He was losing the officers, dropping them behind. Apparently they were not much good at running. He climbed a hill and made his way down the other side. In a moment he would be back at the ship. But where to, this time? He slowed down, stopping. He could see the ship already, outlined against the sky, where he had parked it. The settlement was behind him; he was on the outskirts of the wilderness between the inhabited places, where the forests and desolation began. He crossed a barren field and entered the trees.

As he came toward it, the door of the ship opened.

Peters stepped out, framed against the light. In his arms was a heavy boris-gun. Olham stopped, rigid. Peters stared around him, into the darkness. 'I know you're there, some place,' he said. 'Come on up here, Olham. There are Security men all around you.'

Olham did not move.

'Listen to me. We will catch you very shortly. Apparently you still do not believe you're the robot. Your call to the woman indicates that you are still under the illusion created by your artificial memories.

'But you *are* the robot. You are the robot, and inside you is the bomb. Any moment the trigger phrase may be spoken, by you, by someone else, by anyone. When that happens the bomb will destroy everything for miles around. The Project, the woman, all of us will be killed. Do you understand?'

Olham said nothing. He was listening. Men were moving toward him, slipping through the woods.

'If you don't come out, we'll catch you. It will be only a matter of time. We no longer plan to remove you to the Moon-base. You will be destroyed on sight and we will have to take the chance that the bomb will detonate. I have ordered every available Security officer into the area. The whole county is being searched, inch by inch. There is no place you can go. Around this wood is a cordon of armed men. You have about six hours left before the last inch is covered.'

Olham moved away. Peters went on speaking; he had not seen him at all. It was too dark to see anyone. But Peters was right. There was no place he could go. He was beyond the settlement, on the outskirts where the woods began. He could hide for a time, but eventually they would catch him.

Only a matter of time.

Olham walked quietly through the wood. Mile by mile, each part of the county was being measured off, laid bare, searched, studied, examined. The cordon was coming all the time, squeezing him into a smaller and smaller space.

What was there left? He had lost the ship, the one hope of escape. They were at his home; his wife was with them, believing, no doubt, that the real Olham had been killed. He clenched his fists. Some place there was a wrecked Outspace needle-ship, and in it the remains of the robot. Somewhere nearby the ship had crashed, crashed and broken up.

And the robot lay inside, destroyed.

A faint hope stirred him. What if he could find the remains? If he could show them the wreckage, the remains of the ship, the robot—

But where? Where would he find it?

He walked on, lost in thought. Some place, not too far off, probably. The ship would have landed close to the Project; the robot would have expected to go the rest of the way on foot. He went up the side of a hill and looked around. Crashed and burned. Was there some clue, some hint? Had he read anything, heard anything? Some place close by, within walking distance. Some wild place, a remote spot where there would be no people.

Suddenly Olham smiled. Crashed and burned—

Sutton Wood.

He increased his pace.

It was morning. Sunlight filtered down through the broken trees on to the man crouching at the edge of the clearing. Olham glanced up from time to time, listening. They were not far off, only a few minutes away. He smiled.

Down below him, strewn across the clearing and into the charred stumps that had been Sutton Wood, lay a tangled mass of wreckage. In the sunlight it glittered a little, gleaming darkly. He had not had too much trouble finding it. Sutton Wood was a place he knew well; he had climbed around it many times in his life, when he was younger. He had known where he would find the remains. There was one peak that jutted up suddenly, without warning.

A descending ship, unfamiliar with the Wood, had little chance of missing it. And now he squatted, looking down at the ship, or what remained of it.

Olham stood up. He could hear them, only a little distance away, coming together, talking in low tones. He tensed himself. Everything depended on who first saw him. If it were Nelson, he had no chance. Nelson would fire at once. He would be dead before they saw the ship. But if he had time to call out, hold them off for a moment—That was all he needed. Once they saw the ship he would be safe.

But if they fired first—

A charred branch cracked. A figure appeared, coming forward uncertainly. Olham took a deep breath. Only a few seconds remained, perhaps the last seconds in his life. He raised his arms, peering intently.

It was Peters.

'Peters!' Olham waved his arms. Peters lifted his gun, aiming. 'Don't fire!' His voice shook. 'Wait a minute. Look past me, across the clearing.'

'I've found him,' Peters shouted. Security men came pouring out of the burned woods around him.

'Don't shoot. Look past me. The ship, the needle-ship. The Outspace ship. Look!'

Peters hesitated. The gun wavered.

'It's down there,' Olham said rapidly. 'I knew I'd find it here. The burned wood. Now you believe me. You'll find the remains of the robot in the ship. Look, will you?'

'There is something down there,' one of the men said nervously.

'Shoot him!' a voice said. It was Nelson.

'Wait.' Peters turned sharply. 'I'm in charge. Don't anyone fire. Maybe he's telling the truth.'

'Shoot him,' Nelson said. 'He killed Olham. Any minute he may kill us all. If the bomb goes off——'

'Shut up.' Peters advanced toward the slope. He stared down. 'Look at that.' He waved two men up to him. 'Go down there and see what that is.'

The men raced down the slope, across the clearing. They bent down, poking in the ruins of the ship.

'Well?' Peters called.

Olham held his breath. He smiled a little. It must be there; he had not had time to look, himself, but it had to be there. Suddenly doubt assailed him. Suppose the robot had lived long enough to wander away? Suppose his body had been completely destroyed, burned to ashes by the fire?

He licked his lips. Perspiration came out on his forehead. Nelson was staring at him, his face still livid. His chest rose and fell.

'Kill him,' Nelson said. 'Before he kills us.'

The two men stood up.

'What have you found?' Peters said. He held the gun steady. 'Is there anything there?'

'Looks like something. It's a needle-ship, all right. There's something beside it.'

'I'll look.' Peters strode past Olham. Olham watched him go down the hill and up to the men. The others were following after him, peering to see.

'It's a body of some sort,' Peters said. 'Look at it!'

Olham came along with them. They stood around in a circle, staring down.

On the ground, bent and twisted into a strange shape, was a grotesque form. It looked human, perhaps; except that it was bent so strangely, the arms and legs flung off in all directions. The mouth was open, the eyes stared glassily.

'Like a machine that's run down,' Peters murmured.

Olham smiled feebly. 'Well?' he said.

Peters looked at him. 'I can't believe it. You were telling the truth all the time.'

'The robot never reached me,' Olham said. He took out a cigarette and lit it. 'It was destroyed when the ship crashed. You were all too busy with the war to wonder why an out-of-the-way woods would suddenly catch fire and burn. Now you know.'

He stood smoking, watching the men. They were dragging the grotesque remains from the ship. The body was stiff, the arms and legs rigid.

'You'll find the bomb, now,' Olham said. The men laid the body on the ground. Peters bent down.

'I think I see the corner of it.' He reached out, touching the body.

The chest of the corpse had been laid open. Within the gaping tear something glinted, something metal. The men stared at the metal without speaking.

'That would have destroyed us all, if it had lived,' Peters said. 'That metal box, there.'

There was silence.

'I think we owe you something,' Peters said to Olham. 'This must have been a nightmare to you. If you hadn't escaped, we would have—' He broke off.

Olham put out his cigarette. 'I knew, of course, that the robot had never reached me. But I had no way of proving it. Sometimes it isn't possible to prove a thing right away. That was the whole trouble. There wasn't any way I could demonstrate that I was myself.'

'How about a vacation?' Peters said. 'I think we might work out a month's vacation for you. You could take it easy, relax.'

'I think right now I want to go home,' Olham said.

'All right, then,' Peters said. 'Whatever you say.'

Nelson had squatted down on the ground, beside the corpse. He reached out toward the glint of metal visible within the chest.

'Don't touch it,' Olham said. 'It might still go off. We'd better let the demolition squad take care of it later on.'

Nelson said nothing. Suddenly he grabbed hold of the metal, reaching his hand inside the chest. He pulled.

'What are you doing?' Olham cried.

Nelson stood up. He was holding on to the metal object. His face was blank with terror. It was a metal knife, an Outspace needle-knife, covered with blood.

'This killed him,' Nelson whispered. 'My friend was killed with this.' He looked at Olham. 'You killed him with this and left him beside the ship.'

Olham was trembling. His teeth chattered. He looked from the knife to the body. 'This can't be Olham,' he said. His mind spun, everything was whirling. 'Was I wrong?'

He gaped.

'But if that's Olham, then I must be—'

He did not complete the sentence, only the first phrase. The blast was visible all the way to Alpha Centauri.

Albert Camus *born Mondovi, Algeria, 1913. He won a scholarship to high school and was an outstanding student of philosophy at the University of Algiers. In his late teens and early twenties, several crises upset Camus's preparation for a career in college teaching—his first serious attack of tuberculosis; a short-lived marriage ending in divorce a year later; and brief membership of the Communist Party, with which he soon became disenchanted. Work as a journalist and as actor-director-playwright in his own theatre preceded his departure from Algeria in 1942 to join the French Resistance movement and editorship of the underground newspaper,* COMBAT. *Following a second, happier marriage in 1940 he wrote and published more prolifically, though still worried by recurrent bouts of tuberculosis. In 1957 he received the Nobel Prize for 'his important literary production, which with clearsighted earnestness illuminates the human conscience of our time.' He was killed in a car accident in 1960.*

Essays, short stories, novels: all Camus's major works are related to Algeria. 'THE GUEST' *is no exception. In common with other works this story centres on the making of a decision and raises questions about justice and the individual conscience.*

The terse, disciplined style in this faithful translation of the French original, is an effective vehicle in conveying with absolute clarity the story's unsolved dilemmas.

Suggested further reading: 'THE RENEGADE', 'THE SILENT MEN', *in* EXILE AND THE KINGDOM. *Novels:* THE STRANGER, THE PLAGUE, THE REBEL.

THE GUEST

Albert Camus

THE SCHOOLMASTER WAS WATCHING THE TWO MEN CLIMB TOWARDS HIM.
One was on horseback, the other on foot. They had not yet tackled the
abrupt rise leading to the schoolhouse built on the hillside. They were
toiling onwards, making slow progress in the snow, among the stones, on
the vast expanse of the high, deserted plateau. From time to time the horse
stumbled. Without hearing anything yet, he could see the breath issuing
from the horse's nostrils. One of the men, at least, knew the region. They
were following the trail although it had disappeared days ago under a
layer of dirty white snow. The schoolmaster calculated that it would take
them half an hour to get onto the hill. It was cold; he went back into the
school to get a sweater.

He crossed the empty, frigid classroom. On the blackboard the four
rivers of France, drawn with four different coloured chalks, had been
flowing towards their estuaries for the past three days. Snow had suddenly
fallen in mid-October after eight months of drought without the transition
of rain, and the twenty pupils, more or less, who lived in the villages
scattered over the plateau had stopped coming. With fair weather they
would return. Daru now heated only the single room that was his lodging,
adjoining the classroom and giving also onto the plateau to the east. Like
the class windows, his window looked to the south too. On that side the
school was a few kilometres from the point where the plateau began to
slope towards the south. In clear weather could be seen the purple mass of
the mountain range where the gap opened onto the desert.

Somewhat warmed, Daru returned to the window from which he had
first seen the two men. They were no longer visible. Hence they must
have tackled the rise. The sky was not so dark, for the snow had stopped
falling during the night. The morning had opened with a dirty light which
had scarcely become brighter as the ceiling of clouds lifted. At two in the
afternoon it seemed as if the day were merely beginning. But still this was
better than those three days when the thick snow was falling amidst
unbroken darkness with little gusts of wind that rattled the double door
of the classroom. Then Daru had spent long hours in his room, leaving it
only to go to the shed and feed the chickens or get some coal. Fortunately
the delivery truck from Tadjid, the nearest village to the north, had
brought his supplies two days before the blizzard. It would return in
forty-eight hours.

Besides, he had enough to resist a siege, for the little room was cluttered
with bags of wheat that the administration left as a stock to distribute to
those of his pupils whose families had suffered from the drought. Actually
they had all been victims because they were all poor. Every day Daru

would distribute a ration to the children. They had missed it, he knew, during these bad days. Possibly one of the fathers or big brothers would come this afternoon and he could supply them with grain. It was just a matter of carrying them over to the next harvest. Now shiploads of wheat were arriving from France and the worst was over. But it would be hard to forget that poverty, that army of ragged ghosts wandering in the sunlight, the plateaus burned to a cinder month after month, the earth shrivelled up little by little, literally scorched, every stone bursting into dust under one's foot. The sheep had died then by thousands and even a few men, here and there, sometimes without anyone's knowing.

In contrast with such poverty, he who lived almost like a monk in his remote schoolhouse, none the less satisfied with the little he had and with the rough life, had felt like a lord with his whitewashed walls, his narrow couch, his unpainted shelves, his well, and his weekly provision of water and food. And suddenly this snow, without warning, without the fore-taste of rain. This is the way the region was, cruel to live in, even without men—who didn't help matters either. But Daru had been born here. Everywhere else, he felt exiled.

He stepped out onto the terrace in front of the schoolhouse. The two men were now half-way up the slope. He recognized the horseman as Balducci, the old gendarme he had known for a long time. Balducci was holding on the end of a rope an Arab who was walking behind him with hands bound and head lowered. The gendarme waved a greeting to which Daru did not reply, lost as he was in contemplation of the Arab dressed in a faded blue jellaba, his feet in sandals but covered with socks of heavy raw wool, his head surmounted by a narrow, short *chèche*. They were approaching. Balducci was holding back his horse in order not to hurt the Arab, and the group was advancing slowly.

Within earshot, Balducci shouted: 'One hour to do the three kilo-metres from El Ameur!' Daru did not answer. Short and square in his thick sweater, he watched them climb. Not once had the Arab raised his head. 'Hello,' said Daru when they got up onto the terrace. 'Come in and warm up.' Balducci painfully got down from his horse without letting go the rope. From under his bristling moustache he smiled at the schoolmaster. His little dark eyes, deep-set under a tanned forehead, and his mouth surrounded with wrinkles made him look attentive and studious. Daru took the bridle, led the horse to the shed, and came back to the two men, who were now waiting for him in the school. He led them into his room. 'I am going to heat up the classroom,' he said. 'We'll be more comfortable there.' When he entered the room again, Balducci was on the couch. He had undone the rope tying him to the Arab, who had squatted near the stove. His hands still bound, the *chèche* pushed back on his head, he was looking towards the window. At first Daru noticed only his huge lips, fat, smooth, almost negroid; yet his nose was straight, his eyes were dark and full of fever. The *chèche* revealed an obstinate forehead and, under the weathered skin now rather discoloured by the cold, the whole face had a restless and rebellious look that struck Daru when the Arab, turning his face towards him, looked him straight in the eyes. 'Go into the other room,' said the schoolmaster, 'and I'll make you some mint tea.' 'Thanks,' Balducci said. 'What a nuisance! How I long for retirement.' And addressing his prisoner in Arabic: 'Come on, you.' The Arab got up and, slowly, holding his bound wrists in front of him, went into the classroom.

With the tea, Daru brought a chair. But Balducci was already enthroned on the nearest pupil's desk and the Arab had squatted against the teacher's platform facing the stove, which stood between the desk and the window. When he held out the glass of tea to the prisoner, Daru hesitated at the sight of his bound hands. 'He might perhaps be untied.' 'Certainly,' said Balducci. 'That was for the journey.' He started to get to his feet. But Daru, setting the glass on the floor, had knelt beside the Arab. Without saying anything, the Arab watched him with his feverish eyes. Once his hands were free, he rubbed his swollen wrists against each other, took the glass of tea, and sucked up the burning liquid in swift little sips.

'Good,' said Daru. 'And where are you headed for?'

Balducci withdrew his moustache from the tea. 'Here, my boy.'

'Odd pupils! And you're spending the night?'

'No. I'm going back to El Ameur. And you will deliver this fellow to Tinguit. He is expected at police headquarters.'

Balducci was looking at Daru with a friendly little smile.

'What's this story?' asked the schoolmaster. 'Are you pulling my leg?'

'No, my boy. Those are the orders.'

'The orders? I'm not . . .' Daru hesitated, not wanting to hurt the old Corsican. 'I mean, that's not my job.'

'What! What's the meaning of that? In wartime people do all kinds of jobs.'

'Then I'll wait for the declaration of war!'

Balducci nodded.

'O.K. But the orders exist and they concern you too. Things are brewing, it appears. There is talk of a forthcoming revolt. We are mobilized, in a way.'

Daru still had his obstinate look.

'Listen, my boy,' Balducci said. 'I like you and you must understand. There's only a dozen of us at El Ameur to patrol throughout the whole territory of a small department and I must get back in a hurry. I was told to hand this man over to you and return without delay. He couldn't be kept there. His village was beginning to stir; they wanted to take him back. You must take him to Tinguit tomorrow before the day is over. Twenty kilometres shouldn't worry a husky fellow like you. After that, all will be over. You'll come back to your pupils and your comfortable life.'

Behind the wall the horse could be heard snorting and pawing the earth. Daru was looking out of the window. Decidedly, the weather was clearing and the light was increasing over the snowy plateau. When all the snow was melted, the sun would take over again and once more would burn the fields of stone. For days, still, the unchanging sky would shed its dry light on the solitary expanse where nothing had any connection with man.

'After all,' he said, turning around towards Balducci, 'what did he do?' And, before the gendarme had opened his mouth, he asked: 'Does he speak French?'

'No, not a word. We had been looking for him for a month, but they were hiding him. He killed his cousin.'

'Is he against us?'

'I don't think so. But you can never be sure.'

'Why did he kill?'

'A family squabble, I think. One owed the other grain, it seems. It's not at all clear. In short, he killed his cousin with a billhook. You know, like a sheep, *kreezk*!'

Balducci made the gesture of drawing a blade across his throat and the Arab, his attention attracted, watched him with a sort of anxiety. Daru felt a sudden wrath against the man, against all men with their rotten spite, their tireless hates, their blood lust.

But the kettle was singing on the stove. He served Balducci more tea, hesitated, then served the Arab again, who, a second time, drank avidly. His raised arms made the jellaba fall open and the schoolmaster saw his thin, muscular chest.

'Thanks, my boy,' Balducci said. 'And now, I'm off.'

He got up and went towards the Arab, taking a small rope from his pocket.

'What are you doing?' Daru asked dryly.

Balducci, disconcerted, showed him the rope.

'Don't bother.'

The old gendarme hesitated. 'It's up to you. Of course, you are armed?'

'I have my shot gun.'

'Where?'

'In the trunk.'

'You ought to have it near your bed.'

'Why? I have nothing to fear.'

146

'You're mad. If there's an uprising, no one is safe, we're all in the same boat.'

'I'll defend myself. I'll have time to see them coming.'

Balducci began to laugh, then suddenly the moustache covered the white teeth.

'You'll have time? O.K. That's just what I was saying. You have always been a little cracked. That's why I like you, my son was like that.'

At the same time he took out his revolver and put in on the desk.

'Keep it; I don't need two weapons from here to El Ameur.'

The revolver shone against the black paint of the table. When the gendarme turned towards him, the schoolmaster caught the smell of leather and horseflesh.

'Listen, Balducci,' Daru said suddenly, 'every bit of this disgusts me, and most of all your fellow here. But I won't hand him over. Fight, yes, if I have to. But not that.'

The old gendarme stood in front of him and looked at him severely.

'You're being a fool,' he said slowly. 'I don't like it either. You don't get used to putting a rope on a man even after years of it, and you're even ashamed—yes, ashamed. But you can't let them have their way.'

'I won't hand him over,' Daru said again.

'It's an order, my boy, and I repeat it.'

'That's right. Repeat to them what I've said to you: I won't hand him over.'

Balducci made a visible effort to reflect. He looked at the Arab and at Daru. At last he decided.

'No, I won't tell them anything. If you want to drop us, go ahead; I'll not denounce you. I have an order to deliver the prisoner and I'm doing so. And now you'll just sign this paper for me.'

'There's no need. I'll not deny that you left him with me.'

'Don't be mean with me. I know you'll tell the truth. You're from hereabouts and you are a man. But you must sign, that's the rule.'

Daru opened his drawer, took out a little square bottle of purple ink, the red wooden penholder with the 'sergeant-major' pen he used for making models of penmanship, and signed. The gendarme carefully folded the paper and put it into his wallet. Then he moved towards the door.

'I'll see you off,' Daru said.

'No,' said Balducci. 'There's no use being polite. You insulted me.'

He looked at the Arab, motionless in the same spot, sniffed peevishly, and turned away towards the door. 'Good-bye, son,' he said. The door shut behind him. Balducci appeared suddenly outside the window and then disappeared. His footsteps were muffled by the snow. The horse stirred on the other side of the wall and several chickens fluttered in fright.

A moment later Balducci reappeared outside the window leading the horse by the bridle. He walked towards the little rise without turning round and disappeared from sight with the horse following him. A big stone could be heard bouncing down. Daru walked back towards the prisoner, who, without stirring, never took his eyes off him. 'Wait,' the schoolmaster said in Arabic and went towards the bedroom. As he was going through the door, he had a second thought, went to the desk, took the revolver, and stuck it in his pocket. Then, without looking back, he went into his room.

For some time he lay on his couch watching the sky gradually close over, listening to the silence. It was this silence that had seemed painful to him during the first days here, after the war. He had requested a post in the little town at the base of the foothills separating the upper plateaus from the desert. There, rocky walls, green and black to the north, pink and lavender to the south, marked the frontier of eternal summer. He had been named to a post farther north, on the plateau itself. In the beginning, the solitude and the silence had been hard for him on these wastelands peopled only by stones. Occasionally, furrows suggested cultivation, but they had been dug to uncover a certain kind of stone good for building. The only ploughing here was to harvest rocks. Elsewhere a thin layer of soil accumulated in the hollows would be scraped out to enrich paltry village gardens. This is the way it was: bare rock covered three-quarters of the region. Towns sprang up, flourished, then disappeared; men came by, loved one another or fought bitterly, then died. No one in this desert, neither he nor his guest, mattered. And yet, outside this desert neither of them, Daru knew, could have really lived.

When he got up, no noise came from the classroom. He was amazed at the unmixed joy he derived from the mere thought that the Arab might have fled and that he would be alone with no decision to make. But the prisoner was there. He had merely stretched out between the stove and the desk. With eyes open, he was staring at the ceiling. In that position, his thick lips were particularly noticeable, giving him a pouting look. 'Come,' said Daru. The Arab got up and followed him. In the bedroom, the schoolmaster pointed to a chair near the table under the window. The Arab sat down without taking his eyes off Daru.

'Are you hungry?'

'Yes,' the prisoner said.

Daru set the table for two. He took flour and oil, shaped a cake in a frying-pan, and lighted the little stove that functioned on bottled gas. While the cake was cooking, he went out to the shed to get cheese, eggs, dates, and condensed milk. When the cake was done he set it on the window sill to cool, heated some condensed milk diluted with water, and beat up the eggs into an omelet. In one of his motions he knocked against the revolver stuck in his right pocket. He set the bowl down, went into the classroom, and put the revolver in his desk drawer. When he came back to the room, night was falling. He put on the light and served the Arab. 'Eat,' he said. The Arab took a piece of the cake, lifted it eagerly to his mouth, and stopped short.

'And you?' he asked.

'After you. I'll eat too.'

The thick lips opened slightly. The Arab hesitated, then bit into the cake determinedly.

The meal over, the Arab looked at the schoolmaster. 'Are you the judge?'

'No, I'm simply keeping you until tomorrow.'

'Why do you eat with me?'

'I'm hungry.'

The Arab fell silent. Daru got up and went out. He brought back a folding bed from the shed, set it up between the table and the stove, at right-angles to his own bed. From a large suitcase which, upright in a corner, served as a shelf for papers, he took two blankets and arranged them on the camp bed. Then he stopped, felt useless, and sat down on his bed. There was nothing more to do or to get ready. He had to look at this man. He looked at him, therefore, trying to imagine his face bursting with rage. He couldn't do so. He could see nothing but the dark yet shining eyes and the animal mouth.

'Why did you kill him?' he asked in a voice whose hostile tone surprised him.

The Arab looked away.

'He ran away. I ran after him.'

He raised his eyes to Daru again and they were full of a sort of woeful interrogation. 'Now what will they do to me?'

'Are you afraid?'

He stiffened, turning his eyes away.

'Are you sorry?'

The Arab stared at him open-mouthed. Obviously he did not understand. Daru's annoyance was growing. At the same time he felt awkward and self-conscious with his big body wedged between the two beds.

'Lie down there,' he said impatiently. 'That's your bed.'

The Arab didn't move. He called to Daru:

'Tell me!'

The schoolmaster looked at him.

'Is the gendarme coming back tomorrow?'

'I don't know.'

'Are you coming with us?'

'I don't know. Why?'

The prisoner got up and stretched out on top of the blankets, his feet towards the window. The light from the electric bulb shone straight into his eyes and he closed them at once.

'Why?' Daru repeated, standing beside the bed.

The Arab opened his eyes under the blinding light and looked at him, trying not to blink.

'Come with us,' he said.

In the middle of the night, Daru was still not asleep. He had gone to bed after undressing completely; he generally slept naked. But when he suddenly realized that he had nothing on, he hesitated. He felt vulnerable and the temptation came to him to put on his clothes again. Then he shrugged his shoulders; after all, he wasn't a child and, if need be, he could break his adversary in two. From his bed he could observe him, lying on his back, still motionless with his eyes closed under the harsh light. When Daru turned out the light, the darkness seemed to coagulate all of a sudden. Little by little, the night came back to life in the window where the starless sky was stirring gently. The schoolmaster soon made out the body lying at his feet. The Arab still did not move, but his eyes seemed open. A faint wind was prowling around the schoolhouse. Perhaps it would drive away the clouds and the sun would reappear.

During the night the wind increased. The hens fluttered a little and then were silent. The Arab turned over on his side with his back to Daru, who thought he heard him moan. Then he listened for his guest's breathing, become heavier and more regular. He listened to that breath so close to him and mused without being able to go to sleep. In this room where he had been sleeping alone for a year, this presence bothered him. But it bothered him also by imposing on him a sort of brotherhood he knew well but refused to accept in the present circumstances. Men who share the same rooms, soldiers or prisoners, develop a strange alliance as if, having cast off their armour with their clothing, they fraternized every evening, over and above their differences, in the ancient community of dream and fatigue. But Daru shook himself; he didn't like such musings, and it was essential to sleep.

A little later, however, when the Arab stirred slightly, the schoolmaster was still not asleep. When the prisoner made a second move, he stiffened, on the alert. The Arab was lifting himself slowly on his arms with almost the motion of a sleepwalker. Seated upright in bed, he waited motionless without turning his head towards Daru, as if he were listening attentively. Daru did not stir; it had just occurred to him that the revolver was still in the drawer of his desk. It was better to act at once. Yet he continued to observe the prisoner, who, with the same slithery motion, put his feet on the ground, waited again, then began to stand up slowly. Daru was about to call out to him when the Arab began to walk, in a quite natural but extraordinarily silent way. He was heading towards the door at the end of the room that opened into the shed. He lifted the latch with precaution and went out, pushing the door behind him but without shutting it. Daru had not stirred. 'He is running away,' he merely thought. 'Good riddance!' Yet he listened attentively. The hens were not fluttering; the guest must be on the plateau. A faint sound of water reached him, and he didn't know what it was until the Arab again stood framed in the doorway, closed the door carefully, and came back to bed without a sound. Then Daru turned his back on him and fell asleep. Still later he seemed, from the depths of his sleep, to hear furtive steps around the schoolhouse. 'I'm dreaming! I'm dreaming!' he repeated to himself. And he went on sleeping.

When he awoke, the sky was clear; the loose window let in a cold, pure air. The Arab was asleep, hunched up under the blankets now, his mouth open, utterly relaxed. But when Daru shook him, he started dreadfully, staring at Daru with wild eyes as if he had never seen him and such a frightened expression that the schoolmaster stepped back. 'Don't be afraid. It's me. You must eat.' The Arab nodded his head and said yes. Calm had returned to his face, but his expression was vacant and listless.

The coffee was ready. They drank it seated together on the folding bed as they munched their pieces of the cake. Then Daru led the Arab under the shed and showed him the tap where he washed. He went back into the room, folded the blankets and the bed, made his own bed and put the room in order. Then he went through the classroom and out onto the terrace. The sun was already rising in the blue sky; a soft, bright light was bathing the deserted plateau. On the ridge the snow was melting in spots. The stones were about to reappear. Crouched on the edge of the plateau, the schoolmaster looked at the deserted expanse. He thought of Balducci. He had hurt him, for he had sent him off in a way as if he didn't want to be associated with him. He could still hear the gendarme's farewell and, without knowing why, he felt strangely empty and vulnerable. At that moment, from the other side of the schoolhouse, the prisoner coughed. Daru listened to him almost despite himself and then, furious, threw a pebble that whistled through the air before sinking into the snow. That man's stupid crime revolted him, but to hand him over was contrary to honour. Merely thinking of it made him smart with humiliation. And he cursed at one and the same time his own people who had sent him this Arab and the Arab too who had dared to kill and not managed to get away. Daru got up, walked in a circle on the terrace, waited motionless, and then went back into the schoolhouse.

The Arab, leaning over the cement floor of the shed, was washing his teeth with two fingers. Daru looked at him and said: 'Come.' He went back into the room ahead of the prisoner. He slipped a hunting-jacket on over his sweater and put on walking-shoes. Standing, he waited until the Arab had put on his *chèche* and sandals. They went into the classroom and the schoolmaster pointed to the exit, saying: 'Go ahead.' The fellow didn't budge. 'I'm coming,' said Daru. The Arab went out. Daru went back into the room and made a package of pieces of rusk, dates, and sugar. In the classroom, before going out, he hesitated a second in front of his desk, then crossed the threshold and locked the door. 'That's the way,' he said. He started towards the east, followed by the prisoner. But, a short distance from the schoolhouse, he thought he heard a slight sound behind them. He retraced his steps and examined the surroundings of the house; there was no one there. The Arab watched him without seeming to understand. 'Come on,' said Daru.

They walked for an hour and rested beside a sharp peak of limestone. The snow was melting faster and faster and the sun was drinking up the puddles at once, rapidly cleaning the plateau, which gradually dried and vibrated like the air itself. When they resumed walking, the ground rang under their feet. From time to time a bird rent the space in front of them with a joyful cry. Daru breathed in deeply the fresh morning light. He felt a sort of rapture before the vast familiar expanse, now almost entirely yellow under its dome of blue sky. They walked an hour more, descending towards the south. They reached a level height made up of crumbly rocks. From there on, the plateau sloped down, eastward, towards a low plain where there were a few spindly trees and, to the south, towards out-croppings of rock that gave the landscape a chaotic look.

Daru surveyed the two directions. There was nothing but the sky on the horizon. Not a man could be seen. He turned towards the Arab, who was looking at him blankly. Daru held out the package to him. 'Take it,' he said. 'There are dates, bread, and sugar. You can hold out for two days. Here are a thousand francs too.' The Arab took the package and the money but kept his full hands at chest level as if he didn't know what to do with what was being given him. 'Now look,' the schoolmaster said as he pointed in the direction of the east, 'there's the way to Tinguit. You have a two-hour walk. At Tinguit you'll find the administration and the police. They are expecting you.' The Arab looked towards the east, still holding the package and the money against his chest. Daru took his elbow and turned him rather roughly towards the south. At the foot of the height on which they stood could be seen a faint path. 'That's the trail across the plateau. In a day's walk from here you'll find pasture lands and the first nomads. They'll take you in and shelter you according to their law.' The Arab had now turned towards Daru and a sort of panic was visible in his expression. 'Listen,' he said. Daru shook his head: 'No, be quiet. Now I'm leaving you.' He turned his back on him, took two long steps in the direction of the school, looked hesitantly at the motionless Arab, and started off again. For a few minutes he heard nothing but his own step resounding on the cold ground and did not turn his head. A moment later, however, he turned around. The Arab was still there on the edge of the hill, his arms hanging now, and he was looking at the schoolmaster. Daru felt something rise in his throat. But he swore with impatience, waved vaguely, and started off again. He had already gone some distance when he again stopped and looked. There was no longer anyone on the hill.

Daru hesitated. The sun was now rather high in the sky and was beginning to beat down on his head. The schoolmaster retraced his steps, at first somewhat uncertainly, then with decision. When he reached the little hill, he was bathed in sweat. He climbed it as fast as he could and stopped, out of breath, at the top. The rockfields to the south stood out sharply against the blue sky, but on the plain to the east a steamy heat was already rising. And in that slight haze, Daru, with heavy heart, made out the Arab walking slowly on the road to prison.

A little later, standing before the window of the classroom, the schoolmaster was watching the clear light bathing the whole surface of the plateau, but he hardly saw it. Behind him on the blackboard, among the winding French rivers, sprawled the clumsily chalked-up words he had just read: 'You handed over our brother. You will pay for this.' Daru looked at the sky, the plateau, and, beyond, the invisible lands stretching all the way to the sea. In this vast landscape he had loved so much, he was alone.

Daniel Keyes *born in Brooklyn in 1927. After completing an M.A. at Brooklyn College he worked as a seaman and as a purser before becoming a University English lecturer. Much of his work has been based upon extensions of the story 'FLOWERS FOR ALGERNON', which was expanded into a novel, in 1966, then into a television play, and finally, a film, CHARLY. The diary form, used much earlier by Defoe, in parts of ROBINSON CRUSOE, by Goethe, in THE SORROWS OF YOUNG WERTHER, and by Gide, in PASTORAL SYMPHONY, gives the illusion of objective reportage, but the diarist continually reveals, or betrays, his own prejudices, giving a particular bias to the narrative. Into this complex form Keyes weaves dialect speech, and references to real and imaginary techniques of experimental psychology.*

At present he is living in Michigan, working on his second novel.

FLOWERS FOR ALGERNON

Daniel Keyes

progris riport 1—martch 5 1965

DR STRAUSS SAYS I SHUD RITE DOWN WHAT I THINK AND EVREY THING THAT
happins to me from now on. I dont know why but he says its importint
so they will see if they will use me. I hope they use me. Miss Kinnian says
maybe they can make me smart. I want to be smart. My name is Charlie
Gordon. I am 37 years old and 2 weeks ago was my brithday. I have
nuthing more to rite now so I will close for today.

progris riport 2—martch 6

I had a test today. I think I faled it. and I think that may be now they
wont use me. What happind is a nice young man was in the room and he
had some white cards with ink spilled all over them. He sed Charlie what
do you see on this card. I was very skared even tho I had my rabits foot
in my pockit because when I was a kid I always faled tests in school and
I spillled ink to.

I told him I saw a inkblot. He said yes and it made me feel good. I thot
that was all but when I got up to go he stopped me. He said now sit down
Charlie we are not thru yet. Then I don't remember so good but he
wantid me to say what was in the ink. I dint see nuthing in the ink but he
said there was picturs there other pepul saw some picturs. I coudnt see any
picturs. I reely tryed to see. I held the card close up and then far away. Then
I said if I had my glases I coud see better I usally only ware my glases in
the movies or TV but I said they are in the closit in the hall. I got them.
Then I said let me see that card agen I bet Ill find it now.

I tryed hard but I still coudnt find the picturs I only saw the ink. I told
him may be I need new glases. He rote somthing down on a paper and I
got skared of faling the test. I told him it was a very nice inkblot with
littel points all around the edges. He looked very sad so that wasnt it. I
said please let me try agen. Ill get it in a few minits becaus Im not so fast
somtimes. Im a slow reeder too in Miss Kinnians class for slow adults but
Im trying very hard.

He gave me a chance with another card that had 2 kinds of ink spilled
on it red and blue.

He was very nice and talked slow like Miss Kinnian does and he
explaned it to me that it was a *raw shok*. He said pepul see things in the ink.
I said show me where. He said think. I told him I think a inkblot but that
wasn't rite eather. He said what does it remind you—pretend something.
I closd my eyes for a long time to pretend. I told him I pretned a fowntan
pen with ink leeking all over a table cloth. Then he got up and went out.

I dont think I passd the *raw shok* test.

155

progris riport 3—martch 7

Dr Strauss and Dr Nemur say it dont matter about the inkblots. I told them I dint spill the ink on the cards and I coudn't see anything in the ink. They said that maybe they will still use me. I said Miss Kinnian never gave me tests like that one only spellin and reading. They said Miss Kinnian told that I was her bestist pupil in the adult nite scool becaus I tryed the hardist and I reely wantid to lern. They said how come you went to the adult nite scool all by yourself Charlie. How did you find it. I said I askd pepul and sumbldy told me where I shud go to lern to read and spell good. They said why did you want to. I told them becaus all my life I wantid to be smart and not dumb. But its very hard to be smart. They said you know it will probly be tempirery. I said yes. Miss Kinnian told me. I dont care if it herts.

Later I had more crazy tests today. The nice lady who gave it me told me the name and I asked her how do you spellit so I can rite it in my progris riport. THEMATIC APPERCEPTION TEST. I dont know the frist 2 words but I know what *test* means. You got to pass it or you get bad marks. This test looked easy becaus I coud see the picturs. Only this time she dint want me to tell her the picturs. That mixd me up. I said the man yesterday said I shoud tell him what I saw in the ink she said that dont make no difrence. She said make up storys about the pepul in the picturs.

I told her how can you tell storys about pepul you never met. I said why shud I make up lies. I never tell lies any more becaus I always get caut.

She told me this test and the other one the raw-shok was for getting personalty. I laffed so hard. I said how can you get that thing from from inkblots and fotos. She got sore and put her picturs away. I dont care. It was sily. I gess I faled that test too.

Later some men in white coats took me to a difernt part of the hospitil and gave me a game to play. It was like a race with a white mouse. They called the mouse Algernon. Algernon was in a box with a lot of twists and turns like all kinds of walls and they gave me a pencil and a paper with lines and lots of boxes. On one side it said START and on the other end it said FINISH. They said it was *amazed* and that Algernon and me had the same *amazed* to do. I dint see how we could have the same *amazed* if Algernon had a box and I had a paper but I dint say nothing. Anyway there wasnt time because the race started.

One of the men had a watch he was trying to hide so I wouldnt see it so I tryed not to look and that made me nervus.

Anyway that test made me feel worser than all the others because they did it over 10 times with difernt *amazeds* and Algernon won every time. I dint know that mice were so smart. Maybe thats because Algernon is a white mouse. Maybe white mice are smarter then other mice.

progris riport 4—Mar 8

Their going to use me! Im so exited I can hardly write. Dr Nemur and
Dr Strauss had a argament about it first. Dr Nemur was in the office when
Dr Strauss brot me in. Dr Nemur was worryed about using me but
Dr Strauss told him Miss Kinnian rekemmended me the best from all the
people who she was teaching. I like Miss Kinnian becaus shes a very smart
teacher. And she said Charlie your going to have a second chance. If you
volenteer for this experament you mite get smart. They dont know if it
will be perminint but theirs a chance. Thats why I said ok even when I
was scared because she said it was an operashun. She said dont be scared
Charlie you done so much with so little I think you deserv it most of all.

So I got scaird when Dr Nemur and Dr Strauss argud about it. Dr
Strauss said I had something that was very good. He said I had a good
motor-vation. I never even knew I had that. I felt proud when he said that
not every body with an eye-q of 68 had that thing. I dont know what it is
or where I got it but he said Algernon had it too. Algernons *motor-vation*
is the cheese they put in his box. But it cant be that because I didnt eat any
cheese this week.

Then he told Dr Nemur something I dint understand so while they were
talking I wrote down some of the words.

He said Dr Nemur I know Charlie is not what you had in mind as the
first of your new brede of intelek** (coudnt get the word) superman. But
most people of his low ment** are host** and uncoop** they are usualy
dull apath** and hard to reach. He has a good natcher hes intristed and
eager to please.

Dr Nemur said remember he will be the first human beeng ever to have
his intelijence trippled by surgicle meens.

Dr Strauss said exakly. Look at how well hes lerned to read and write
for his low mentel age its as grate an acheve** as you and I lerning
einstines therey of **vity without help. That shows the intenss motor-
vation. Its comparat** a tremen** achev** I say we use Charlie.

I dint get all the words and they were talking to fast but it sounded like
Dr Strauss was on my side and like the other one wasnt.

Then Dr Nemur nodded he said all right maybe your right. We will
use Charlie. When he said that I got so exited I jumped up and shook his
hand for being so good to me. I told him thank you doc you wont be
sorry for giving me a second chance. And I mean it like I told him. After
the operashun Im gonna try to be smart. Im gonna try awful hard.

progris ript 5—Mar 10

Im skared. Lots of people who work here and the nurses and the people
who gave me the tests came to bring me candy and wish me luck. I hop
I have luck. I got my rabits foot and my lucky penny and my horse shoe.

Only a black cat crossed me when I was comming to the hospital. Dr Strauss says dont be supersitis Charlie this is sience. Anyway Im keeping my rabits foot with me.

I asked Dr Strauss if Ill beat Algernon in the race after the operashun and he said may be. If the operashun works Ill show that mouse I can be as smart as he is. Maybe smarter. Then Ill be abel to read better and spell the words good and know lots of things and be like other people. I want to be smart like other people. If it works perminint they will make everybody smart all over the wurld.

They dint give me anything to eat this morning. I dont know what that eating has to do with getting smart. Im very hungry and Dr Nemur took away my box of candy. That Dr Nemur is a grouch. Dr Strauss says I can have it back after the operashun. You cant eat befor a operashun . . .

Progress Report 6—Mar 15

The operashun dint hurt. He did it while I was sleeping. They took off the bandijis from my eyes and my head today so I can make a PROGRESS REPORT. Dr Nemur who looked at some of my other ones says I spell PROGRESS wrong and he told me how to spell it and REPORT too. I got to try and remember that.

I have a very bad memary for spelling. Dr Strauss says its ok to tell about all the things that happin to me but he says I shoud tell more about what I feel and what I think. When I told him I dont know how to think he said try. All the time when the bandijis were on my eyes I tryed to think. Nothing happened. I dont know what to think about. Maybe if I ask him he will tell me how I can think now that Im suppose to get smart. What do smart people think about. Fancy things I suppose. I wish I knew some fancy things alredy.

Progress Report 7—mar 19

Nothing is happining. I had lots of tests and different kinds of races with Algernon. I hate that mouse. He always beats me. Dr Strauss said I got to play those games. And he said some time I got to take those tests over again. Thse inkblots are stupid. And those pictures are stupid too. I like to draw a picture of a man and a woman but I wont make up lies about people.

I got a headache from trying to think so much. I thot Dr Strauss was my frend but he dont help me. He dont tell me what to think or when Ill get smart. Miss Kinnian dint come to see me. I think writing these progress reports are stupid too.

Progress Report 8—Mar 23

Im going back to work at the factery. They said it was better I shud go back to work but I cant tell anyone what the operashun was for and I have to come to the hospitil for an hour evry night after work. They are gonna pay me mony every month for lerning to be smart.

Im glad Im going back to work because I miss my job and all my frends and all the fun we have there.

Dr Strauss says I shud keep writing things down but I dont have to do it every day just when I think of something or something speshul happins. He says dont get discoridged because it takes time and it happins slow. He says it took a long time with Algernon before he got 3 times smarter then he was before. Thats why Algernon beats me all the time because he had that operashun too. That makes me feel better. I coud probly do that *amazed* faster than a reglar mouse. Maybe some day Ill beat Algernon. Boy that would be something. So far Algernon looks like he mite be smart perminent.

Mar 25 (I dont have to write PROGRESS REPORT on top any more just when I hand it in once a week for Dr Nemur to read. I just have to put the date on. That saves time)

We had a lot of fun at the factery today. Joe Carp said hey look where Charlie had his operashun what did they do Charlie put some brains in. I was going to tell him but I remembered Dr Strauss said no. Then Frank Reilly said what did you do Charlie forget your key and open your door the hard way. That made me laff. Their really my frends and they like me.

Sometimes somebody will say hey look at Joe or Frank or George he really pulled a Charlie Gordon. I don't know why they say that but they always laff. This morning Amos Borg who is the 4 man at Donnegans used my name when he shouted at Ernie the office boy. Ernie lost a packige. He said Ernie for godsake what are you trying to be a Charlie Gordon. I dont understand why he said that. I never lost any packiges.

Mar 28 Dr Strauss came to my room tonight to see why I dint come in like I was suppose to. I told him I dont like to race with Algernon any more. He said I dont have to for a while but I shud come in. He had a present for me only it wasnt a present but just for lend. I thot it was a little television but it wasnt. He said I got to turn it on when I go to sleep. I said your kidding why shud I turn it on when Im going to sleep. Who ever herd of a thing like that. But he said if I want to get smart I got to do what he says. I told him I dint think I was going to get smart and he put his hand on my sholder and said Charlie you dont know it yet but your getting smarter all the time. You wont notice for a while. I think he was just being nice to make me feel good because I dont look any smarter.

Oh yes I almost forgot. I asked him when I can go back to the class at Miss Kinnian school. He said I wont go their. He said that soon Miss Kinnian will come to the hospitil to start and teach me speshul. I was mad at her for not comming to see me when I got the operashun but I like her so may be we will be frends again.

Mar 29 That crazy TV kept me up all night. How can I sleep with something yelling crazy things all night in my ears. And the nutty pictures. Wow. I dont know what it says when Im up so how am I going to know when Im sleeping.

Dr Strauss says its ok. He says my brains are lerning when I sleep and that will help me when Miss Kinnian starts my lessons in the hospitl (only I found out it isnt a hospitil its a labatory). I think its all crazy. If you can get smart when your sleeping why do people go to school. That thing I dont think will work. I use to watch the late show and the late late show on TV all the time and it never made me smart. Maybe you have to sleep while you watch it.

PROGRESS REPORT 9—April 3

Dr Strauss showed me how to keep the TV turned low so now I can sleep. I dont hear a thing. And I still dont understand what it says. A few times I play it over in the morning to find out what I lerned when I was sleeping and I dont think so. Miss Kinnian says Maybe its another langwidge or something. But most times it sounds american. It talks so fast faster than even Miss Gold who was my teacher in 6 grade and I remember she talked so fast I coudnt understand her.

I told Dr Strauss what good is it to get smart in my sleep. I want to be smart when Im awake. He says its the same thing and I have two minds. Theres the *subconscious* and the *conscious* (thats how you spell it). And one dont tell the other one what its doing. They dont even talk to each other. Thats why I dream. And boy have I been having crazy dreams. Wow. Ever since that night TV. The late late late late late show.

I forgot to ask him if it was only me or if everybody had those two minds.

(I just looked up the word in the dictionary Dr Strauss gave me. The word is *subconscious. adj. Of the nature of mental operations yet not present in consciousness; as, subconscious conflict of desires.*) Theres more but I still dont know what it means. This isnt a very good dictionary for dumb people like me.

Anyway the headache is from the party. My frends from the factery Joe Carp and Frank Reilly invited me to go with them to Muggsys Saloon for some drinks. I dont like to drink but they said we will have lots of fun. I had a good time.

Joe Carp said I shoud show the girls how I mop out the toilet in the factory and he got me a mop. I showed them and everyone laffed when I told that Mr Donnegan said I was the best janiter he ever had because I like my job and do it good and never come late or miss a day except for my operashun.

I said Miss Kinnian always said Charlie be proud of your job because you do it good.

Everybody laffed and we had a good time and they gave me lots of drinks and Joe said Charlie is a card when hes potted. I dont know what that means but everybody likes me and we have fun. I cant wait to be smart like my best frends Joe Carp and Frank Reilly.

I dont remember how the party was over but I think I went out to buy a newspaper and coffe for Joe and Frank and when I came back there was no one their. I looked for them all over till late. Then I dont remember so good but I think I got sleepy or sick. A nice cop brot me back home. Thats what my landlady Mrs Flynn says.

But I got a headache and a big lump on my head and black and blue all over. I think maybe I fell but Joe Carp says it was the cop they beat up drunks some times. I dont think so. Miss Kinnian says cops are to help people. Anyway I got a bad headache and Im sick and hurt all over. I dont think Ill drink anymore.

April 6   I beat Algernon! I dint even know I beat him until Burt the tester told me. Then the second time I lost because I got so exited I fell off the chair before I finished. But after that I beat him 8 more times. I must be getting smart to beat a smart mouse like Algernon. But I dont *feel* smarter.

I wanted to race Algernon some more but Burt said thats enough for one day. They let me hold him for a minit. Hes not so bad. Hes soft like a ball of cotton. He blinks and when he opens his eyes their black and pink on the eges.

I said can I feed him because I felt bad to beat him and I wanted to be nice and make frends. Burt said no Algernon is a very specshul mouse with an operashun like mine, and he was the first of all the animals to stay smart so long. He told me Algernon is so smart that every day he has to solve a test to get his food. Its a thing like a lock on a door that changes every time Algernon goes in to eat so he has to lern something new to get his food. That made me sad because if he couldnt lern he would be hungry.

I dont think its right to make you pass a test to eat. How woud Dr Nemur like it to have to pass a test every time he wants to eat. I think Ill be frends with Algernon.

April 9   Tonight after work Miss Kinnian was at the laboratory. She looked like she was glad to see me but scared. I told her dont worry Miss Kinnian Im not smart yet and she laffed. She said I have confidence in you Charlie the way you struggled so hard to read and right better than all the others. At werst you will have it for a littel wile and your doing somthing for sience.

We are reading a very hard book. I never read such a hard book before. Its called *Robinson Crusoe* about a man who gets merooned on a dessert Iland. Hes smart and figers out all kinds of things so he can have a house and food and hes a good swimmer. Only I feel sorry because hes all alone and has no frends. But I think their must be somebody else on the iland because theres a picture with his funny umbrella looking at footprints. I hope he gets a frend and not be lonely.

April 10 Miss Kinnian teaches me to spell better. She says look at a word and close your eyes and say it over and over until you remember. I have lots of truble with *through* that you say *threw* and *enough* and *tough* that you dont say *enew* and *tew*. You got to say *enuff* and *tuff*. Thats how I use to write it before I started to get smart. Im confused but Miss Kinnian says theres no reason in spelling.

Apr 14 Finished *Robinson Crusoe*. I want to find out more about what happens to him but Miss Kinnian says that's all there is. *Why.*

Apr 15 Miss Kinnian says Im lerning fast. She read some of the Progress Reports and she looked at me kind of funny. She says Im a fine person and Ill show them all. I asked her why. She said never mind but I shoudnt feel bad if I find out that everybody inst nice like I think. She said for a person who god gave so little to you done more then a lot of people with brains they never even used. I said all my frends are smart people but there good. They like me and they never did anything that wasnt nice. Then she got something in her eye and she had to run out to the ladys room.

Apr 16 Today, I lerned, the *comma*, this is a comma (,) a period, with a tail, Miss Kinnian, says its important, because, it makes writing better, she said, somebody, coud lose, a lot of money, if a comma, isnt, in the, right place, I dont have, any money, and I dont see, how a comma, keeps you from losing it,

But she says, everybody, uses commas, so Ill use, them too,

Apr 17 I used the comma wrong. Its punctuation. Miss Kinnian told me to look up long words in the dictionary to lern to spell them. I said whats the difference if you can read it anyway. She said its part of your education so now on Ill look up all the words Im not sure how to spell. It takes a long time to write that way but I think Im remembering. I only have to look up once and after that I get it right. Anyway thats how come I got the word *punctuation* right. (Its that way in the dictionary). Miss Kinnian says a period is punctuation too, and there are lots of other marks to lern. I told her I thot all the periods had to have tails but she said no.

You got to mix them up, she showed? me" how. to mix! them (up,. and now; I can! mix up all kinds" of punctuation, in! my writing? There, are lots! of rules? to lern; but Im gettin'g them in my head.

One thing I? like about, Dear Miss Kinnian: (thats the way it goes in a business letter if I ever go into business) is she, always gives me' a reason" when—I ask. She's a gen'ius! I wish! I cou'd be smart' like, her;

(Punctuation, is; fun!)

April 18 What a dope I am! I didn't even understand what she was talking about. I read the grammar book last night and it explanes the whole thing. Then I saw it was the same way as Miss Kinnian was trying to tell me, but I didn't get it. I got up in the middle of the night, and the whole thing straightened out in my mind.

Miss Kinnian said that the TV working in my sleep helped out. She said I reached a plateau. Thats like the flat top of a hill.

After I figgered out how punctuation worked, I read over all my old Progress Reports from the beginning. Boy, did I have crazy spelling and punctuation! I told Miss Kinnian I ought to go over the pages and fix all the mistakes but she said, 'No, Charlie, Dr Nemur wants them just as they are. That's why he let you keep them after they were photostated, to see your own progress. You're coming along fast, Charlie.'

That made me feel good. After the lesson I went down and played with Algernon. We don't race any more.

April 20 I feel sick inside. Not sick like for a doctor, but inside my chest it feels empty like getting punched and a heartburn at the same time.

I wasn't going to write about it, but I guess I got to, because it's important. Today was the first time I ever stayed home from work.

Last night Joe Carp and Frank Reilly invited me to a party. There were lots of girls and some men from the factory. I remembered how sick I got last time I drank too much, so I told Joe I didn't want anything to drink. He gave me a plain Coke instead. It tasted funny, but I thought it was just a bad taste in my mouth.

We had a lot of fun for a while. Joe said I should dance with Ellen and she would teach me the steps. I fell a few times and I couldn't understand why because no one else was dancing besides Ellen and me. And all the time I was tripping because somebody's foot was always sticking out.

Then when I got up I saw the look on Joe's face and it gave me a funny feeling in my stomack. 'He's a scream,' one of the girls said. Everybody was laughing.

Frank said, 'I ain't laughed so much since we sent him off for the newspaper that night at Muggsy's and ditched him.'

'Look at him. His face is red.'

'He's blushing. Charlie is blushing.'

'Hey, Ellen, what'd you do to Charlie? I never saw him act like that before.'

I didn't know what to do or where to turn. Everyone was looking at me and laughing and I felt naked. I wanted to hide myself. I ran out into the street and I threw up. Then I walked home. It's a funny thing I never knew that Joe and Frank and the others liked to have me around all the time to make fun of me.

Now I know what it means when they say 'to pull a Charlie Gordon.' I'm ashamed.

PROGRESS REPORT 11

April 21 Still didn't go into the factory. I told Mrs. Flynn my landlady to call and tell Mr. Donnegan I was sick. Mrs. Flynn looks at me very funny lately like she's scared of me.

I think it's a good thing about finding out how everybody laughs at me. I thought about it a lot. It's because I'm so dumb and I don't even know when I'm doing something dumb. People think it's funny when a dumb person can't do things the same way they can.

Anyway, now I know I'm getting smarter every day. I know punctuation and I can spell good. I like to look up all the hard words in the dictionary and I remember them. I'm reading a lot now, and Miss Kinnian says I read very fast. Sometimes I even understand what I'm reading about, and it stays in my mind. There are times when I can close my eyes and think of a page and it all comes back like a picture.

Besides history, geography, and arithmetic, Miss Kinnian said I should start to learn a few foreign languages. Dr. Strauss gave me some more tapes to play while I sleep. I still don't understand how that conscious and unconscious mind works, but Dr. Strauss says not to worry yet. He asked me to promise that when I start learning college subjects next week I wouldn't read any books on psychology—that is, until he gives me permission.

I feel a lot better today, but I guess I'm still a little angry that all the time people were laughing and making fun of me because I wasn't so smart. When I become intelligent like Dr. Strauss says, with three times my I.Q. of 68, then maybe I'll be like everyone else and people will like me and be friendly.

I'm not sure what an I.Q. is. Dr. Nemur said it was something that measured how intelligent you were—like a scale in the drug-store weighs pounds. But Dr. Strauss had a big argument with him and said an I.Q. didn't weigh intelligence at all. He said an I.Q. showed how much intelligence you could get, like the numbers on the outside of a measuring cup. You still had to fill the cup up with stuff.

Then when I asked Burt, who gives me my intelligence tests and works with Algernon, he said that both of them were wrong (only I had to promise not to tell them he said so). Burt says that the I.Q. measures a lot of different things including some of the things you learned already, and it really isn't any good at all.

So I still don't know what I.Q. is except that mine is going to be over 200 soon. I didn't want to say anything, but I don't see how if they don't know *what* it is, or *where* it is—I don't see how they know *how much* of it you've got.

Dr. Nemur says I have to take a *Rorschach Test* tomorrow. I wonder what *that* is.

April 22 I found out what a *Rorschach* is. It's the test I took before the operation—the one with the inkblots on the pieces of carbdoard. The man who gave me the test was the same one.

I was scared to death of those inkblots. I knew he was going to ask me to find the pictures and I knew I wouldn't be able to. I was thinking to myself, if only there was some way of knowing what kind of pictures were hidden there. Maybe there weren't any pictures at all. Maybe it was just a trick to see if I was dumb enough to look for something that wasn't there. Just thinking about that made me sore at him.

'All right, Charlie,' he said, 'you've seen these cards before, remember?'
'Of course I remember.'

The way I said it, he knew I was angry, and he looked surprised. 'Yes, of course. Now I want you to look at this one. What might this be? What do you see on this card? People see all sorts of things in these inkblots. Tell me what it might be for you—what it makes you think of.'

I was shocked. That wasn't what I had expected him to say at all. 'You mean there are no pictures hidden in those inkblots?'

He frowned and took off his glasses. 'What?'

'Pictures. Hidden in the inkblots. Last time you told me that everyone could see them and you wanted me to find them too.'

He explained to me that the last time he had used almost the exact same words he was using now. I didn't believe it, and I still have the suspicion that he misled me at the time just for the fun of it. Unless—I don't know any more—could I have been *that* feebleminded?

We went through the cards slowly. One of them looked like a pair of bats tugging at something. Another one looked like two men fencing with swords. I imagined all sorts of things. I guess I got carried away. But I didn't trust him any more, and I kept turning them around and even looking on the back to see if there was anything there I was supposed to catch. While he was making his notes, I peeked out of the corner of my eye to read it. But it was all in code that looked like this:

WF + A Ddf—Ad orig. WF—A SF + obj

The test still doesn't make sense to me. It seems to me that anyone could make up lies about things that they didn't really see. How could he know I wasn't making a fool of him by mentioning things that I didn't really imagine? Maybe I'll understand it when Dr. Strauss lets me read up on psychology.

April 25 I figured out a new way to line up the machines in the factory, and Mr. Donnegan says it will save him ten thousand dollars a year in labor and increased production. He gave me a twenty-five-dollar bonus.

I wanted to take Joe Carp and Frank Reilly out to lunch to celebrate, but Joe said he had to buy some things for his wife, and Frank said he was meeting his cousin for lunch. I guess it'll take a little time for them to get used to the changes in me. Everybody seems to be frightened of me. When I went over to Amos Borg and tapped him on the shoulder, he jumped up in the air.

People don't talk to me much any more or kid around the way they used to. It makes the job kind of lonely.

April 27 I got up the nerve today to ask Miss Kinnian to have dinner with me tomorrow night to celebrate my bonus.

At first she wasn't sure it was right, but I asked Dr. Strauss and he said it was okay. Dr. Strauss and Dr. Nemur don't seem to be getting along so well. They're arguing all the time. This evening when I came in to ask Dr. Strauss about having dinner with Miss Kinnian, I heard them shouting. Dr. Nemur was saying that it was *his* experiment and *his* research, and Dr. Strauss was shouting back that he contributed just as much, because he found me through Miss Kinnian and he performed the operation. Dr. Strauss said that someday thousands of neurosurgeons might be using his technique all over the world.

Dr. Nemur wanted to publish the results of the experiment at the end of this month. Dr. Strauss wanted to wait a while longer to be sure. Dr. Strauss said that Dr. Nemur was more interested in the Chair of Psychology at Princeton than he was in the experiment. Dr. Nemur said that Dr. Strauss was nothing but an opportunist who was trying to ride to glory on *his* coattails.

When I left afterwards, I found myself trembling. I don't know why for sure, but it was as if I'd seen both men clearly for the first time. I remember hearing Burt say that Dr. Nemur had a shrew of a wife who was pushing him all the time to get things published so that he could become famous. Burt said that the dream of her life was to have a big-shot husband.

Was Dr. Strauss really trying to ride on his coattails?

April 28 I don't understand why I never noticed how beautiful Miss Kinnian really is. She has brown eyes and feathery brown hair that comes to the top of her neck. She's only thirty-four! I think from the beginning I had the feeling that she was an unreachable genius—and very, very old. Now, every time I see her she grows younger and more lovely.

We had dinner and a long talk. When she said that I was coming along so fast that soon I'd be leaving her behind, I laughed.

'It's true, Charlie. You're already a better reader than I am. You can read a whole page at a glance while I can take in only a few lines at a time. And you remember every single thing you read. I'm lucky if I can recall the main thoughts and the general meaning.'

'I don't feel intelligent. There are so many things I don't understand.'

She took out a cigarette and I lit it for her. 'You've got to be a *little* patient. You're accomplishing in days and weeks what it takes normal people to do in half a lifetime. That's what makes it so amazing. You're like a giant sponge now, soaking things in. Facts, figures, general knowledge. And soon you'll begin to connect them, too. You'll see how the different branches of learning are related. There are many levels, Charlie, like steps on a giant ladder that take you up higher and higher to see more and more of the world around you.

'I can see only a little bit of that, Charlie, and I won't go much higher than I am now, but you'll keep climbing up and up, and see more and more, and each step will open new worlds that you never even knew existed.' She frowned. 'I hope . . . I just hope to God—'

'What?'

'Never mind, Charles. I just hope I wasn't wrong to advise you to go into this in the first place.'

I laughed. 'How could that be? It worked, didn't it? Even Algernon is still smart.'

We sat there silently for a while and I knew what she was thinking about as she watched me toying with the chain of my rabbit's foot and my keys. I didn't want to think of that possibility any more than elderly people want to think of death. I *knew* that this was only the beginning. I knew what she meant about levels because I'd seen some of them already. The thought of leaving her behind made me sad.

I'm in love with Miss Kinnian.

PROGRESS REPORT 12
April 30 I've quit my job with Donnegan's Plastic Box Company. Mr. Donnegan insisted that it would be better for all concerned if I left. What did I do to make them hate me so?

The first I knew of it was when Mr. Donnegan showed me the petition. Eight hundred and forty names, everyone connected with the factory, except Fanny Girden. Scanning the list quickly, I saw at once that hers was the only missing name. All the rest demanded that I be fired.

Joe Carp and Frank Reilly wouldn't talk to me about it. No one else would either, except Fanny. She was one of the few people I'd known who set her mind to something and believed it no matter what the rest of the world proved, said, or did—and Fanny did not believe that I should have been fired. She had been against the petition on principle and despite the pressure and threats she'd held out.

'Which don't mean to say,' she remarked, 'that I don't think there's something mighty strange about you, Charlie. Them changes. I don't know. You used to be a good, dependable, ordinary man—not too bright maybe, but honest. Who knows what you done to yourself to get so smart all of a sudden. Like everybody around here's been saying, Charlie, it's not right.'

'But how can you say that, Fanny? What's wrong with a man becoming intelligent and wanting to acquire knowledge and understanding of the world around him?'

She stared down at her work and I turned to leave. Without looking at me, she said: 'It was evil when Eve listened to the snake and ate from the tree of knowledge. It was evil when she saw that she was naked. If not for that none of us would ever have to grow old and sick, and die.'

Once again now I have the feeling of shame burning inside me. This intelligence has driven a wedge between me and all the people I once knew and loved. Before, they laughed at me and despised me for my ignorance and dullness; now, they hate me for my knowledge and understanding. What in God's name do they want of me?

They've driven me out of the factory. Now I'm more alone than ever before. . . .

May 15 Dr. Strauss is very angry at me for not having written any progress reports in two weeks. He's justified because the lab is now paying me a regular salary. I told him I was too busy thinking and reading. When I pointed out that writing was such a slow process that it made me impatient with my poor handwriting, he suggested that I learn to type. It's much easier to write now because I can type nearly seventy-five words a minute. Dr. Strauss continually reminds me of the need to speak and write simply so that people will be able to understand me.

I'll try to review all the things that happened to me during the last two weeks. Algernon and I were presented to the American Psychological Association sitting in convention with the World Psychological Association last Tuesday. We created quite a sensation. Dr. Nemur and Dr. Strauss were proud of us.

I suspect that Dr. Nemur, who is sixty—ten years older than Dr. Strauss —finds it necessary to see tangible results of his work. Undoubtedly the result of pressure by Mrs. Nemur.

Contrary to my earlier impressions of him, I realize that Dr. Nemur is not at all a genius. He has a very good mind, but it struggles under the specter of self-doubt. He wants people to take him for a genius. Therefore, it is important for him to feel that his work is accepted by the world. I believe that Dr. Nemur was afraid of further delay because he worried that someone else might make a discovery along these lines and take the credit from him.

Dr. Strauss on the other hand might be called a genius, although I feel that his areas of knowledge are too limited. He was educated in the tradition of narrow specialization; the broader aspects of background were neglected far more than necessary—even for a neuro-surgeon.

I was shocked to learn that the only ancient languages he could read were Latin, Greek, and Hebrew, and that he knows almost nothing of mathematics beyond the elementary levels of the calculus of variations. When he admitted this to me, I found myself almost annoyed. It was as if he'd hidden this part of himself in order to deceive me, pretending—as do many people I've discovered—to be what he is not. No one I've ever known is what he appears to be on the surface.

Dr. Nemur appears to be uncomfortable around me. Sometimes when I try to talk to him, he just looks at me strangely and turns away. I was angry at first when Dr. Strauss told me I was giving Dr. Nemur an inferiority complex. I thought he was mocking me and I'm oversensitive at being made fun of.

How was I to know that a highly respected psychoexperimentalist like Nemur was unacquainted with Hindustani and Chinese? It's absurd when you consider the work that is being done in India and China today in the very field of his study.

I asked Dr. Strauss how Nemur could refute Rahajamati's attack on his method and results if Nemur couldn't even read them in the first place. That strange look on Dr. Strauss' face can mean only one of two things. Either he doesn't want to tell Nemur what they're saying in India, or else—and this worries me—Dr. Strauss doesn't know either. I must be careful to speak and write clearly and simply so that people won't laugh.

May 18 I am very disturbed. I saw Miss Kinnian last night for the first time in over a week. I tried to avoid all discussions of intellectual concepts and to keep the conversation on a simple, everyday level, but she just stared at me blankly and asked me what I meant about the mathematical variance equivalent in Dorbermann's *Fifth Concerto*.

When I tried to explain she stopped me and laughed. I guess I got angry, but I suspect I'm approaching her on the wrong level. No matter what I try to discuss with her, I am unable to communicate. I must review Vrostadt's equations on *Levels of Semantic Progression*. I find that I don't communicate with people much any more. Thank God for books and music and things I can think about. I am alone in my apartment at Mrs. Flynn's boardinghouse most of the time and seldom speak to anyone.

May 20 I would not have noticed the new dishwasher, a boy of about sixteen, at the corner diner where I take my evening meals if not for the incident of the broken dishes.

They crashed to the floor, shattering and sending bits of white china under the tables. The boy stood there, dazed and frightened, holding the empty tray in his hand. The whistles and catcalls from the customers (the cries of 'hey, there go the profits!' . . . '*Mazeltov!*' . . . and 'well, *he* didn't work here very long . . .' which invariably seems to follow the breaking of glass or dishware in a public restaurant) all seemed to confuse him.

When the owner came to see what the excitement was about, the boy cowered as if he expected to be struck and threw up his arms as if to ward off the blow.

'All right! All right, you dope,' shouted the owner, 'don't just stand there! Get the broom and sweep that mess up. A broom . . . a broom, you idiot! It's in the kitchen. Sweep up all the pieces.'

The boy saw that he was not going to be punished. His frightened expression disappeared and he smiled and hummed as he came back with the broom to sweep the floor. A few of the rowdier customers kept up the remarks, amusing themselves at his expense.

'Here, sonny, over here there's a nice piece behind you. . . .'
'C'mon, do it again. . . .'
'He's not so dumb. It's easier to break 'em than to wash 'em. . . .'

As his vacant eyes moved across the crowd of amused onlookers, he slowly mirrored their smiles and finally broke into an uncertain grin at the joke which he obviously did not understand.

I felt sick inside as I looked at his dull, vacuous smile, the wide, bright eyes of a child, uncertain but eager to please. They were laughing at him because he was mentally retarded.

And I had been laughing at him too.

Suddenly, I was furious at myself and all those who were smirking at him. I jumped up and shouted, 'Shut up! Leave him alone! It's not his fault he can't understand! He can't help what he is! But for God's sake . . . he's still a human being!'

The room grew silent. I cursed myself for losing control and creating a scene. I tried not to look at the boy as I paid my check and walked out without touching my food. I felt ashamed for both of us.

How strange it is that people of honest feelings and sensibility, who would not take advantage of a man born without arms or legs or eyes— how such people think nothing of abusing a man born with low intelligence. It infuriated me to think that not too long ago I, like this boy, had foolishly played the clown.

And I had almost forgotten.

I'd hidden the picture of the old Charlie Gordon from myself because now that I was intelligent it was something that had to be pushed out of my mind. But today in looking at that boy, for the first time I saw what I had been. *I was just like him!*

Only a short time ago, I learned that people laughed at me. Now I can see that unknowingly I joined with them in laughing at myself. That hurts most of all.

I have often reread my progress reports and seen the illiteracy, the childish naïveté, the mind of low intelligence peering from a dark room, through the keyhole, at the dazzling light outside. I see that even in my dullness I knew that I was inferior, and that other people had something I lacked—something denied me. In my mental blindness, I thought that it was somehow connected with the ability to read and write, and I was sure that if I could get those skills I would automatically have intelligence too.

Even a feeble-minded man wants to be like other men.

A child may not know how to feed itself, or what to eat, yet it knows of hunger.

This then is what I was like, I never knew. Even with my gift of intellectual awareness, I never really knew.

This day was good for me. Seeing the past more clearly, I have decided to use my knowledge and skills to work in the field of increasing human intelligence levels. Who is better equipped for this work? Who else has lived in both worlds? These are my people. Let me use my gift to do something for them.

Tomorrow, I will discuss with Dr. Strauss the manner in which I can work in this area. I may be able to help him work out the problems of widespread use of the technique which was used on me. I have several good ideas of my own.

There is so much that might be done with this technique. If I could be made into a genius, what about thousands of others like myself? What fantastic levels might be achieved by using this technique on normal people? On *geniuses?*

There are so many doors to open. I am impatient to begin.

PROGRESS REPORT 13

May 23 It happened today. Algernon bit me. I visited the lab to see him as I do occasionally, and when I took him out of his cage, he snapped at

Daniel Keyes

my hand. I put him back and watched him for a while. He was unusually
disturbed and vicious.

May 24 Burt, who is in charge of the experimental animals, tells me that
Algernon is changing. He is less co-operative, he refuses to run the maze
any more; general motivation has decreased. And he hasn't been eating.
Everyone is upset about what this may mean.

May 25 They've been feeding Algernon, who now refuses to work the
shifting-lock problem. Everyone identifies me with Algernon. In a way
we're both the first of our kind. They're all pretending that Algernon's
behaviour is not necessarily significant for me. But it's hard to hide the
fact that some of the other animals who were used in this experiment are
showing strange behavior.

Dr. Strauss and Dr. Nemur have asked me not to come to the lab any
more. I know what they're thinking but I can't accept it. I am going ahead
with my plans to carry their research forward. With all due respect to
both of these fine scientists, I am well aware of their limitations. If there
is an answer, I'll have to find it out for myself. Suddenly, time has become
very important to me.

May 29 I have been given a lab of my own and permission to go ahead
with the research. I'm on to something. Working day and night. I've had
a cot moved into the lab. Most of my writing time is spent on the notes
which I keep in a separate folder, but from time to time I feel it necessary
to put down my moods and my thoughts out of sheer habit.

I find the *calculus of intelligence* to be a fascinating study. Here is the
place for the application of all the knowledge I have acquired. In a sense
it's the problem I've been concerned with all my life.

May 31 Dr. Strauss thinks I'm working too hard. Dr. Nemur says I'm
trying to cram a lifetime of research and thought into a few weeks. I know
I should rest, but I'm driven on by something inside that won't let me
stop. I've got to find the reason for the sharp regression in Algernon. I've
got to know *if* and *when* it will happen to me.

June 4 LETTER TO DR. STRAUSS (*copy*)
Dear Dr. Strauss:

Under separate cover I am sending you a copy of my report entitled,
'The Algernon-Gordon Effect: A Study of Structure and Function of
Increased Intelligence,' which I would like to have you read and have
published.

As you see, my experiments are completed. I have included in my

172

report all of my formulae, as well as mathematical analysis in the appendix. Of course, these should be verified.

Because of its importance to both you and Dr. Nemur (and need I say to myself, too?) I have checked and re-checked my results a dozen times in the hope of finding an error. I am sorry to say the results must stand. Yet for the sake of science, I am grateful for the little bit that I here add to the knowledge of the function of the human mind and of the laws governing the artificial increase of human intelligence.

I recall your once saying to me that an experimental *failure* or the *disproving* of a theory was as important to the advancement of learning as a success would be. I know now that this is true. I am sorry, however, that my own contribution to the field must rest upon the ashes of the work of two men I regard so highly.

Yours truly,
Charles Gordon

encl.: rept.

June 5 I must not become emotional. The facts and the results of my experiments are clear, and the more sensational aspects of my own rapid climb cannot obscure the fact that the tripling of intelligence by the surgical technique developed by Drs. Strauss and Nemur must be viewed as having little or no practical applicability (at the present time) to the increase of human intelligence.

As I review the records and data on Algernon, I see that although he is still in his physical infancy, he has regressed mentally. Motor activity is impaired; there is a general reduction of glandular activity; there is an accelerated loss of co-ordination.

There are also strong indications of progressive amnesia.

As will be seen by my report, these and other physical and mental deterioration syndromes can be predicted with statistically significant results by the application of my formula.

The surgical stimulus to which we were both subjected has resulted in an intensification and acceleration of all mental processes. The unforeseen development, which I have taken the liberty of calling the *Algernon-Gordon Effect*, is the logical extension of the entire intelligence speed-up. The hypothesis here proven may be described simply in the following terms: Artificially increased intelligence deteriorates at a rate of time directly proportional to the quantity of the increase.

I feel that this, in itself, is an important discovery.

As long as I am able to write, I will continue to record my thoughts in these progress reports. It is one of my few pleasures. However, by all indications, my own mental deterioration will be very rapid.

I have already begun to notice signs of emotional instability and forgetfulness, the first symptoms of the burnout.

June 10 Deterioration progressing. I have become absent-minded. Algernon died two days ago. Dissection shows my predictions were right. His brain had decreased in weight and there was a general smoothing out of cerebral convolutions as well as a deepening and broadening of brain fissures.

I guess the same thing is or will soon be happening to me. Now that it's definite, I don't want it to happen.

I put Algernon's body in a cheese box and buried him in the back yard. I cried.

June 15 Dr. Strauss came to see me again. I wouldn't open the door and I told him to go away. I want to be left to myself. I have become touchy and irritable. I feel the darkness closing in. It's hard to throw off thoughts of suicide. I keep telling myself how important this introspective journal will be.

It's a strange sensation to pick up a book that you've read and enjoyed just a few months ago and discover that you don't remember it. I remembered how great I thought John Milton was, but when I picked up *Paradise Lost* I couldn't understand it at all. I got so angry I threw the book across the room.

I've got to try to hold on to some of it. Some of the things I've learned. Oh, God, please don't take it all away.

June 19 Sometimes, at night, I go out for a walk. Last night I couldn't remember where I lived. A policeman took me home. I have the strange feeling that this has all happened to me before—a long time ago. I keep telling myself I'm the only person in the world who can describe what's happening to me.

June 21 Why can't I remember? I've got to fight. I lie in bed for days and I don't know who or where I am. Then it all comes back to me in a flash. Fugues of amnesia. Symptoms of senility—second childhood. I can watch them coming on. It's so cruelly logical. I learned so much and so fast. Now my mind is deteriorating rapidly. I won't let it happen. I'll fight it. I can't help thinking of the boy in the restaurant, the blank expression, the silly smile, the people laughing at him. No—please—not that again. . . .

June 22 I'm forgetting things that I learned recently. It seems to be following the classic pattern—the last things learned are the first things forgotten. Or is that the pattern? I'd better look it up again. . . .

I reread my paper on the *Algernon-Gordon Effect* and I get the strange feeling that it was written by someone else. There are parts I don't even understand.

Motor activity impaired. I keep tripping over things, and it becomes increasingly difficult to type.

June 23   I've given up using the typewriter completely. My co-ordination is bad. I feel that I'm moving slower and slower. Had a terrible shock today. I picked up a copy of an article I used in my research, Krueger's *Uber psychische Ganzheit*, to see if it would help me understand what I had done. First I thought there was something wrong with my eyes. Then I realized I could no longer read German. I tested myself in other languages. All gone.

June 30   A week since I dare to write again. It's slipping away like sand through my fingers. Most of the books I have are too hard for me now. I get angry with them because I know that I read and understood them just a few weeks ago.

I keep telling myself I must keep writing these reports so that somebody will know what is happening to me. But it gets harder to form the words and remember spellings. I have to look up even simple words in the dictionary now and it makes me impatient with myself.

Dr. Strauss comes around almost every day, but I told him I wouldn't see or speak to anybody. He feels guilty. They all do. But I don't blame anyone. I knew what might happen. But how it hurts.

July 7   I don't know where the week went. Todays Sunday I know because I can see through my window people going to church. I think I stayed in bed all week but I remember Mrs. Flynn bringing food to me a few times. I keep saying over and over Ive got to do something but then I forget or maybe its just easier not to do what I say Im going to do.

I think of my mother and father a lot these days. I found a picture of them with me taken at a beach. My father has a big ball under his arm and my mother is holding me by the hand. I dont remember them the way they are in the picture. All I remember is my father drunk most of the time and arguing with mom about money.

He never shaved much and he used to scratch my face when he hugged me. My mother said he died but Cousin Miltie said he heard his mom and dad say that my father ran away with another woman. When I asked my mother she slapped my face and said my father was dead. I dont think I ever found out which was true but I dont care much. (He said he was going to take me to see cows on a farm once but he never did. He never kept his promises. . . .)

July 10 My landlady Mrs Flynn is very worried about me. She says the way I lay around all day and dont do anything I remind her of her son before she threw him out of the house. She said she doesn't like loafers. If Im sick its one thing, but if Im a loafer thats another thing and she wont have it. I told her I think Im sick.

I try to read a little bit every day, mostly stories, but sometimes I have to read the same thing over and over again because I dont know what it means. And its hard to write. I know I should look up all the words in the dictionary but its so hard and Im so tired all the time.

Then I got the idea that I would only use the easy words instead of the long hard ones. That saves time. I put flowers on Algernons grave about once a week. Mrs. Flynn thinks Im crazy to put flowers on a mouses grave but I told her that Algernon was special.

July 14 Its sunday again. I dont have anything to do to keep me busy now because my television set is broke and I dont have any money to get it fixed. (I think I lost this months check from the lab. I dont remember)

I get awful headaches and asperin doesnt help me much. Mrs Flynn knows Im really sick and she feels very sorry for me. Shes a wonderful woman whenever someone is sick.

July 22 Mrs Flynn called a strange doctor to see me. She was afraid I was going to die. I told the doctor I wasnt too sick and that I only forget sometimes. He asked me did I have any friends or relatives and I said no I dont have any. I told him I had a friend called Algernon once but he was a mouse and we used to run races together. He looked at me kind of funny like he thought I was crazy.

He smiled when I told him I used to be a genius. He talked to me like I was a baby and he winked at Mrs Flynn. I got mad and chased him out because he was making fun of me the way they all used to.

July 24 I have no more money and Mrs Flynn says I got to go to work somewhere and pay the rent because I havent paid for over two months. I dont know any work but the job I used to have at Donnegans Plastic Box Company. I dont want to go back there because they all knew me when I was smart and maybe theyll laugh at me. But I don't know what else to do to get money.

July 25 I was looking at some of my old progress reports and its very funny but I cant read what I wrote. I can make out some of the words but they dont make sense.

Miss Kinnian came to the door but I said go away I dont want to see you. She cried and I cried too but I wouldnt let her in because I didn't want her to laugh at me. I told her I didn't like her any more. I told her I didnt want to be smart any more. Thats not true. I still love her and I still want to be smart but I had to say that so shed go away. She gave Mrs Flynn money to pay the rent. I dont want that. I got to get a job.

Please . . . please let me not forget how to read and write. . . .

July 27 Mr Donnegan was very nice when I came back and asked him for my old job of janitor. First he was very suspicious but I told him what happened to me then he looked very sad and put his hand on my shoulder and said Charlie Gordon you got guts.

Everybody looked at me when I came downstairs and started working in the toilet sweeping it out like I used to. I told myself Charlie if they make fun of you dont get sore because you remember their not so smart as you once thot they were. And besides they were once your friends and if they laughed at you that doesnt mean anything because they liked you too.

One of the new men who came to work there after I went away made a nasty crack he said hey Charlie I hear your a very smart fella a real quiz kid. Say something intelligent. I felt bad but Joe Carp came over and grabbed him by the shirt and said leave him alone you lousy cracker or Ill break your neck. I didnt expect Joe to take my part so I guess hes really my friend.

Later Frank Reilly came over and said Charlie if anybody bothers you or trys to take advantage you call me or Joe and we will set em straight. I said thanks Frank and I got choked up so I had to turn around and go into the supply room so he wouldn't see me cry. Its good to have friends.

July 28 I did a dumb thing today I forgot I wasnt in Miss Kinnians class at the adult center any more like I use to be. I went in and sat down in my old seat in the back of the room and she looked at me funny and she said Charles. I dint remember she ever called me that before only Charlie so I said hello Miss Kinnian Im redy for my lesin today only I lost my reader that we was using. She startid to cry and run out of the room and everybody looked at me and I saw they wasnt the same pepul who used to be in my class.

Then all of a suddin I remembered some things about the operashun and me getting smart and I said holy smoke I reely pulled a Charlie Gordon that time. I went away before she come back to the room.

Thats why Im going away from New York for good. I dont want to do nothing like that agen. I dont want Miss Kinnian to feel sorry for me. Evry body feels sorry at the factery and I dont want that eather so Im going someplace where nobody knows that Charlie Gordon was once a genus and now he cant even reed a book or rite good.

Im taking a cuple of books along and even if I cant reed them Ill practise hard and maybe I wont forget every thing I lerned. If I try reel hard maybe Ill be a littel bit smarter then I was before the operashun. I got my rabits foot and my luky penny and maybe they will help me.

If you ever reed this Miss Kinnian dont be sorry for me Im glad I got a second chanse to be smart becaus I lerned a lot of things that I never even new were in this world and Im grateful that I saw it all for a littel bit. I dont know why Im dumb agen or what I did wrong maybe its becaus I dint try hard enuff. But if I try and practis very hard maybe Ill get a littl smarter and know what all the words are. I remember a littel bit how nice I had a feeling with the blue book that has the torn cover when I red it. Thats why Im gonna keep trying to get smart so I can have that feeling agen. Its a good feeling to know things and be smart. I wish I had it rite now if I did I would sit down and reed all the time. Anyway I bet Im the first dumb person in the world who ever found out somthing importent for sience. I remember I did somthing but I dont remember what. So I gess its like I did it for all the dumb pepul like me.

Good-by Miss Kinnian and Dr Strauss and evreybody. And P.S. please tell Dr Nemur not to be such a grouch when pepul laff at him and he woud have more frends. Its easy to make frends if you let pepul laff at you. Im going to have lots of frends where I go.

P.P.S. Please if you get a chanse put some flowrs on Algernons grave in the bak yard. . . .

Joseph Conrad born (*Josef Korzeniovsky*) at *Bergdyczev, Poland,* *in 1857. His father was imprisoned and exiled as a Polish Nationalist leader,* *in 1863, and his mother died in Russia for assisting her husband's struggles.* *Conrad became a seaman and political activist after leaving university, travelling* *to Martinique and the West Indies, and gun-running off Marseilles. He settled* *in England, became a sailor off the Norfolk coast, and became a British subject.* *In 1886, following voyages to Sydney, Bangkok and the Mediterranean, he* *became a master mariner, and in 1890 took his first command, the Otago,* *down the Congo to central Africa.*

Although he did not speak English until he was twenty one, he had begun his *first novel before 1890. He married in 1896, and spent his life writing in* *English, for which he felt 'a subtle accord of my emotional nature with its genius.'* *The sea, which he knew profoundly, and which he prized for 'an isolation from* *all land entanglements' is the setting for some of his finest early stories,* *including* THE NIGGER OF THE NARCISSUS, LORD JIM, THE HEART OF *DARKNESS, and* TYPHOON. *The writings of his middle period, including* NOSTROMO, THE SECRET SHARER, *and* UNDER WESTERN EYES *are concerned* *with what he calls 'moral discovery', and take as their province the area where* *human isolation and loneliness come into conflict with social necessity. His later* *writings:* CHANCE, VICTORY, THE SHADOW LINE, *and* THE SECRET SHARER *return, partially, to the sea setting, but reflect the tragic irony which characterizes* *his major novels.*

'AMY FOSTER', *a tale or* novella: *exceeds the normal conventions of the* *short story in both length and complexity of structure. A basically simple story* *is told by means of a complex narrative in which Dr Kennedy recounts an action* *which took place in the past, and the author's persona, the 'I' in the story,* *retells it for us. The essence of the story is inarticulateness, yet it is told with* *memorable clarity. The themes of isolation, alienation, and responsibility are* *raised again.*

Conrad died in 1924. His achievements led F. R. Leavis to include him *among the finest exponents of the great tradition of English prose fiction.*

AMY FOSTER

Joseph Conrad

KENNEDY IS A COUNTRY DOCTOR, AND LIVES IN COLEBROOK, ON THE SHORES of Eastbay. The high ground rising abruptly behind the red roofs of the little town crowds the quaint High Street against the wall which defends it from the sea. Beyond the sea wall there curves for miles in a vast and regular sweep the barren beach of shingle, with the village of Brenzett standing out darkly across the water, a spire in a clump of trees; and still farther out the perpendicular column of a lighthouse, looking in the distance no bigger than a lead pencil, marks the vanishing point of the land. The country at the back of Brenzett is low and flat; but the bay is fairly well sheltered from the seas, and occasionally a big ship, windbound or through stress of weather, makes use of the anchoring ground a mile and a half due north from you as you stand at the back door of the 'Ship Inn' in Brenzett. A dilapidated windmill nearby, lifting its shattered arms from a mound no loftier than a rubbish heap, and a Martello tower squatting at the water's edge half a mile to the south of the Coastguard cottages, are familiar to the skippers of small craft. These are the official seamarks for the patch of trustworthy bottom represented on the Admiralty charts by an irregular oval of dots enclosing several figure sixes, with a tiny anchor engraved among them and the legend 'mud and shells' over all.

The brow of the upland overtops the square tower of the Colebrook Church. The slope is green and looped by a white road. Ascending along this road, you open a valley broad and shallow, a wide green trough of pastures and hedges merging inland into a vista of purple tints and flowing lines closing the view.

In this valley down to Brenzett and Colebrook and up to Darnford, the market town fourteen miles away, lies the practice of my friend Kennedy. He had begun life as surgeon in the Navy, and afterwards had been the companion of a famous traveller, in the days when there were continents with unexplored interiors. His papers on the fauna and flora made him known to scientific societies. And now he had come to a country practice—from choice. The penetrating power of his mind, acting like a corrosive fluid, had destroyed his ambition, I fancy. His intelligence is of a scientific order, of an investigating habit, and of that unappeasable curiosity which believes that there is a particle of a general truth in every mystery.

A good many years ago now, on my return from abroad, he invited me to stay with him. I came readily enough, and as he could not neglect his patients to keep me company, he took me on his rounds—thirty miles or so of an afternoon, sometimes. I waited for him on the roads;

the horse reached after the leafy twigs, and, sitting high in the dogcart I could hear Kennedy's laugh through the half-open door of some cottage. He had a big, hearty laugh that would have fitted a man twice his size, a brisk manner, a bronzed face, and a pair of gray, profoundly attentive eyes. He had the talent of making people talk to him freely, and an inexhaustible patience in listening to their tales.

One day, as we trotted out of a large village into a shady bit of road, I saw on our left hand a low, black cottage, with diamond panes in the windows, a creeper on the end wall, a roof of shingle, and some roses climbing on the rickety trelliswork of the tiny porch. Kennedy pulled up to a walk. A woman, in full sunlight, was throwing a dripping blanket over a line stretched between two old apple trees. And as the bobtailed, long-necked chestnut, trying to get his head, jerked the left hand, covered by a thick dogskin glove, the doctor raised his voice over the hedge: 'How's your child, Amy?'

I had time to see her dull face, red, not with a mantling blush, but as if her flat cheeks had been vigorously slapped, and to take in the squat figure, the scanty, dusty brown hair drawn into a tight knot at the back of the head. She looked quite young. With a distinct catch in her breath, her voice sounded low and timid.

'He's well, thank you.'

We trotted again. 'A young patient of yours,' I said; and the doctor, flicking the chestnut absently, muttered, 'Her husband used to be.'

'She seems a dull creature,' I remarked, listlessly.

'Precisely,' said Kennedy. 'She is very passive. It's enough to look at the red hands hanging at the end of those short arms, at those slow, prominent brown eyes, to know the inertness of her mind—an inertness that one would think made it everlastingly safe from all the surprises of imagination. And yet which of us is safe? At any rate, such as you see her, she had enough imagination to fall in love. She's the daughter of one Isaac Foster, who from a small farmer has sunk into a shepherd; the beginning of his misfortunes dating from his runaway marriage with the cook of his widowed father—a well-to-do, apoplectic grazier, who passionately struck his name off his will, and had been heard to utter threats against his life. But this old affair, scandalous enough to serve as a motive for a Greek tragedy, arose from the similarity of their characters. There are other tragedies, less scandalous and of a subtler poignancy, arising from irreconcilable differences and from that fear of the Incomprehensible that hangs over all our heads—over all our heads . . .'

The tired chestnut dropped into a walk; and the rim of the sun, all red in a speckless sky, touched familiarly the smooth top of a plowed rise near the road as I had seen it times innumerable touch the distant horizon of the sea. The uniform brownness of the harrowed field glowed with a rose tinge, as though the powdered clods had sweated out in minute pearls of blood the toil of uncounted plowmen. From the edge of a copse a wagon with two horses was rolling gently along the ridge. Raised above our heads upon the skyline, it loomed up against the red sun, triumphantly big, enormous, like a chariot of giants drawn by two slow-stepping steeds of legendary proportions. And the clumsy figure of the man plodding at the head of the leading horse projected itself on the background of the Infinite with a heroic uncouthness. The end of his carter's whip quivered high up in the blue. Kennedy discoursed.

'She's the eldest of a large family. At the age of fifteen they put her out to service at the New Barns Farm. I attended Mrs Smith, the tenant's wife, and saw that girl there for the first time. Mrs Smith, a genteel person with a sharp nose, made her put on a black dress every afternoon. I don't know what induced me to notice her at all. There are faces that call your attention by a curious want of definiteness in their whole aspect, as, walking in a mist, you peer attentively at a vague shape which, after all, may be nothing more curious or strange than a signpost. The only peculiarity I perceived in her was a slight hesitation in her utterance, a sort of preliminary stammer which passes away with the first word. When sharply spoken to, she was apt to lose her head at once; but her heart was of the kindest. She had never been heard to express a dislike for a single human being, and she was tender to every living creature. She was devoted to Mrs Smith, to Mr Smith, to their dogs, cats, canaries; and as to Mrs Smith's gray parrot, its peculiarities exercised upon her a positive fascination. Nevertheless, when that outlandish bird, attacked by the cat, shrieked for help in human accents, she ran out into the yard stopping her ears, and did not prevent the crime. For Mrs Smith this was another evidence of her stupidity; on the other hand, her want of charm, in view of Smith's well-known frivolousness, was a great recommendation. Her shortsighted eyes would swim with pity for a poor mouse in a trap, and she had been seen once by some boys on her knees in the wet grass helping a toad in difficulties. If it's true, as some German fellow has said, that without phosphorus there is no thought, it is still more true that there is no kindness of heart without a certain amount of imagination. She had some. She had even more than is necessary to understand suffering and to be moved by pity. She fell in love under circumstances that leave no room for doubt in the matter; for you need imagination to form a notion of beauty at all, and still more to discover your ideal in an unfamiliar shape.

'How this aptitude came to her, what it did feed upon, is an inscrutable mystery. She was born in the village, and had never been farther away from it than Colebrook or perhaps Darnford. She lived for four years with the Smiths. New Barns is an isolated farmhouse a mile away from

Joseph Conrad

the road, and she was content to look day after day at the same fields, hollows, rises; at the trees and the hedgerows; at the faces of the four men about the farm, always the same—day after day, month after month, year after year. She never showed a desire for conversation, and, as it seemed to me, she did not know how to smile. Sometimes of a fine Sunday afternoon she would put on her best dress, a pair of stout boots, a large gray hat trimmed with a black feather (I've seen her in that finery), seize an absurdly slender parasol, climb over two stiles, tramp over three fields and along two hundred yards of road—never farther. There stood Foster's cottage. She would help her mother to give their tea to the younger children, wash up the crockery, kiss the little ones, and go back to the farm. That was all. All the rest, all the change, all the relaxation. She never seemed to wish for anything more. And then she fell in love. She fell in love silently, obstinately—perhaps helplessly. It came slowly, but when it came it worked like a powerful spell; it was love as the ancients understood it: an irresistible and fateful impulse—a possession! Yes, it was in her to become haunted and possessed by a face, by a presence, fatally, as though she had been a pagan worshipper of form under a joyous sky—and to be awakened at last from that mysterious forgetfulness of self, from that enchantment, from that transport, by a fear resembling the unaccountable terror of a brute. . . .'

With the sun hanging low on its western limit, the expanse of the grasslands framed in the counterscarps of the rising ground took on a gorgeous and somber aspect. A sense of penetrating sadness, like that inspired by a grave strain of music, disengaged itself from the silence of the fields. The men we met walked past, slow, unsmiling, with downcast eyes, as if the melancholy of an overburdened earth had weighted their feet, bowed their shoulders, borne down their glances.

'Yes,' said the doctor to my remark, 'one would think the earth is under a curse, since of all her children these that cling to her the closest are uncouth in body and as leaden of gait as if their very hearts were loaded with chains. But here on this same road you might have seen amongst these heavy men a being lithe, supple and long-limbed, straight like a pine, with something striving upwards in his appearance as though the heart within him had been buoyant. Perhaps it was only the force of the contrast, but when he was passing one of these villagers here, the soles of his feet did not seem to me to touch the dust of the road. He vaulted over the stiles, paced these slopes with a long elastic stride that made him noticeable at a great distance, and had lustrous black eyes. He was so different from the mankind around that, with his freedom of movement, his soft—a little startled—glance, his olive complexion and graceful bearing, his humanity suggested to me the nature of a woodland creature. He came from there.'

The doctor pointed with his whip, and from the summit of the descent

184

seen over the rolling tops of the trees in a park by the side of the road, appeared the level sea far below us, like the floor of an immense edifice inlaid with bands of dark ripple, with still trails of glitter, ending in a belt of glassy water at the foot of the sky. The light blur of smoke, from an invisible steamer, faded on the great clearness of the horizon like the mist of a breath on a mirror; and, inshore, the white sails of a coaster, with the appearance of disentangling themselves slowly from under the branches, floated clear of the foliage of the trees.

'Shipwrecked in the bay?' I said.

'Yes; he was a castaway. A poor emigrant from Central Europe bound to America and washed ashore here in a storm. And for him, who knew nothing of the earth, England was an undiscovered country. It was some time before he learned its name; and for all I know he might have expected to find wild beasts or wild men here, when, crawling in the dark over the sea wall, he rolled down the other side into a dyke, where it was another miracle he didn't get drowned. But he struggled instinctively like an animal under a net, and this blind struggle threw him out into a field. He must have been, indeed, of a tougher fiber than he looked to withstand without expiring such buffetings, the violence of his exertions, and so much fear. Later on, in his broken English that resembled curiously the speech of a young child, he told me himself that he put his trust in God, believing he was no longer in this world. And truly—he would add—how was he to know? He fought his way against the rain and the gale on all fours, and crawled at last among some sheep huddled close under the lee of a hedge. They ran off in all directions, bleating in the darkness, and he welcomed the first familiar sound he heard on these shores. It must have been two in the morning then. And this is all we know of the manner of his landing, though he did not arrive unattended by any means. Only his grisly company did not begin to come ashore till much later in the day. . . .'

The doctor gathered the reins, clicked his tongue; we trotted down the hill. Then turning, almost directly, a sharp corner into High Street, we rattled over the stones and were home.

Late in the evening Kennedy, breaking a spell of moodiness that had come over him, returned to the story. Smoking his pipe, he paced the long room from end to end. A reading lamp concentrated all its light upon the papers on his desk; and, sitting by the open window, I saw, after the windless, scorching day, the frigid splendor of a hazy sea lying motionless under the moon. Not a whisper, not a splash, not a stir of the shingle, not a footstep, not a sigh came up from the earth below—never a sign of life but the scent of climbing jasmine; and Kennedy's voice, speaking behind me, passed through the wide casement, to vanish outside in a chill and sumptuous stillness.

'. . . The relations of shipwrecks in the olden times tell us of much suffering. Often the castaways were only saved from drowning to die miserably from starvation on a barren coast; others suffered violent death or else slavery, passing through years of precarious existence with people to whom their strangeness was an object of suspicion, dislike or fear. We read about these things, and they are very pitiful. It is indeed hard upon a man to find himself a lost stranger, helpless, incomprehensible, and of a mysterious origin, in some obscure corner of the earth. Yet amongst all the adventurers shipwrecked in all the wild parts of the world, there is not one, it seems to me, that ever had to suffer a fate so simply tragic as the man I am speaking of, the most innocent of adventurers cast out by the sea in the bight of this bay, almost within sight from this very window.

'He did not know the name of his ship. Indeed, in the course of time we discovered he did not even know that ships had names—"like Christian people"; and when, one day, from the top of Talfourd Hill, he beheld the sea lying open to his view, his eyes roamed afar, lost in an air of wild surprise, as though he had never seen such a sight before. And probably he had not. As far as I could make out, he had been hustled together with many others on board an emigrant ship at the mouth of the Elbe, too bewildered to take note of his surroundings, too weary to see anything, too anxious to care. They were driven below into the 'tween-deck and battened down from the very start. It was a low timber dwelling —he would say—with wooden beams overhead, like the houses in his country, but you went into it down a ladder. It was very large, very cold, damp and somber, with places in the manner of wooden boxes where people had to sleep one above another, and it kept on rocking all ways at once all the time. He crept into one of these boxes and lay down there in the clothes in which he had left his home many days before, keeping his bundle and his stick by his side. People groaned, children cried, water dripped, the lights went out, the walls of the place creaked and everything was being shaken so that in one's little box one dared not lift one's head. He had lost touch with his only companion (a young man from the same valley, he said), and all the time a great noise of wind went on outside and heavy blows fell—boom! boom! An awful sickness overcame him, even to the point of making him neglect his prayers. Besides, one could not tell whether it was morning or evening. It seemed always to be night in that place.

'Before that he had been travelling a long, long time on the iron track. He looked out of the window, which had a wonderfully clear glass in it, and the trees, the houses, the fields, and the long roads seemed to fly round and round about him till his head swam. He gave me to understand that he had on his passage beheld uncounted multitudes of people— whole nations—all dressed in such clothes as the rich wear. Once he was made to get out of the carriage, and slept through a night on a bench in a house of bricks with his bundle under his head; and once for many hours he had to sit on a floor of flat stones, dozing, with his knees up and with his bundle between his feet. There was a roof over him, which seemed made of glass, and was so high that the tallest mountain pine he had ever seen would have had room to grow under it. Steam machines rolled in at one end and out at the other. People swarmed more than you can see on a feast day round the miraculous Holy Image in the yard of the Carmelite Convent down in the plains where, before he left his home, he drove his mother in a wooden cart—a pious old woman who wanted to offer prayers and make a vow for his safety. He could not give me an idea of how large and lofty and full of noise and smoke and gloom, and clang of iron, the place was, but someone had told him it was called Berlin. Then they rang a bell, and another steam machine came in, and again he was taken on and on through a land that wearied his eyes by its flatness without a single bit of a hill to be seen anywhere. One more night he spent shut up in a building like a good stable with a litter of straw on the floor, guarding his bundle amongst a lot of men, of whom not one could understand a single word he said. In the morning they were all led down to the stony shores of an extremely broad muddy river, flowing not between hills but between houses that seemed immense. There was a steam machine that went on the water, and they all stood upon it packed tight, only now there were with them many women and children who made much noise. A cold rain fell, the wind blew in his face; he was wet through, and his teeth chattered. He and the young man from the same valley took each other by the hand.

'They thought they were being taken to America straight away, but suddenly the steam machine bumped against the side of a thing like a great house on the water. The walls were smooth and black, and there uprose, growing from the roof as it were, bare trees in the shape of crosses, extremely high. That's how it appeared to him then, for he had never seen a ship before. This was the ship that was going to swim all the way to America. Voices shouted, everything swayed; there was a ladder dipping up and down. He went up on his hands and knees in mortal fear of falling into the water below, which made a great splashing. He got separated from his companion, and when he descended into the bottom of that ship his heart seemed to melt suddenly within him.

'It was then also, as he told me, that he lost contact for good and all with one of those three men who the summer before had been going about through all the little towns in the foothills of his country. They would arrive on market days driving in a peasant's cart, and would set up an office in an inn or some other Jew's house. There were three of them, of whom one with a long beard looked venerable; and they had red cloth collars round their necks and gold lace on their sleeves like Government officials. They sat proudly behind a long table; and in the next room, so that the common people shouldn't hear, they kept a cunning telegraph machine, through which they could talk to the Emperor of America. The fathers hung about the door, but the young men of the mountains would crowd up to the table asking many questions, for there was work to be got all the year round at three dollars a day in America, and no military service to do.

'But the American Kaiser would not take everybody. Oh, no! He himself had great difficulty in getting accepted, and the venerable man in uniform had to go out of the room several times to work the telegraph on his behalf. The American Kaiser engaged him at last at three dollars, he being young and strong. However, many able young men backed out, afraid of the great distance; besides, those only who had some money could be taken. There were some who sold their huts and their land because it cost a lot of money to get to America; but then, once there, you had three dollars a day, and if you were clever you could find places where true gold could be picked up on the ground. His father's house was getting over-full. Two of his brothers were married and had children. He promised to send money home from America by post twice a year. His father sold an old cow, a pair of piebald mountain ponies of his own raising, and a cleared plot of fair pasture land on the sunny slope of a pineclad pass to a Jew innkeeper, in order to pay the people of the ship that took men to America to get rich in a short time.

'He must have been a real adventurer at heart, for how many of the greatest enterprises in the conquest of the earth had for their beginning just such a bargaining away of the paternal cow for the mirage or true gold far away! I have been telling you more or less in my own words what I learned fragmentarily in the course of two or three years, during which I seldom missed an opportunity of a friendly chat with him. He told me this story of his adventure with many flashes of white teeth and lively glances of black eyes, at first in a sort of anxious baby-talk, then, as he acquired the language, with great fluency, but always with that singing, soft, and at the same time vibrating intonation that instilled a strangely penetrating power into the sound of the most familiar English words, as if they had been the words of an unearthly language. And he always would come to an end, with many emphatic shakes of his head, upon that awful sensation of his heart melting within him directly he set foot on board that ship. Afterwards there seemed to come for him a period of blank ignorance, at any rate as to facts. No doubt he must have been abominably seasick and abominably unhappy—this soft and passionate adventurer, taken thus out of his knowledge, and feeling bitterly as he lay in his emigrant bunk his utter loneliness; for his was a highly sensitive nature. The next thing we know of him for certain is that he had been hiding in Hammond's pig-pound by the side of the road to Norton, six miles, as the crow flies, from the sea. Of these experiences he was unwilling to speak: they seemed to have seared into his soul a somber sort of wonder and indignation. Through the rumors of the countryside, which lasted for a good many days after his arrival, we know that the fishermen of West Colebrook had been disturbed and startled by heavy knocks against the walls of weatherboard cottages, and by a voice crying piercingly strange words in the night. Several of them turned out even, but, no doubt, he had fled in sudden alarm at their rough angry tones hailing each other in the darkness. A sort of frenzy must have helped him up the steep Norton hill. It was he, no doubt, who early the following morning had been seen lying (in a swoon, I should say) on the roadside grass by the Brenzett carrier, who actually got down to have a nearer look, but drew back, intimidated by the perfect immobility, and by something queer in the aspect of that tramp, sleeping so still under the showers. As the day advanced, some children came dashing into school at Norton in such a fright that the school-mistress went out and spoke indignantly to a "horrid-looking man" on the road. He edged away, hanging his head, for a few steps, and then suddenly ran off with extraordinary fleetness. The driver of Mr Bradley's milk cart made no secret of it that he had lashed with his whip at a hairy sort of gypsy fellow who, jumping up at a turn of the road by the Vents, made a snatch at the pony's bridle. And he caught him a good one, too, right over the face, he said, that made him drop down in the mud a jolly sight quicker than he had jumped up; but it was a good half a mile before he could stop the pony. Maybe that in his desperate endeavours to get help, and in his need to get in touch with someone, the poor devil had tried to stop the cart. Also three boys confessed afterwards to throwing stones at a funny tramp, knocking about all wet and muddy, and, it seemed, very drunk, in the narrow deep lane by the limekilns. All this was the talk of three villages for days; but we have Mrs Finn's (the wife of Smith's wagoner) unimpeachable testimony that she saw him get over the low wall of Hammond's pig-pound and lurch straight at her, babbling aloud in a voice that was enough to make one die of fright. Having the baby with her in a perambulator, Mrs Finn called out to him to go away, and as he persisted in coming nearer, she hit him courageously with her umbrella over the head, and, without once looking back, ran like the wind with the perambulator as far as the first house in the village. She stopped then, out of breath, and spoke to old Lewis, hammering there at a heap of stones; and the old chap, taking off his immense black wire goggles, got up on his shaky legs to look where she pointed. Together they followed with their eyes the figure of the man running over a field;

they saw him fall down, pick himself up, and run on again, staggering and waving his long arms above his head, in the direction of the New Barns Farm. From that moment he is plainly in the toils of his obscure and touching destiny. There is no doubt after this of what happened to him. All is certain now: Mrs Smith's intense terror; Amy Foster's stolid conviction held against the other's nervous attack, that the man "meant no harm"; Smith's exasperation (on his return from Darnford Market) at finding the dog barking himself into a fit, the back door locked, his wife in hysterics; and all for an unfortunate dirty tramp, supposed to be even then lurking in his stackyard. Was he? He would teach him to frighten women.

'Smith is notoriously hot-tempered, but the sight of some nondescript and miry creature sitting cross-legged amongst a lot of loose straw, and swinging itself to and fro like a bear in a cage, made him pause. Then this tramp stood up silently before him, one mass of mud and filth from head to foot. Smith, alone amongst his stacks with this apparition, in the stormy twilight ringing with the infuriated barking of the dog, felt the dread of an inexplicable strangeness. But when that being, parting with his black hands the long matted locks that hung before his face, as you part the two halves of a curtain, looked out at him with glistening, wild, black-and-white eyes, the weirdness of this silent encounter fairly staggered him. He has admitted since (for the story has been a legitimate subject of conversation about here for years) that he made more than one step backwards. Then a sudden burst of rapid, senseless speech persuaded him at once that he had to do with an escaped lunatic. In fact, that impression never wore off completely. Smith has not in his heart given up his secret conviction of the man's essential insanity to this very day.

'As the creature approached him, jabbering in a most discomposing manner, Smith (unaware that he was being addressed as "gracious lord," and adjured in God's name to afford food and shelter) kept on speaking firmly but gently to it, and retreating all the time into the other yard. At last, watching his chance, by a sudden charge he bundled him headlong into the wood-lodge, and instantly shot the bolt. Thereupon he wiped his brow, though the day was cold. He had done his duty to the community by shutting up a wandering and probably dangerous maniac. Smith isn't a hard man at all, but he had room in his brain only for that one idea of lunacy. He was not imaginative enough to ask himself whether the man might not be perishing with cold and hunger. Meantime, at first, the maniac made a great deal of noise in the lodge. Mrs Smith was screaming upstairs, where she had locked herself in her bedroom; but Amy Foster sobbed piteously at the kitchen door, wringing her hands and muttering, "Don't! don't!" I daresay Smith had a rough time of it that evening with one noise and another, and this insane, disturbing voice crying obstinately through the door only added to his irritation. He couldn't possibly have connected this troublesome lunatic with the sinking of a ship in Eastbay, of which there had been a rumor in the Darnford market place. And I dare say the man inside had been very near to insanity on that night. Before his excitement collapsed and he became unconscious he was throwing himself violently about in the dark, rolling on some dirty sacks, and biting his fists with rage, cold, hunger, amazement, and despair.

'He was a mountaineer of the eastern range of the Carpathians, and the vessel sunk the night before in Eastbay was the Hamburg emigrant ship *Herzogin Sophia-Dorothea*, of appalling memory.

'A few months later we could read in the papers the accounts of the bogus "Emigration Agencies" among the Slavic peasantry in the more remote provinces of Austria. The object of these scoundrels was to get hold of the poor ignorant people's homesteads, and they were in league with the local usurers. They exported their victims through Hamburg mostly. As to the ship, I had watched her out of this very window, reaching close-hauled under short canvas into the bay on a dark, threatening afternoon. She came to an anchor, correctly by the chart, off the Brenzett Coastguard station. I remember before the night fell looking out again at the outlines of her spars and rigging that stood out dark and pointed on a background of ragged, slaty clouds like another and a slighter spire to the left of the Brenzett churchtower. In the evening the wind rose. At midnight I could hear in my bed the terrific gusts and the sounds of a driving deluge.

'About that time the Coastguardmen thought they saw the lights of a steamer over the anchoring ground. In a moment they vanished; but it is clear that another vessel of some sort had tried for shelter in the bay on that awful, blind night, had rammed the German ship amidships ("a breach"—as one of the divers told me afterwards—"that you could sail a Thames barge through"), and then had gone out either scatheless or damaged, who shall say; but had gone out, unknown, unseen, and fatal, to perish mysteriously at sea. Of her nothing ever came to light, and yet the hue and cry that was raised all over the world would have found her out if she had been in existence anywhere on the face of the waters.

'A completeness without a clue, and a stealthy silence as of a neatly executed crime, characterize, this murderous disaster which, as you may remember, had its gruesome celebrity. The wind would have prevented the loudest outcries from reaching the shore; there had been evidently no time for signals of distress. It was death without any sort of fuss. The Hamburg ship, filling all at once, capsized as she sank, and at daylight there was not even the end of a spar to be seen above water. She was missed, of course, and at first the Coastguardsmen surmised that she had either dragged her anchor or parted her cable sometime during the night, and had been blown out to sea. Then, after the tide turned, the wreck must have shifted a little and released some of the bodies, because a child— a little fair-haired child in a red frock—came ashore abreast of the Martello tower. By the afternoon you could see along three miles of beach dark figures with bare legs dashing in and out of the tumbling foam, and rough-looking men, women with hard faces, children, mostly fair-haired were being carried, stiff and dripping, on stretchers, on wattles, on ladders, in a long procession past the door of the "Ship Inn," to be laid out in a row under the north wall of the Brenzett Church.

'Officially, the body of the little girl in the red frock is the first thing that came ashore from that ship. But I have patients amongst the sea-faring population of West Colebrook, and, unofficially, I am informed that very early that morning two brothers, who went down to look after their cobble hauled up on the beach, found a good way from Brenzett, an ordinary ship's hencoop, lying high and dry on the shore, with eleven drowned ducks inside. Their families ate the birds, and the hencoop was split into firewood with a hatchet. It is possible that a man (supposing he happened to be on deck at the time of the accident) might have floated ashore on that hencoop. He might. I admit it is improbable, but there was the man—and for days, nay, for weeks—it didn't enter our heads that we had amongst us the only living soul that had escaped from that disaster. The man himself, even when he learned to speak intelligibly, could tell us very little. He remembered he had felt better (after the ship had anchored, I suppose), and that the darkness, the wind, and the rain took his breath away. This looks as if he had been on deck sometime during that night. But we mustn't forget he had been taken out of his knowledge, that he had been seasick and battened down below for four days, that he had no general notion of a ship or of the sea, and therefore could have no definite idea of what was happening to him. The rain, the wind, the darkness he knew; he understood the bleating of the sheep, and he remembered the pain of his wretchedness and misery, his heart-broken astonishment that it was neither seen nor understood, his dismay at finding all the men angry and all the women fierce. He had approached them as a beggar, it is true, he said; but in his country, even if they gave nothing, they spoke gently to beggars. The children in his country were not taught to throw stones at those who asked for compassion. Smith's strategy overcame him completely. The wood-lodge presented the horrible aspect of a dungeon. What would be done to him next? . . . No wonder that Amy Foster appeared to his eyes with the aureole of an angel of light. The girl had not been able to sleep for thinking of the poor man, and in the morning, before the Smiths were up, she slipped out across the back yard. Holding the door of the wood-lodge ajar, she looked in and extended to him half a loaf of white bread—"such bread as the rich eat in my country," he used to say.

'At this he got up slowly from amongst all sorts of rubbish, stiff, hungry, trembling, miserable, and doubtful. "Can you eat this?" she asked in her soft and timid voice. He must have taken her for a "gracious lady." He devoured ferociously, and tears were falling on the crust. Suddenly he dropped the bread, seized her wrist, and imprinted a kiss on her hand. She was not frightened. Through his forlorn condition she had observed that he was good-looking. She shut the door and walked back slowly to the kitchen. Much later on, she told Mrs Smith, who shuddered at the bare idea of being touched by that creature.

'Through this act of impulsive pity he was brought back again within the pale of human relations with his new surroundings. He never forgot it—never.

'That very same morning old Mr Swaffer (Smith's nearest neighbour) came over to give his advice, and ended by carrying him off. He stood, unsteady on his legs, meek, and caked over in half-dried mud, while the two men talked around him in an incomprehensible tongue. Mrs Smith had refused to come downstairs till the madman was off the premises; Amy Foster, far from within the dark kitchen, watched through the open back door; and he obeyed the signs that were made to him to the best of his ability. But Smith was full of mistrust. "Mind, sir! It may be all his cunning," he cried repeatedly in a tone of warning. When Mr Swaffer started the mare, the deplorable being sitting humbly by his side, through weakness, nearly fell out over the back of the high two-wheeled cart. Swaffer took him straight home. And it is then that I come upon the scene.

'I was called in by the simple process of the old man beckoning to me with his forefinger over the gate of his house as I happened to be driving past. I got down, of course.

'"I've got something here," he mumbled, leading way to an outhouse at a little distance from his other farm buildings.

'It was there that I saw him first, in a long, low room taken upon the space of that sort of coach house. It was bare and whitewashed, with a small square aperture glazed with one cracked, dusty pane at its further end. He was lying on his back upon a straw pallet; they had given him a couple of horse blankets, and he seemed to have spent the remainder of his strength in the exertion of cleaning himself. He was almost speechless; his quick breathing under the blankets pulled up to his chin, his glittering restless black eyes reminded me of a wild bird caught in a snare. While I was examining him, old Swaffer stood silently by the door, passing the tips of his fingers along his shaven upper lip. I gave some directions, promised to send a bottle of medicine, and naturally made some enquiries.

'"Smith caught him in the stackyard at New Barns," said the old chap in his deliberate, unmoved manner, and as if the other had been indeed a sort of wild animal. "That's how I came by him. Quite a curiosity, isn't he? Now tell me, doctor—you've been all over the world—don't you think that's a bit of a Hindu we've got hold of here?"

'I was greatly surprised. His long black hair scattered over the straw bolster contrasted with the olive pallor of his face. It occurred to me he might be a Basque. It didn't necessarily follow that he should understand Spanish; but I tried him with the few words I know, and also with some French. The whispered sounds I caught by bending my ear to his lips puzzled me utterly. That afternoon the young ladies from the rectory (one of them read Goethe with a dictionary, and the other had struggled with Dante for years), coming to see Miss Swaffer, tried their German and Italian on him from the doorway. They retreated, just the least bit scared by the flood of passionate speech which, turning on his pallet, he let out at them. They admitted that the sound was pleasant, soft, musical—but, in conjunction with his looks perhaps, it was startling—so excitable, so utterly unlike anything one had ever heard. The village boys climbed up the bank to have a peep through the little square aperture. Everybody was wondering what Mr Swaffer would do with him.

'He simply kept him.

'Swaffer would be called eccentric were he not so much respected. They will tell you that Mr Swaffer sits up as late as ten o'clock at night to read books, and they will tell you also that he can write a check for two hundred pounds without thinking twice about it. He himself would tell you that the Swaffers had owned land between this and Darnford for these three hundred years. He must be eighty-five today, but he does not look a bit older than when I first came here. He is a great breeder of sheep, and deals extensively in cattle. He attends market days for miles around in every sort of weather, and drives sitting bowed low over the reins, his lank gray hair curling over the collar of his warm coat, and with a green plaid rug round his legs. The calmness of advanced age gives a solemnity to his manner. He is clean-shaved; his lips are thin and sensitive; something rigid and monachal in the set of his features lends a certain elevation to the character of his face. He has been known to drive miles in the rain to see a new kind of rose in somebody's garden, or a monstrous cabbage grown by a cottager. He loves to hear tell of or to be shown something that he calls "outlandish." Perhaps it was just that outlandishness of the man which influenced old Swaffer. Perhaps it was only an inexplicable caprice. All I know is that at the end of three weeks I caught sight of Smith's lunatic digging in Swaffer's kitchen garden. They had found out he could use a spade. He dug barefooted.

'His black hair flowed over his shoulders. I suppose it was Swaffer who had given him the striped old cotton shirt; but he wore still the national brown cloth trousers (in which he had been washed ashore) fitting to the leg almost like tights; was belted with a broad leather belt studded with little brass discs; and had never yet ventured into the village. The land he looked upon seemed to him kept neatly, like the grounds round a land-owner's house; the size of the cart horses struck him with astonishment; the roads resembled garden walks, and the aspect of the people, especially on Sundays, spoke of opulence. He wondered what made them so hard-hearted and their children so bold. He got his food at the back door, carried it in both hands, carefully, to his outhouse, and, sitting alone on his pallet, would make the sign of the cross before he began. Beside the same pallet, kneeling in the early darkness of the short days, he recited aloud the Lord's Prayer before he slept. Whenever he saw old Swaffer he would bow with veneration from the waist, and stand erect while the old man, with his fingers over his upper lip, surveyed him silently. He bowed also to Miss Swaffer, who kept house frugally for her father— a broad-shouldered, big-boned woman of forty-five, with the pocket of her dress full of keys, and a gray, steady eye. She was Church—as people said (while her father was one of the trustees of the Baptist Chapel)—and wore a little steel cross at her waist. She dressed severely in black, in memory of one of the innumerable Bradleys of the neighbourhood, to whom she had been engaged some twenty-five years ago—a young farmer who broke his neck out hunting on the eve of the wedding day. She had the unmoved countenance of the deaf, spoke very seldom, and her lips, thin like her father's, astonished one sometimes by a mysteriously ironic curl.

'These were the people to whom he owed allegiance, and an over-whelming loneliness seemed to fall from the leaden sky of that winter without sunshine. All the faces were sad. He could talk to no one, and had no hope of ever understanding anybody. It was as if these had been the faces of people from the other world—dead people—he used to tell me years afterwards. Upon my word, I wonder he did not go mad. He didn't know where he was. Somewhere very far from his mountains— somewhere over the water. Was this America, he wondered?

'If it hadn't been for the steel cross at Miss Swaffer's belt he would not he confessed, have known whether he was in a Christian country at all. He used to cast stealthy glances at it, and feel comforted. There was nothing here the same as in his country! The earth and the water were different; there were no images of the Redeemer by the roadside. The very grass was different, and the trees. All the trees but the three old Norway pines on the bit of lawn before Swaffer's house, and these re-minded him of his country. He had been detected once, after dusk, with his forehead against the trunk of one of them, sobbing, and talking to himself. They had been like brothers to him at that time, he affirmed. Everything else was strange. Conceive you the kind of an existence over-shadowed, oppressed, by the everyday material appearances, as if by the visions of a nightmare. At night, when he could not sleep he kept on thinking of the girl who gave him the first piece of bread he had eaten in this foreign land. She had been neither fierce nor angry, nor frightened. Her face he remembered as the only comprehensible face amongst all these faces that were as closed, as mysterious, and as mute as the faces of the dead who are possessed of a knowledge beyond the comprehension of the living. I wonder whether the memory of her compassion pre-vented him from cutting his throat. But there! I suppose I am an old sentimentalist, and forget the instinctive love of life which it takes all the strength of an uncommon despair to overcome.

'He did the work which was given him with an intelligence which surprised old Swaffer. By and by it was discovered that he could help at the plowing, could milk the cows, feed the bullocks in the cattle-yard, and was of some use with the sheep. He began to pick up words, too, very fast; and suddenly, one fine morning in spring, he rescued from an untimely death a grandchild of old Swaffer.

'Swaffer's younger daughter is married to Willcox, a solicitor and the town clerk of Colebrook. Regularly twice a year they come to stay with the old man for a few days. Their only child, a little girl not three years old at the time, ran out of the house alone in her little white pinafore, and, toddling across the grass of a terraced garden, pitched herself over a low wall headfirst into the horse pond in the yard below.

'Our man was out with the wagoner and the plow in the field nearest to the house, and as he was leading the team round to begin a fresh furrow, he saw, through the gap of a gate, what for anybody else would have been a mere flutter of something white. But he had straight-glancing, quick, far-reaching eyes, that only seemed to flinch and lose their amazing power before the immensity of the sea. He was bare-footed, and looking as outlandish as the heart of Swaffer could desire. Leaving the horses on the turn, to the inexpressible disgust of the wagoner he bounded off, going over the plowed ground in long leaps, and suddenly appeared before the mother, thrust the child into her arms, and strode away.

'The pond was not very deep; but still, if he had not had such good eyes, the child would have perished—miserably suffocated in the foot or so of sticky mud at the bottom. Old Swaffer walked out slowly into the field, waited till the plow came over to his side, had a good look at him, and without saying a word went back to the house. But from that time they laid out his meals on the kitchen table; and at first, Miss Swaffer, all in black and with an inscrutable face, would come and stand in the doorway of the living room to see him make a big sign of the cross before he fell to. I believe that from that day, too, Swaffer began to pay him regular wages.

'I can't follow step by step his development. He cut his hair short, was seen in the village and along the road going to and fro to his work like any other man. Children ceased to shout after him. He became aware of social differences, but remained for a long time surprised at the bare poverty of the churches among so much wealth. He couldn't understand either why they were kept shut up on weekdays. There was nothing to steal in them. Was it to keep people from praying too often? The rectory took much notice of him about that time, and I believe the young ladies attempted to prepare the ground for his conversion. They could not, however, break him of his habit of crossing himself, but he went so far as to take off the string with a couple of brass medals the size of a sixpence, a tiny metal cross, and a square sort of scapulary which he wore round his neck. He hung them on the wall by the side of his bed, and he was still to be heard every evening reciting the Lord's Prayer, in incomprehensible words and in a slow, fervent tone, as he had heard his old father do at the head of all the kneeling family, big and little, on every evening of his life. And though he wore corduroys at work, and a slop-made pepper-and-salt suit on Sundays, strangers would turn round to look after him on the road. His foreignness had a peculiar and indelible stamp. At last people became used to seeing him. But they never became used to him. His rapid, skimming walk; his swarthy complexion; his hat cocked on the left ear; his habit, on warm evenings, of wearing his coat over one shoulder, like a hussar's dolman; his manner of leaping over the stiles, not as a feat of agility, but in the ordinary course of progression —all these peculiarities were, as one may say, so many causes of scorn and offense to the inhabitants of the village. *They* wouldn't in their dinner hour lie flat on their backs on the grass to stare at the sky. Neither did they go about the fields screaming dismal tunes. Many times have I heard his high-pitched voice from behind the ridge of some sloping sheepwalk, a voice light and soaring, like a lark's, but with a melancholy human note, over our fields that hear only the song of birds. And I would be startled myself. Ah! He was different; innocent of heart, and full of good will, which nobody wanted, this castaway, that, like a man transplanted into another planet, was separated by an immense space from his past and by an immense ignorance from his future. His quick, fervent utterance positively shocked everybody. "An excitable devil," they called him. One evening, in the taproom of the Coach and Horses (having drunk some whisky), he upset them all by singing a love song of his country. They hooted him down, and he was pained; but Preble, the lame wheelwright, and Vincent, the fat blacksmith, and the other notables, too, wanted to drink their evening beer in peace. On another occasion he tried to show them how to dance. The dust rose in clouds from the sanded floor; he leaped straight up amongst the deal tables, struck his heels together, squatted on one heel in front of old Preble, shooting out the other leg, uttered wild and exulting cries, jumped up to whirl on one foot, snapping his fingers above his head—and a strange carter who was having a drink in there began to swear, and cleared out with his half-pint in his hand into the bar. But when suddenly he sprang upon a table and continued to dance among the glasses, the landlord interfered. He didn't want any "acrobat tricks in the taproom." They laid their hands on him. Having had a glass or two, Mr Swaffer's foreigner tried to expostulate: was ejected forcibly: got a black eye.

'I believe he felt the hostility of his human surroundings. But he was tough—tough in spirit, too, as well as in body. Only the memory of the sea frightened him, with that vague terror that is left by a bad dream. His home was far away; and he did not want now to go to America. I had often explained to him that there is no place on earth where true gold can be found lying ready and to be got for the trouble of the picking up. How, then, he asked, could he ever return home with empty hands when there had been sold a cow, two ponies, and a bit of land to pay for his going? His eyes would fill with tears, and, averting them from the immense shimmer of the sea, he would throw himself face down on the grass. But sometimes, cocking his hat with a little conquering air, he would defy my wisdom. He had found his bit of true gold. That was Amy Foster's heart; which was "a golden heart, and soft to people's misery," he would say in the accents of over-whelming conviction.

'He was called Yanko. He had explained that this meant Little John; but as he would also repeat very often that he was a mountaineer (some word sounding in the dialect of his country like Goorall) he got it for his surname. And this is the only trace of him that the succeeding ages may find in the marriage register of the parish. There it stands—Yanko Goorall—in the rector's handwriting. The crooked cross made by the castaway, a cross whose tracing no doubt seemed to him the most solemn part of the whole ceremony, is all that remains now to perpetuate the memory of his name.

'His courtship had lasted some time—ever since he got his precarious footing in the community. It began by his buying for Amy Foster a green satin ribbon in Darnford. This was what you did in his country. You bought a ribbon at a Jew's stall on a fair-day. I don't suppose the girl knew what to do with it, but he seemed to think that his honorable intentions could not be mistaken.

'It was only when he declared his purpose to get married that I fully understood how, for a hundred futile and inappreciable reasons, how—shall I say odious?— he was to all the countryside. Every old woman in the village was up in arms. Smith, coming upon him near the farm, promised to break his head for him if he found him about again. But he twisted his little black moustache with such a bellicose air and rolled such big, black fierce eyes at Smith that this promise came to nothing. Smith, however, told the girl that she must be mad to take up with a man who was surely wrong in his head. All the same, when she heard him in the gloaming whistle from beyond the orchard a couple of bars of a weird and mournful tune, she would drop whatever she had in her hand— she would leave Mrs Smith in the middle of a sentence—and she would run out to his call. Mrs Smith called her a shameless hussy. She answered nothing. She said nothing at all to anybody, and went on her way as if she had been deaf. She and I alone in all the land, I fancy, could see his very real beauty. He was very good-looking, and most graceful in his bearing, with that something wild as of a woodland creature in his aspect. Her mother moaned over her dismally whenever the girl came to see her on her day out. The father was surly, but pretended not to know; and Mrs Finn once told her plainly that "this man, my dear, will do you some harm some day yet." And so it went on. They could be seen on the roads, she tramping stolidly in her finery—gray dress, black feather, stout boots, prominent white cotton gloves that caught your eye a hundred yards away; and he, his coat slung picturesquely over one shoulder, pacing by her side, gallant of bearing and casting tender glances upon the girl with the golden heart. I wonder whether he saw how plain she was. Perhaps among types so different from what he had ever seen, he had not the power to judge; or perhaps he was seduced by the divine quality of her pity.

'Yanko was in great trouble meantime. In his country you get an old man for an ambassador in marriage affairs. He did not know how to proceed. However, one day in the midst of sheep in a field (he was now Swaffer's under-shepherd with Foster) he took off his hat to the father and declared himself humbly. "I daresay she's fool enough to marry you," was all Foster said. "And then," he used to relate, "he puts his hat on his head, looks black at me as if he wanted to cut my throat, whistles the dog, and off he goes, leaving me to do the work." The Fosters, of course, didn't like to lose the wages the girl earned: Amy used to give all her money to her mother. But there was in Foster a very genuine aversion to that match. He contended that the fellow was very good with sheep, but was not fit for any girl to marry. For one thing, he used to go along the hedges muttering to himself like a dam' fool; and then, these foreigners behave very queerly to women sometimes. And perhaps he would want to carry her off somewhere—or run off himself. It was not safe. He preached it to his daughter that the fellow might ill-use her in some way. She made no answer. It was, they said in the village, as if the man had done something to her. People discussed the matter. It was quite an excitement, and the two went on "walking out" together in the face of opposition. Then something unexpected happened.

'I don't know whether old Swaffer ever understood how much he was regarded in the light of a father by his foreign retainer. Anyway the relation was curiously feudal. So when Yanko asked formally for an interview—"and the Miss, too" (he called the severe, deaf Miss Swaffer simply *Miss*)—it was to obtain their permission to marry. Swaffer heard him unmoved, dismissed him by a nod, and then shouted the intelligence into Miss Swaffer's best ear. She showed no surprise, and only remarked grimly, in a veiled voice, "He certainly won't get any other girl to marry him."

'It is Miss Swaffer who has all the credit for the munificence: but in a very few days it came out that Mr Swaffer had presented Yanko with a cottage (the cottage you've seen this morning) and something like an acre of ground—had made it over to him in absolute property. Willcox expedited the deed, and I remember him telling me he had a great pleasure in making it ready. It recited: "In consideration of saving the life of my beloved grandchild, Bertha Willcox."

'Of course, after that no power on earth could prevent them from getting married.

'Her infatuation endured. People saw her going out to meet him in the evening. She stared with unblinking, fascinated eyes up the road where he was expected to appear, walking freely, with a swing from the hip, and humming one of the love tunes of his country. When the boy was born, he got elevated at the "Coach and Horses," essayed again a song and a dance, and was again ejected. People expressed their commiseration for a woman married to that jack-in-the-box. He didn't care. There was a man now (he told me boastfully) to whom he could sing and talk in the language of his country, and show how to dance by and by.

'But I don't know. To me he appeared to have grown less springy of step, heavier in body, less keen of eye. Imagination, no doubt; but it seems to me now as if the net of fate had been drawn closer round him already.

'One day I met him on the footpath over the Talfourd Hill. He told me that "women were funny." I had heard already of domestic differences. People were saying that Amy Foster was beginning to find out what sort of man she had married. He looked upon the sea with indifferent, unseeing eyes. His wife had snatched the child out of his arms one day as he sat on the doorstep crooning to it a song such as the mothers sing to babies in his mountains. She seemed to think he was doing it some harm. Women are funny. And she had objected to him praying aloud in the evening. Why? He expected the boy to repeat the prayer aloud after him by and by, as he used to do after his old father when he was a child—in his own country. And I discovered he longed for their boy to grow up so that he could have a man to talk with in that language that to our ears sounded so disturbing, so passionate, and so bizarre. Why his wife should dislike the idea he couldn't tell. But that would pass, he said. And tilting his head knowingly, he tapped his breastbone to indicate that she had a good heart: not hard, not fierce, open to compassion, charitable to the poor!

'I walked away thoughtfully; I wondered whether his difference, his strangeness, were not penetrating with repulsion that dull nature they had begun by irresistibly attracting. I wondered. . . .'

The doctor came to the window and looked out at the frigid splendor of the sea, immense in the haze, as if enclosing all the earth with all the hearts lost among the passions of love and fear.

'Physiologically, now,' he said, turning away abruptly, 'it was possible. It was possible.'

He remained silent. Then went on—

'At all events, the next time I saw him he was ill—lung trouble. He was tough, but I dare say he was not acclimatized as well as I had supposed. It was a bad winter; and, of course, these mountaineers do get fits of homesickness; and a state of depression would make him vulnerable. He was lying half dressed on a couch downstairs.

'A table covered with a dark oilcloth took up all the middle of the little room. There was a wicker cradle on the floor, a kettle spouting steam on the hob, and some child's linen lay drying on the fender. The room was warm, but the door opens right into the garden, as you noticed perhaps.

'He was very feverish, and kept on muttering to himself. She sat on a chair and looked at him fixedly across the table with her brown, blurred eyes. "Why don't you have him upstairs?" I asked. With a start and a confused stammer she said, "Oh! ah! I couldn't sit with him upstairs, sir."

'I gave her certain directions; and going outside, I said again that he ought to be in bed upstairs. She wrung her hands. "I couldn't. I couldn't. He keeps on saying something—I don't know what." With the memory of all the talk against the man that had been dinned into her ears, I looked at her narrowly. I looked into her shortsighted eyes, at her dumb eyes that once in her life had seen an enticing shape, but seemed, staring at me, to see nothing at all now. But I saw she was uneasy.

'"What's the matter with him?" she asked in a sort of vacant trepidation. "He doesn't look very ill. I never did see anybody look like this before. . . ."

'"Do you think," I asked indignantly, "he is shamming?"

'"I can't help it, sir," she said, stolidly. And suddenly she clapped her hands and looked right and left. "And there's the baby. I am so frightened. He wanted me just now to give him the baby. I can't understand what he says to it."

'"Can't you ask a neighbour to come in tonight?" I asked.

'"Please, sir, nobody seems to care to come," she muttered, dully resigned all at once.

'I impressed upon her the necessity of the greatest care, and then had to go. There was a good deal of sickness that winter. "Oh, I hope he won't talk!" she exclaimed softly just as I was going away.

'I don't know how it is I did not see—but I didn't. And yet, turning in my trap, I saw her lingering before the door, very still, and as if meditating a flight up the miry road.

'Towards the night his fever increased.

'He tossed, moaned, and now and then muttered a complaint. And she sat with the table between her and the couch, watching every movement and every sound, with the terror, the unreasonable terror, of that man she could not understand creeping over her. She had drawn the wicker cradle close to her feet. There was nothing in her now but the maternal instinct and that unaccountable fear.

'Suddenly coming to himself, parched, he demanded a drink of water. She did not move. She had not understood, though he may have thought he was speaking in English. He waited, looking at her, burning with fever, amazed at her silence and immobility, and then he shouted impatiently, "Water! Give me water!"

'She jumped to her feet, snatched up the child, and stood still. He spoke to her, and his passionate remonstrances only increased her fear of that strange man. I believe he spoke to her for a long time, entreating, wondering, pleading, ordering, I suppose. She says she bore it as long as she could. And then a gust of rage came over him.

'He sat up and called out terribly one word—some word. Then he got up as though he hadn't been ill at all, she says. And as in fevered dismay, indignation, and wonder he tried to get to her round the table, she simply opened the door and ran out with the child in her arms. She heard him call twice after her down the road in a terrible voice—and fled. . . . Ah! but you should have seen stirring behind the dull, blurred glance of those eyes the specter of the fear which had hunted her on that night three miles and a half to the door of Foster's cottage! I did the next day.

'And it was I who found him lying face down and his body in a puddle, just outside the little wicker gate.

'I had been called out that night to an urgent case in the village, and on my way home at daybreak passed by the cottage. The door stood open. My man helped me to carry him in. We laid him on the couch. The lamp smoked, the fire was out, the chill of the stormy night oozed from the cheerless yellow paper on the wall. "Amy!" I called aloud, and my voice seemed to lose itself in the emptiness of this tiny house as if I had cried in a desert. He opened his eyes. "Gone!" he said, distinctly. "I had only asked for water—only for a little water. . . ."

'He was muddy. I covered him up and stood waiting in silence, catching a painfully gasped word now and then. They were no longer in his own language. The fever had left him, taking with it the heat of life. And with his panting breast and lustrous eyes he reminded me again of a wild creature under the net; of a bird caught in a snare. She had left him. She had left him—sick—helpless—thirsty. The spear of the hunter had entered his very soul. "Why?" he cried, in the penetrating and indignant voice of a man calling to a responsible Maker. A gust of wind and a swish of rain answered.

'And as I turned away to shut the door he pronounced the word "Merciful!" and expired.

'Eventually I certified heart failure as the immediate cause of death. His heart must have indeed failed him, or else he might have stood this night of storm and exposure, too. I closed his eyes and drove away. Not very far from the cottage I met Foster walking sturdily between the dripping hedges with his collie at his heels.

'"Do you know where your daughter is?" I asked.

'"Don't I!" he cried. "I am going to talk to him a bit. Frightening a poor woman like this."

'"He won't frighten her any more," I said. "He is dead."

'He struck with his stick at the mud.

'"And there's the child."

'Then, after thinking deeply for a while—

'"I don't know that it isn't for the best."

'That's what he said. And she says nothing at all now. Not a word of him. Never. Is his image as utterly gone from her mind as his lithe and striding figure, his caroling voice are gone from our fields? He is no longer before her eyes to excite her imagination into a passion of love or fear; and his memory seems to have vanished from her dull brain as a shadow passes away upon a white screen. She lives in the cottage and works for Miss Swaffer. She is Amy Foster for everybody, and the child is "Amy Foster's boy." She calls him Johnny—which means Little John.

'It is impossible to say whether this name recalls anything to her. Does she ever think of the past? I have seen her hanging over the boy's cot in a very passion of maternal tenderness. The little fellow was lying on his back, a little frightened at me, but very still, with his big black eyes, with his fluttered air of a bird in a snare. And looking at him I seemed to see again the other one—the father, cast out mysteriously by the sea to perish in the supreme disaster of loneliness and despair.'